VENGEANCE BOUND

Also by Justina Ireland
Promise of Shadows

JUSTINA IRELAND

VENGEANCE BOUND

SIMON & SCHUSTER BFYR

New York   London   Toronto   Sydney   New Delhi

SIMON & SCHUSTER BFYR

An imprint of Simon & Schuster Children's Publishing Division
1230 Avenue of the Americas, New York, New York 10020

For information about special discounts for bulk purchases, please contact
Simon & Schuster Special Sales at 1-866-506-1949 or business@simonandschuster.com.
The Simon & Schuster Speakers Bureau can bring authors to your live event.
For more information or to book an event, contact
the Simon & Schuster Speakers Bureau at 1-866-248-3049
or visit our website at www.simonspeakers.com.
Also available in a SIMON & SCHUSTER BFYR hardcover edition
Book design by Lucy Ruth Cummins
The text for this book is set in Seria.
Manufactured in the United States of America
First SIMON & SCHUSTER BFYR paperback edition March 2014
2 4 6 8 10 9 7 5 3 1
The Library of Congress has cataloged the hardcover edition as follows:
Ireland, Justina.
Vengeance bound / Justina Ireland.
p. cm.
Summary: Amelie Ainsworth longs to graduate from high school and live a normal
life, but as an abused child she became one of the Furies, driven to mete out justice
on the Guilty, and lives on the run from the murders they commit.
ISBN 978-1-4424-4462-1 (hc)
[1. Justice—Fiction. 2. Murder—Fiction. 3. Erinyes (Greek mythology)—Fiction.
4. Mythology, Greek—Fiction. 5. High schools—Fiction. 6. Schools—Fiction.
7. Orphans—Fiction. 8. Mental illness—Fiction.] I. Title.
PZ7.I6274Ven 2013
[Fic]—dc23
2012006779
ISBN 978-1-4424-4463-8 (pbk)
ISBN 978-1-4424-5356-2 (eBook)

For Mom, who always believed.

And for Eric, who maybe didn't . . .

NOW will you read it?

VENGEANCE BOUND

BEFORE

ANNIE SHAKES MY ARM FRANTICALLY, startling me awake from a nightmare of blood and nameless terror. I blink away my lingering fear as she peers down at me, her eyes wide.

"We leave tonight," she whispers. "I got it." In one hand is an access card from one of the orderlies. In the other is a set of car keys.

"How?" I say, sitting up in bed. Her eyes slide away from mine, and I don't want to know how she got them. "Is he still alive?" I ask.

"For now."

I nod and swing my legs over the side of the hospital bed. The room spins, and I clutch the mattress. I'm still a little wobbly from Dr. Goodhart's meds. It's only with Annie's help that I've been able to avoid taking the pills over the past few days. She learned sleight of hand from a friend who worked the tourist crowds on River Street, picking pockets or doing magic, whichever paid better. Without her I'd still be comatose from the good doctor's experimental treatments.

Annie throws me a set of scrubs. There are no real clothes in Saint Dymphna's, just pajamas for the patients. I guess they figure jeans and T-shirts will make us think that we're real boys and girls.

I pull the scrubs on over my pajamas. I've lost a lot of weight, and my hip bones jut out under the loose-fitting cotton. How long have I been here? Six months? A year? Time loses all meaning inside these walls.

Once I'm dressed, Annie leads the way out of the building. The escape was her plan all along. I think she feels like she's rescuing me. I guess she is. Without her I'd still be a vegetable.

I trail my hand down the wall, using the connection to steady myself. I'm woozy, and my head feels like it's filled with helium. There's still too much of the meds in my system. Otherwise I would've started hearing the Furies' whispers by now.

That's not good. I'm going to need Their help to kill Dr. Goodhart.

Annie stops suddenly, and I almost run into her. Her eyes are wide with fear, and she has started shaking.

"What's wrong?" I whisper.

"He's here." Her voice is hoarse, and I don't have to ask who she's talking about. I lean around her to look down the hall. The door to Dr. Goodhart's office is open, golden light shining out into the otherwise dark hallway. Annie takes a step back.

"This was a bad idea," she says. Annie has good reason to be afraid.

She's here only because her father is a close, personal friend of Dr. Goodhart's. She told me her story one night in a hushed voice, as though whispering about the horrors made them less real. Annie's dad seemed to think it was her job to help supplement the family income. Her father is a local car dealer, and his daughters are just another asset to be sold and bartered.

But Annie wasn't so keen on the idea. She'd had enough of being used. The night she found one of her father's friends in her bedroom, she stabbed him in the thigh with a pair of scissors. The guy almost bled to death. Daddy sent her to Saint Dymphna's in response.

It has to be painful for her. I know the things Dr. Goodhart has done to me, and I'm here only because there's no one left to speak for me. I can't imagine what it would be like to have my family knowingly subject me to such treatment.

I put my hand on Annie's shoulder, and she jumps. She pushes her too red hair out of her face, which looks bruised. I'm not sure if it's the lights or actual damage.

"Go get the car. I'm going to take care of him," I say.

She clutches at my upper arm. "You can't go in there. It's too dangerous."

I pat her hand and disentangle myself from her fingers. "I'll be fine. Take the access card and get the car running. I'll meet you outside."

"But how are you going to get out? The security system requires a badge."

Hello, dear. We've missed you.

The voice in my brain fills me with a terrible kind of excitement, like waiting for an ice-skater to fall. I haven't heard Them for so long that I was half-afraid They'd left me. I smile, and Annie draws back.

"Oh, I'll figure out something."

I move down the hallway without looking back to see if Annie is following my instructions. It takes only a few strides to reach Dr. Goodhart's office, and the more I move the better I feel. Once there I slip inside on silent feet. My heart pounds with excitement. I've dreamed of this moment so many times, it hardly seems real.

The doctor sits at his desk, head bent over paperwork. He can't be working on anything honest this late at night. Is he falsifying test results, or writing a glowing review about one of his experimental procedures? Either way just the sight of him is enough to fill me with rage. I close the door, locking it behind me. He looks up, his expression of surprise quickly hidden by bland disinterest.

"Hello, Amelie. Is there something I can help you with?"

I take a step forward, willing Them to manifest. I can feel the Furies deep in the back of my mind. They want to appear, but They're sluggish and slow to respond. There are still a few too many drugs in my system.

We're trying, *dear heart*, the hawk woman coos. A rustle of wings in the back of my mind indicates that They are close. But I don't know if I can keep Dr. Goodhart occupied that long.

"I'm here to hand down your judgment," I say, although it feels awkward to say the words without the Furies flanking me. I'm Their Third, but I'm used to acting as more of a mouthpiece than a leader.

Dr. Goodhart leans back in his chair, amusement crinkling the corners of his eyes behind his glasses. His blond hair is mussed and his tie loose, giving him a slightly rumpled look. He has the dashing good looks of a soap opera doctor, but it's all a lie. Underneath his handsome exterior is a soul as black as tar. "Amelie, have you been taking your medicine?"

I hiss in anger just as someone begins pounding on the door behind me. An expression of smug satisfaction appears on Dr. Goodhart's face, and I realize with a start that I forgot about the panic button under his desk. This isn't the first time he's used it on me. The doctor and I go way back.

But it ends tonight.

A sudden pressure on the inside of my skull makes me clutch my head. The room heats, and the Furies break free with a scream, mine and Theirs. It's like surfacing after being underwater for too long. Essentially female, They are barely human. Tisiphone, whose name rhymes with "epiphany," stands to my left, her giant hawk wings folded close in the small space. On my right is Megaera, snakes writhing where her hair should be. They are terrifying in Their beauty, and the look of fear on Dr. Goodhart's face fills me with a manic glee.

I point at him. The silver chains that bind Them to me, invisible up to now, hang low on my arms. "You will pay for what you've done to me."

I take a step forward. Before I can reach him, the door explodes inward behind me. I spin around. Two of the larger orderlies stand silhouetted in the doorway. They draw back when they see the Furies.

"Holy fuck!" One of the orderlies takes a step back out into the hallway. I look between them and Dr. Goodhart. I can't kill with witnesses around. That's how I ended up here in the first place.

Tisiphone screams in rage, the sound of a hawk hunting. I turn in time to see Dr. Goodhart lunge for me, syringe in hand. Before he can get me, Tisiphone reaches out with her talons and rakes them down his face. He screams and falls back. Blood wells up in the long gashes, and I have to fight back my nausea. I don't do so well with blood.

One of the orderlies goes running down the hallway, screaming for a Taser. The other orderly keeps looking from me to his fleeing friend, as though he can't decide between duty and saving his ass. I make the decision for him. Things are quickly spiraling out of control, and I can see my chances of escape evaporating.

"Window!" I yell, and Megaera is there, knocking out the glass before ripping out the bars and part of the surrounding wall with scaled hands. Concrete dust rains down on me as she throws the window bars over my head at the orderly. He scrambles out of the way just in time to avoid being crushed. With him gone I can focus on my true goal.

Dr. Goodhart is on the floor holding his injured face. Blood seeps between his fingers, but I ignore it. I want to hurt him so much that it's a physical pain, a slight cramping in my middle.

I settle for picking up the syringe and jamming it into his thigh. He whimpers a little as the meds flood his system. "This isn't over," I hiss. People are running toward us, shouts of alarm echoing down the hallway. There's no more time. I launch myself out the window.

Luckily, we're on the first floor. I roll as I land on the grass, but it still hurts. The Furies retreat into the back of my mind, but They've been denied justice. They gnash Their teeth in frustration, and it's all I can do not to mimic Them. I've waited so long for this moment, and now it's gone. I want to scream out my disappointment.

I'll never get this opportunity again.

Patience, Megaera says. We will have our revenge.

I sprint across the lawn, my rage melting away into relief when I see the pickup truck idling with its parking lights on. Annie smiles when I dive into the cab.

"Did you get him?"

I shake my head. "Orderlies."

She gives me a look but doesn't say anything, throwing the truck into gear and peeling out of the parking lot. I wonder if her disappointment is as heavy as mine.

There's a moment of panic when we pass a police car and an ambulance heading toward Saint Dymphna's, but they don't stop or turn around, and we whoop in triumph.

"They must not know that you took the truck," I say.

Annie nods, her lips pursed. We drive along in silence for a while before I put a gentle hand on her arm. Tension rides her shoulders even though we escaped. "What's wrong?"

"Nothing. It's just . . . I have to go home."

"Why?"

She swallows hard, and looks at me with haunted eyes. "My sister. It's the reason I had to get out. Tomorrow's her birthday. She's going to be fifteen." She knows firsthand what happens to the girls in her family on their fifteenth birthday.

"Oh," I say. But in the back of my mind the Furies are screaming in joy. Hurting men like Annie's dad is Their idea of fun.

She looks at me. "You have to help me." She swallows hard and turns back to the road. "I looked at your file. Before I started palming your meds. That's why I had to save you." A heavy pause. "I know what you did."

She's talking about the suspected homicide that landed me in Saint Dymphna's in the first place. I was cleared of the charges because it's hard to convict a fourteen-year-old girl of giving a grown man a heart attack. But the charges were enough to kill my poor grandmother, and for Dr. Goodhart to convince the state of Georgia that I needed specialized "care" after it took over guardianship.

"Yes," I say, even though she has yet to ask the question. The Furies are too hungry for me to say no. And I owe her one, no matter what her reasons for helping me. Without her I'd still be lying comatose on a bunk.

"You'll help me," she says, surprise lacing her voice. I guess she didn't think I'd agree so easily.

"Yes, I'll help you." I look out the window, weighing my words. "Do you have somewhere you and your sister can go?"

She nods. "My aunt's. She's been trying to get custody of us for a while, but Daddy has too many connections." She pauses. "What're you going to do?"

"I'm going to handle it."

She frowns, and I grin at her. It feels strange to smile after being a near vegetable for so long. "Don't worry," I say. "He'll never see it coming, and you and your sister will be safe."

She doesn't say anything, and I look out the window. I've been free for less than an hour, and I'm already back to my same old tricks. The Furies are all I have left.

But I'm not afraid anymore. Not this time.

I know They'll take care of me.

HUGS AND KISSES, YOUR WORST NIGHTMARE

I PUT THE CAR IN PARK AND STARE AT the building before me. I can't believe I'm here. West County, Pennsylvania. Last week it was just a spot on the map, another potential stop on this endless road trip. Now it's home. At least for a little while.

It's been two years since I escaped Saint Dymphna's, and I've been on the road ever since.

I get out of the car and look up at where I'll be living for the next few months. It's a dump. Even rural backwaters like West County have their dark places. This is one of them. From the look of it the oversize house was once magnificent, probably a mansion for a wealthy mine owner back when West County was still coal country. At some point the neighborhood turned the corner, from the place to be, to the place to flee, and someone bought the house and chopped it into minuscule apartments. Very cheap apartments.

I get out of the car and head inside, lugging my trunk up the stairs to my new place. I've stayed in dozens of apartments just like this one. They're a great place to crash for a couple of months. Everyone keeps to themselves, and the landlords look the other way as long as the rent's on time. It's a cheap place to disappear, full of two-bit hustlers, single mothers struggling to get by, and illegal immigrants on a pit stop to the American dream. The kind of people who will mind their own business and won't worry about a blond girl who comes and goes at all hours of the day and night.

As I trudge up the rickety steps to my apartment, a baby cries and is shushed lovingly in Spanish. Rap music blares through a closed apartment door, and a couple argue loudly on the landing about a missing tax return check. I ignore all of it, and let myself into my tiny one-bedroom apartment.

The place is cold enough that I can see my breath, and I fiddle with the knob on the radiator until steams hisses through it. As the metal heats with creaks and knocks, I drag my trunk into my room and kick it into my closet. The apartment is furnished, so after another trip back downstairs to grab Odie's cat carrier and my laptop, I'm all finished moving in. I put everything down and look around the dingy, cramped space. Home sweet home.

I let Odie out and sit on the couch. Tomorrow I will start a new school for the ninth and hopefully last time. This year I will graduate. I've managed to cobble together enough credits that I should be able to finally get a diploma. Rather, my alias Corinne Graff will be able to graduate. Amelie Ainsworth is still in hiding.

I sigh. The thought of school fills me with anxiety. I would stop going altogether, but the one time I did that, I started to lose myself. It was during a short stint in South Carolina, and after two months of nothing but sleeping and justice, I didn't like the person I was becoming. The Furies are violent and bloodthirsty, and being just like Them is the last thing I need. At least with school I have a connection to the human race that doesn't involve killing.

I rest my head in my hands. Exhaustion makes me feel like I weigh a thousand pounds. When I think of school, I inevitably think about the future. But what is my future? Keep killing and living like a nomad, or settle down in a big city and live a double life? College by day, justice by night? That isn't appealing. It just sounds tiring.

I yawn and climb to my feet, trying to shake off my uncertainty. It's too early to worry about all of that. I have a few months until graduation, and I've just arrived in West County. It's a fresh start. No one knows me here, no one suspects what I do for fun, and Dr. Goodhart is somewhere in Pennsylvania. I'll find him, and after I take care of him, I'll focus on the small detail of the future.

I have all the time in the world.

And right now it's time to hunt.

I stick my thumb out and walk slowly along the highway. The blowing snow blinds me and makes my eyes water, so I duck my head into the collar of my jacket to hide my face as much as possible. It doesn't really help. It ain't fit out for man or beast, as my grandmother used to say.

Perfect for me.

I'm busy trying to keep the snow out of my eyes, so the minivan catches me by surprise. It swings onto the shoulder in front of me, appearing from out of nowhere. The passenger door opens, and I run toward the light and jump into the heated interior in relief. About time.

"Thanks," I gasp, holding my half-frozen hands out to the heater vents. The blast of warm air melts the snow on my gloves, and I sigh in relief.

"No problem, sweetheart." The driver pulls out cautiously onto the road, and I study him while he focuses on his task. Early thirties, dark hair, good-looking, probably wearing a wedding ring under his gloves. There's a child's car seat behind me. Family man, as though the minivan weren't already a dead giveaway. I worry for a moment that I have the wrong guy. He has a soft look to his face, like he'd spend his spare time rescuing kittens. This can't be the guy I want.

"So, what's a nice girl like you doing hitchhiking on a night like this?" Laugh lines crinkle as he smiles at me. It would be a nice expression if it weren't for the cruelty glittering in his eyes.

Still, I want to be wrong. I don't want to believe this man with a car seat in the back and an Elmo doll peeking out from behind the driver's seat could be a murderer. He looks harmless. Maybe he's innocent. After two years of this, I want to believe there's still something good in this world.

Maybe this man driving in the middle of a snowstorm is just an average guy going to get milk so his kids can have hot cocoa.

He's thinking how nice it will be to cut out your heart.

The whisper in the back of my mind isn't unexpected, and it puts the brakes on any doubts I may have had about the man driving. The truth is, I've been walking down this road every night for the past week, waiting for him to pick me up. We've been looking for him since I got to West County.

Let's finish him now. I want to watch him squirm.

I mentally silence the voices and turn a wide smile to the man. I haven't yet answered his question, and I hope it seems like I was considering my answer instead of the quality of his sins. "My mom and I had a fight, so I need to get to the bus station. My dad lives out in New York." I notice the way he licks his lips before looking away. I'm a girl that could disappear without anyone knowing about it for a while. Just his type.

"Oh, that's too bad, honey. Well, I don't think the buses are running in this weather, but I'll give you a ride into town anyway."

I give him a wide smile. "Thanks. That's really nice of you."

"Did you want to call your mom and let her know where you are, so she doesn't worry? You can borrow my phone."

"Naw. She'll be passed out by now. She always gets drunk after she gets paid." I look out the window, like I'm fighting back emotion. In another life I could've been an actress.

"Oh, okay. I see." I can almost feel the glee coming off him. In the back of my mind They keep up a constant dialogue, arguing between Themselves.

First we need to find a spot, somewhere off the main road . . . The serpent woman's sibilant voice trails off as she starts to plan. She's interrupted by the hawk's scream.

No. Let's do it now!

Patience, Tisiphone. We must do it right.

The serpent, Megaera, is correct. Rushing ends in disaster.

The car turns down a nearly invisible road, little more than a cut through the woods. I turn to the driver with what I hope is alarm. "This isn't the way into town."

"I have to go by a friend's house first, before I take you to the bus station. You don't mind, do you?"

Not at all, but any girl with half a brain would be a little afraid. "Can't you go by his house on the way back?"

"Nope. Sorry." He turns his well-practiced smile on me once again, his face absent of any apology. Even if I didn't have Them in the back of my mind, I would know there was something off about this man.

But if I were a normal girl, it would be too late.

Snow and darkness hide the road, even with the headlights attempting to cut through the gloom. Trees press in on either side, their branches scraping the glass like the scrabbling hands of vengeful victims. I kind of like the sound.

We ride in silence until the trees open up, revealing a rustic cabin. I lean forward, trying to see through the windshield. "Your friend lives here?"

"Actually, no." He turns off the car and lunges for me. I'm taken by surprise. I expected him to lure me inside the cabin. His hands lock around my throat, and I gasp as my air supply is cut off. I pry ineffectively at his fingers for a few heart-pounding seconds, but already there are dark spots at the edges of my vision.

Time to call for backup.

I release the hold I have on Them, and They boil forth, manifesting from the back of my mind. The heat of another realm fills the interior of the van, and the snowflakes sticking to the outside of the windows melt away. There isn't much room for Them in the minivan. Tisiphone's mottled brown wings press against the glass of the windows, and the serpents on Megaera's head brush the roof of the minivan. The sight of Them crammed into the narrow space behind the driver's seat would make me laugh, if I weren't being strangled.

Something must show in my expression, because the man turns just in time for Megaera to grab him with a scaled hand. Whatever he was going to say trails off in a gurgle as the serpent throws him backward. His head hits the driver's side-window with a dull cracking sound.

I cough as air fills my lungs. The man gives me and my companions a wide-eyed look and fumbles behind him for the handle. The door flies open, and he flees. I'm in no condition to chase him or control Them. My body is enjoying being able to breathe again, and my throat aches. They take advantage of the freedom, tearing out into the snowy night behind the man. Over the howling of the wind I can hear his screams of terror, and I lurch out of the car to follow the sound, tracking the path of melted snow through the forest while I gasp for breath. I stop when I find Them, the guilty man hunching at the base of a pine tree.

"Don't," I croak as Tisiphone raises one of her talon-hands to swipe at the man. She pauses, hand poised in midair. They would usually burn away a soul if given half the chance, but it has been a while since They were allowed to play. They're savoring his pain and fear. He's a treat, a man with a long history of hurting women. Someone who has caused that much pain deserves to suffer. It's the only reason he's still alive.

But I can't let Them hurt him the way They want to. The coroner won't exactly think it's just a heart attack if this guy looks like he was attacked by an animal.

His eyes light on me, and he lunges forward, Tisiphone's hesitation the opening he needed. He doesn't get far. She grabs him by the throat and jams him against the tree hard enough to dislodge snow from the branches. It evaporates into steam around us. The snow on the ground has already melted from Their presence, revealing a thick carpet of dried pine needles.

While I'm studying the ground, Tisiphone's talon-fingers clench, the black nails cutting into the soft flesh of his neck. At my pointed look she lets him go and steps back. He rubs the bloody spots on his throat. "What are you? What the hell are you?" the man blabbers, and I can't help but smile.

"There are plenty of nightmares that stalk the night. I'm yours."

I step forward, taking my place between the other two with a sigh of relief. Silver chains encircle my arms, leading back to Them and binding us together. My vision splits in three, seeing what They see too. It's like looking at a dressing room mirror, each image slightly different. Tisiphone's vision is bright colors and a flash of images as she reads his past crimes. Megaera's is cast in red, heat vision more than anything. She sees the pain of his past victims clinging to him. I can see only what is in front of me, but my weakness isn't a hindrance.

Three is the right number. Now we are complete.

"Matthew Alders, you are accused of killing women, and keeping their hearts as trophies. How do you plead?"

His eyes are wild, and he looks from Megaera, to me, to Tisiphone. She flaps her wings once and grins at him, and he cowers even more. "What, what are you talking about? What are you?"

I grab Alders by the chin and use Tisiphone's ability to read the sins written on his soul. This works only when the Furies have manifested physically and the silver chains connect us, which is a shame. It would make life a lot easier if I could do it all the time.

It takes seconds to see the parade of his victims. A montage flickers past, Alders on the computer checking out dating sites and e-mailing lonely women while a little girl plays at his feet, him driving along the same road where he found me, picking up random strangers. My stomach turns as I watch him bring all of them here to his cabin. I break the connection after I see what he did to the first girl, who was around my age. I don't need Megaera's special sight to see that this man is a monster.

I swallow my nausea and drop my hand to my side. "Guilty," I whisper.

"Guilty!" the hawk screams, excitement coloring the sound.

"Guilty," the serpent echoes, her low voice solemn. The slightest hint of a smile plays around her thin, scaled lips.

I hold out my hand. The chains looping around my arms flow forward, swirling and coalescing into a silver sword. I don't bother saying anything else to Alders, I'm so disgusted by the things he's done. Men who prey on women are the worst sort of creature. Monsters like Alders deserve to die.

Even if it is wrong to kill them.

I hesitate for a moment. As much as I know that it's the smart thing to do, I don't want to kill Alders. I hate the way his death will eat at me, making me question our actions. Are we truly the ones who should be handing down justice? Wouldn't it be better to hand him over to the police, let the proper authorities deal with him?

But then I think about the next girl he'll pick up on this lonely road, and the chances that the evidence won't be enough to convict him. And I know that I have no other choice.

Besides, it's the price that the Furies demand. What else am I going to do?

I stab him through the chest with the sword, and he stiffens as his heart stops. It's a better death than the one he gave his victims, and I pull the blade out with a grunt. Beside me Tisiphone and Megaera sigh sadly. It went too quickly for Them, and Their disappointment is almost palpable.

With Alders dead I'm able to focus, and I direct my thoughts toward pushing the Furies back into my subconscious. It's a bit like mentally reeling in a fish, but They don't fight me. They aren't always so cooperative.

Once They are sequestered in the back of my mind, I walk back to the minivan, the woods around me eerily silent. The blowing snow has stopped for a moment, and a deep sense of peace settles over me. I don't always enjoy our work, but I have to believe I'm doing good, helping Them. Because of me other women won't have to endure what I did.

But in the end it doesn't really matter if what we do is right or not.

The Furies are all I need. And I would do anything to keep Them happy.

I reach the minivan. The door is still open, and the interior light beckons to me with the promise of heat. I rifle through the inside, finding Alders's wallet and emptying it. I have my own money, an inheritance from my parents and grandmother, but if I touch it, the authorities will know where I am. I'm technically still a ward of the state until I'm eighteen, and I have no intention of ever going back to Georgia. So instead of trying to use my inheritance, I live off the guilty. Tonight's haul is a whopping sixty-eight dollars.

Now that I'm done handing down Matthew Alders's justice, I'm tired. I just want to get back to my apartment so I can sleep. I consider taking the van but decide it's better to leave it where it is. No sense in giving the police any reason to suspect foul play. I pull the hood of my coat tight with a sigh. Then I hike back down the road to my car.

It takes me a little more than an hour to make it back. The afterglow of the justice makes it seem like a much shorter trip. Still, by the time I clear the snow off my windshield, I'm half-frozen. I get into my car and wait for the heater to warm up, shivering in the driver's seat like a junkie coming down from a fix. When the hot air starts blowing, I start for home, feeling light even though I'm dog tired.

It's only when I remember that I have school tomorrow that the euphoria of the justice melts away, leaving behind an odd knot of dread and excitement.

THE FIRST THIRD

SECONDS AFTER MY HEAD HITS THE PILLOW, I open my eyes to a bleak landscape, the colors muted like in an old photograph. Rust-colored earth and jagged mountains form geography not of this world. The sky is cloudless, and a heated wind scours my skin, making it feel like it's being baked off. The heat will follow me back to the waking world, leaving my sheets soaked from the sweat of being in this other realm.

The serpent and the hawk are nowhere to be found, only the woman in flowing white. Alekto, the third Fury. The one I've replaced. At times when I've been here, I've watched the three of Them fight, Their words like the screams of wounded animals, unintelligible but filled with rage and sorrow. Mostly I end up here when Alekto wants to chat. She's the one who told me Their true names, who taught me how to bring Them to heel, and how to mitigate the effects of Their bloodlust. Without her I would have gone crazy, truly insane, a long time ago.

Still, for someone who abandoned the cause, she sure does like to interfere a lot, and that makes me despise her.

Unlike the other two, she is human. Well, as human as a mythical creature can be. She isn't like Them, animal parts mashed together with human features. She is beautiful and golden, like a living statue. It's in her image that the Furies remade me, a side effect of Their possession. My hair used to be dark, a brown so deep it was almost black. My eyes were always blue, but a shade closer to gray. Now Alekto and I share the same corn silk ringlets and sapphire-blue eyes. Her skin has a golden hue, the one feature of hers that They either didn't or couldn't copy. I could never mimic the look unless I rolled around in glitter. And that's not happening. She gleams as she walks across the earth toward me, her mouth turned down at the corners. Lecture time.

"Once, the world was ruled by the great gods. They looked down on the earth from their rule on high, and mocked the antics of men and beasts alike. They bore children, and tormented them as they did the rest of their creations. The gods were frivolous and cruel, and the children of the gods balked at the tyranny of their sires but were helpless to stop them. After all, who can challenge the whims of a god?"

I swallow a groan and close my eyes, willing the dream to end. I've heard this story before. She has told it dozens of times. When I open my eyes, the dreamscape is still there, and Alekto continues without missing a beat.

"The youngest child of the king of the gods was given a sickle by his mother, the goddess of the earth. She had a soft spot for the humans and had grown tired of her husband's antics. She knew her husband's death would change the plight of man, who toiled long and hard only to have the gods dash it all away. The sickle was the only thing that could kill the old king of the gods, and the young god did not want to miss his chance. In the early light of dawn, when the day was not yet born, the young god struck. He slew his father, the oldest of the gods. Dying, the old god bled out over the world and swore revenge.

"The first drop of blood landed on a hawk hunting over a meadow. It was the First, born of the surprise of betrayal. Her moods are manic: one minute joyous, the next violent.

"The second drop of blood landed on a serpent sunning itself on a rock. Sly and cunning, the Second is the simmering anger that never fades but simply bides its time, waiting to strike."

I sigh, hoping Alekto will hurry up and get to the point of our meeting. I don't need to hear all of this again. But sometimes what she reveals is useful, so I bite my tongue and wait for her to finish.

"The third drop of blood landed on a maiden sleeping in a meadow, waiting for her beloved to return to her side. The Third was born of all the sorrow of betrayal, and she woke with a start, tears falling ceaselessly. She could not remember anything of her previous life, and she was consumed by the sadness of a now dead god. But that sorrow and despair called to the other two, and when They joined her side, she felt a measure of peace. After all, They were all sisters of the same blood. Together They knew what They had to do—find the guilty and punish them for their crimes. And for a long time that is what They did.

"But one day something changed."

I straighten at this, a new line in the story. Usually she just ends at the point where the three hunt the guilty and hand down justice, like the happily ever after in some twisted fairy tale. I frown at her, even though it's hard since she's so pretty. "What changed?"

She blinks, and looks at me like she has just realized I'm standing here. "You let Them loose again," she begins, without any sort of transition. "How do you expect me to help you if you continually give in to Their demands?"

"I wasn't aware I'd asked for your help." I used to cower in fear when she spoke through my dreams, but she holds even less power than the Furies do. After almost five years of being joined to the Furies, I've figured some things out. They have constant access to me, but she can enter only through my dreams. They leave me the clues that lead me to Their prey. She does nothing but talk.

She purses her lips at me. "Not yet, but you will soon. You have to resist Them. The more you give in to Them, the closer They get to Their goal of ruling your mind completely. Do not let Them gain control of you."

"What other choice do I have?" I snap. I'm tired of having this conversation. She keeps hinting that there's a way to rid myself of Them, has for a long time. But she never gives me a straight answer, and I'm not entirely sure I trust her. After all, the only reason I have Them in my head is because at some point she severed her chains to Them. I can't believe I'm the only person They've ever possessed. Did Alekto "help" that previous person too?

Besides, at least They are honest about Their goals. Alekto is not.

She's unfazed by my outburst. "You always have a choice. That is one of the beautiful things about your kind, the number of options you have." She looks wistful, as though she's remembering a time when she could make her own decisions.

"Uh-huh." I glance around for an exit. I'm not interested in sticking around and listening to her ambiguous threats and prophecies. I pick a spot on the horizon, a place where the mountains bump against one another, and walk toward it. Eventually I'll be able to break the hold she has over the dream, and then I can get some rest.

"If I could tell you how to rid yourself of Them, I would. But I am forbidden. Just know this: He will change everything for Them, and They will do whatever They can to keep you away from him. I am warning you now. It is going to come down to him or Them. And They will not be happy with the answer."

I turn around to ask her who she's talking about, but Alekto has already left the dreamscape. I sigh in resignation as the dream begins to dissolve. When I blink again, I'm lying in bed, staring at the ceiling.

I am completely clueless about what the dream meant, but at least now I can get some sleep.

I roll over, trying to get comfortable. My eyes close, and I don't give the golden goddess's cryptic warning another thought.

IMAGINARY ME

AFTER THE FIRST FIFTEEN MINUTES OF SCHOOL, I'm certain I've made a mistake. Maybe West County wasn't the best choice. It's hard to remember that I need this, the sense of normalcy that school brings. It always seems like a good idea, but right now I'm wondering why I even bother.

I gaze out the window of the guidance counselor's office at the pickup trucks and beat-up family cars pulling into West County High's parking lot. Boys dressed like designer lumberjacks and girls wearing high-end knockoffs bounce out of the vehicles and make their way through the snow and into the building. It all looks so normal. It's different from my last school down in Virginia. There designer labels and expensive foreign cars were the order of the day. But beneath all of that money and wealth was the same darkness I've found everywhere I've been.

Nine schools in the past two years. That has to be some kind of record. And being the new kid still makes me as nervous as a cat on a boat.

So why am I scared? I haven't even gone to a single class, and already my palms are slick with sweat, anxiety twisting my belly into knots. I've done this so many times, it should be easy. But it's not. If I didn't need this so much, this one little connection to the real world, I would leave and never come back. But it's this small shred of normalcy that keeps me from completely becoming a monster.

"Miss Graff, are you listening?"

I blink and turn my attention back to Mr. Hanes and his never-ending welcome speech. He's the school counselor and vice principal, and despite the name, he'd never be a candidate to model underwear. He's a small, blustering mole of a man with a beer paunch and no hair. Judging by the awards proudly displayed on the walls—#1 ADMINISTRATOR, VICE PRINCIPAL OF THE YEAR, STUDENTS' APPRECIATION—at some point in his career he actually convinced himself that he helps kids. Maybe it lets him justify the minuscule pay that doesn't even allow for a new wardrobe. His paisley tie and brown suit are several decades out of fashion. I don't say this, though. Instead I tilt my head slightly to the side and give him a megawatt smile, a testament to what modern dentistry can do.

"I'm sorry, Mr. Hanes. I have to confess that I was staring out the window. Y'know, we just don't get snow like that in the South."

The soft cadence of my voice has the desired effect. Some Northerners just can't get enough of a Southern accent. People up here tend to think their cousins to the South are slow, and slow equals dumb. When people think you're dumb, they underestimate you, and being underestimated is the greatest tool a hunter can have. The Furies taught me that. It's why I adopted the drawl. You can never make things too easy for yourself.

Mr. Hanes looks out the window, and his irritation is forgotten as he studies the snow-covered landscape outside. "Yes, I suppose it must be something to get used to, as if transferring in your senior year weren't hard enough. Snow and college applications. You've got a full plate," he says with a chuckle.

I lean back in the chair and cross my ankles, folding my hands and resting them on my knees. I try to think of what Dr. Goodhart, my old shrink, would do. He was a master of manipulation, and I owe a lot to my time spent with him. "Now, Mr. Hanes, you were speaking of integrating well into my new environment?"

I say it sincerely. Mr. Hanes clears his throat, and I can see I've caught him off guard. No normal, well-adjusted teenager talks like that, at least not without a heavy dose of sarcasm. I mentally swear at myself. *You're supposed to be fitting in.* Instead I've wrested control of the moment and deflected his irritation. Mr. Hanes narrows his eyes as he senses my coup, and I widen my eyes to appear more innocent. The expression would look ridiculous on most people, but I know from practice that it looks authentic on me. I think it's the eyes. They seem bluer every time I look in the mirror.

That's because you're evolving, a husky voice whispers seductively in my mind. A warm breeze caresses my cheek, and my head fills with the soft rustle of wings shifting. Tisiphone. She's always there to soothe, even though she's the crazier of the two. I stiffen but try to remain calm.

Mr. Hanes still studies me, and I sit a little straighter in my chair, thrusting my shoulders back. Out of habit I toss my hair over my shoulder. It's a move They taught me. Like with most men, it distracts Mr. Hanes. He adjusts his tie and licks his lips. Discomfort stirs low in my belly, and I wish I hadn't worn such a tight sweater. Unfortunately, my near strangulation left a mess of bruises on my throat, so I'm in for a week of turtlenecks or awkward questions. I opted for the turtlenecks. The sweater was the only thing clean.

The Furies stir in the back of my mind at his casual regard, a settling of feathers and a slither of scales.

Lustful creature, the serpent hisses.

A girlish giggle echoes in my head. *Let's see if he'll squeal like a pig.*

I blink, mentally pushing Them into the back of my mind. My constant companions, champions of justice and bloodshed, are also very distracting. At my urging They go meekly to the back of my mind, squatting on the edge of my consciousness like fat toads on a log. I smile again, allowing no hint of my inner turmoil to show on my face. Instead there's a slight upturn of my lips. It's meant to put Mr. Hanes at ease, but it has the opposite effect. My eyes must have given away Their thoughts. It happens sometimes, a shifting in the depths of my pupils that sets off the fight or flight response, like the gleam in the eyes of a predator. I thought I was doing a better job of restraining Them.

You only think you're controlling us. Megaera's sibilant whisper is followed by mocking laughter. I fight the urge to rest my head in my hands. I'm not strong enough to do this again. Dr. Goodhart was right. I'm a danger to myself and others. I'll never fit into normal society.

Mr. Hanes watches me silently before he wipes at his suddenly sweaty brow. "I, uh—that is . . . Do you have any questions for me before we go get your class schedule?"

I shake off my melancholy and force a yearbook-worthy grin to my face. "Nope." Maybe I'm smiling too much. How much does the average person smile? Everything hinges on convincing people that I'm ordinary. Too many missteps and people will question my sanity. Again.

I stand up and follow Mr. Hanes out into the school's main office. From Mr. Hanes's welcome speech I've learned that there are precisely 411 students at West County High. The office reflects the school's small size. There is only one harried-looking secretary. Mr. Hanes holds two positions, and the principal, Ms. Halyard, is here only part-time. Her door is closed today, indicating that Monday is one of the days she's at the nearby middle school.

Mr. Hanes hands me a printout detailing my class schedule. The school's layout is pretty straightforward. All of the classrooms are in the single L-shaped building.

Mr. Hanes clears his throat again. "Here's your schedule. Teachers have all the materials you need, so they'll hand those out when you report. Your locker combination is there at the bottom, as well as your locker number."

Mr. Hanes trails off and just watches me, like his brain is trying to process an image it doesn't understand. I watch him, wondering if he has ever acted on his impulses, if there's any sort of justification to kill him on the spot. Then I remember why I'm here. I need to blend in. Another attempt at normalcy, at stopping the slow slide into becoming just like Them.

Good luck with that.

I open my mouth to thank him, but he's still staring at me like I might jump up and bite him. They shift in the back of my mind, and I gnaw my lower lip. "I'm sorry," I mutter. I'm not sure what I'm apologizing for. Making Mr. Hanes nervous? Imagining what it would be like to choke him to death with his necktie? His face registers surprise at my comment, but he nods in acknowledgment anyway. I slip out of the office before Mr. Hanes's mind can figure out what his gut already knows—that there is something very wrong with me.

SET ADRIFT

AFTER FOUR SOUL-CRUSHING CLASSES THAT
make me question the sanity of high school—the history teacher
spends twenty minutes ranting about immigration, and the English
teacher sobs her way through a reading of a Shakespeare sonnet—I
discover that West County High School is one of those archaic institu-
tions where students are forced to eat on campus. I am informed of this
when I try to leave at lunchtime. A fat man in a puffy jacket and orange
safety vest waves me back from my car in the parking lot.

"You got a pass?" It takes me a second to realize it's not a statement
but a question.

"Uh, no. Am I s'posed to have one?" I smile and relax against my car.

The metal of the Toyota is cold, even through my coat. The man does not frighten me. He's the school equivalent of a mall cop.

He sniffs. "You can't leave campus without a pass. Now you get back inside before I report you to Mr. Hanes." He pulls up on his belt to emphasize the statement.

I have the urge to break the man's nose. It'd be so easy. A simple thrust upward with the heel of my hand, to shove the little piece of cartilage so far into his nasal cavity that it utterly destroys his brain. It's what the Furies urge me to do in soft whispers.

Just a quick jab. Who'd notice?

We could be in the car and gone before anyone hears his screams.

Just a little taste, hmm? His pain would be so delicious.

He has to be guilty of something.

My hand reaches out, and I stop it with a start. Already They are taking charge, turning me into little more than a puppet. Their need to destroy life is an ever-present sensation, violence that simmers just below the thin veneer of control I wear.

Normally I'm okay with that. It's not always easy to know where I end and They begin. Sometimes I think I even enjoy the justice They hand down. But I came to West County with a mission: to be normal, live my life the way I want to, and stop the roller coaster of destruction They've put me on. I have to find balance. The past couple years of handing down justice have burned me out, moving from town to town, dodging close calls. Too many schools, too many new faces. I'm just so tired. I need a place to call home, even if it is the backwater of West County.

I pull my hand back and cradle it against my chest while I take a few deep breaths. The cold air braces me and removes the fog that settled over my mind when the Furies urged me toward violence. I flash the confused security guard a smile. "Well, I do apologize. My mistake." I flip my hair over my shoulder and go back the way I came.

I'm not about to screw up everything on the first day.

I've fought hard to retain this part of my life, the average girl. When the Furies began to urge me to justice after my parents died, I dismissed it immediately. True, They'd once saved my life, but that was before I knew Their price.

When They'd first invaded my mind, Their whispers had driven me to the brink of insanity and had made my parents think I needed professional help. After my parents had sent me to Brighter Day, a facility for "troubled teens," I'd been determined to get rid of Them, or at least ignore Them. I didn't need the drama.

Then my parents were killed on their way to see me one weekend. If it hadn't been for the Furies, I wouldn't have been in the hospital. I blamed Them for my parents' deaths, and swore I wouldn't give in to Their demands for justice. No matter what.

After Brighter Day I moved in with my grandma down South. Savannah was warm and predictable and safe. I had a normal life to occupy me, and my grandmother was thrilled to have me around. For the first time in years I felt like I could forget the past and be happy. I ignored the Furies' whispers and focused on meaningless pastimes like dancing, something I'd been into before life had gone so very wrong. When the cravings got too strong, I would run until I fell down from exhaustion, or eat more chocolate than the fat kid from

Willy Wonka. Life was as normal for me as it was ever going to get, and everyone just chalked up my oddities to being a teenager.

But slowly even the chocolate and physical exhaustion weren't enough. I started to have the dreams again, to yearn for the screaming. The killing.

The righteousness.

I pushed the thoughts aside. Those were Their feelings, not mine. I knew despite Their constant whispers that They were wrong, that killing, no matter how justified, was morally repugnant. I tried to focus on what was important. Family. School. Church. Wearing the right clothes and the right hairstyles. Even though I secretly knew it was all so useless, that none of it really mattered. Family could disappear in the skid of tires on wet asphalt. School was pointless. I was always a little ahead, and I already knew all of the answers.

But I was good at being good. Why would I want to ruin that?

And then I saw him in the grocery store. At first I thought it was my imagination. After all, most people are just naturally drawn to cute kids. He wasn't a monster, no matter how Tisiphone howled about his dark deeds. It was just my own overactive imagination that linked this stranger to my nightmares. Too little sleep. Too much time digging through the past with my new psychologist.

But even without Their constant dialogue, something about the man seemed so familiar.

I followed him, picking up items for my grandma out of order so I could track his meandering progress through the store. In the produce section he picked up a shiny red apple and handed it to a little girl crying in a shopping cart, a wide friendly smile on his face. He wasn't my personal demon, but I knew the look of a predator when I saw it. And I knew I had to do something about it.

Four months later my grandmother was dead and I was in Saint Dymphna's, fighting for my life.

I push the memories aside and walk back into the main building. Once inside I head straight to my locker to hang up my coat. When I pull open the metal door, a newspaper clipping, yellowed with age, flutters to the floor. It's one of Their abilities, leaving me messages like this. I have no idea how They do it. I've learned over the years that They don't wholly exist in this world, and that Their presence here is intertwined with mine. But I'm not sure if They place the clippings using some rip in the space-time continuum or if They have free run of this world while I sleep. I've never asked.

I don't really want to know.

I pick up the slip of paper and read the headline: MAN CONVICTED OF FOUR RAPE-MURDERS RELEASED FOR "GOOD BEHAVIOR."

The article goes on to relate how Hank Meacham, a local mechanic, had originally been sentenced to twenty-five years in prison for the murders of several young women. The state paroled him after only ten years, since he had been a model prisoner.

I clench the article in my hand, crumpling the newsprint. The date on the story is from five years ago. The news clipping isn't random. It's Their way of signaling our next target. They weren't happy about quickly dispatching Alders last night, and now They're ready to hunt again.

I could ignore Them like Alekto wants me to, not go out tonight to get rid of the man in the article. Really, I'd like to never hand down another justice, to just live my life like an average girl. But that's the fool's errand, as my grandmother used to say. I tried it once, and the outcome was a hundred times worse than anything before or since. My grandmother might even still be alive if I hadn't lost control so severely.

A little control is better than none at all.

I jam the clipping into my pocket before hanging my coat in the locker. After closing the metal door, I slowly walk to the cafeteria, dreading the half hour I will be forced to spend in the company of West County High's student body.

In the few weeks since I left Virginia, I've forgotten how grueling school can be. The constant attention, the judging and weighing. It's like being under a microscope. They, however, love it.

In my mind They keep up a constant dialogue as I maneuver down the hallway. They can read the sins of any man, and one of Their favorite pastimes is to tell me every little thing a person has done. High school is full of sinners.

Oh, that one cheated on the girl who gave herself to him.

That one's a liar. Liar! And he had lustful thoughts about his teacher. We should punish him.

What about that one? He doesn't pray in church; instead he stares at the breasts of pious women.

Scandalous!

I ignore Them, looking down so I don't have to make eye contact with the boys I pass. There are a few that They don't comment on. Obviously not every guy is bad, but They can make something as small as stealing a cookie sound like a capital offense. For the most part I try to ignore Their whisperings.

They never confess the wrongs of women. Early on I asked Them about this, but Their only answer was to start howling about Alekto's betrayal and the man who stole her away. The sound was loud enough to give me a crippling headache. I never asked Them again.

I'm a little surprised by how noisy They are as we walk to the cafeteria. Usually They're silent the day after justice. But not today. Just being in the building makes Them tremble with agitation.

I shush Them, silencing Their internal dialogue before opening the double doors to the lunchroom. I am immediately assaulted by a wall of sound. Voices raised in excitement, angst, and gossip roll over me. The clanging of trays on the food line provides a background beat. It's enough to make my breath catch, for anxiety to claw its way through my chest.

They flutter in the back of my mind, urging me to leave. *You don't need this. You have us.* They want to quench my nervousness with the sweet screams of justice.

I take a half step backward and stop. It would be so easy to listen to Them, to run away. But I can't. This little bit of normalcy is something I need. I crave it the way They hunger for the fear of the guilty. Hanging around people is the only thing keeping me from being just like Them.

I ignore Their whispers and walk calmly over to the food line, where I select a thick slice of chocolate cake and a bottle of chocolate milk. Chocolate calms Them, and I need all of the help I can get. I grab a bottle of water as well, since good hydration is essential to good health even in cold weather. I pay for my food, courtesy of the money from Alders's wallet, and at the end of the line I turn around and survey the lunchroom. Like every other school in America, or at least the ones on TV, the cafeteria is segregated by coolness. The band geeks sit at one table, the regular geeks at another, the jocks are next to the popular kids, and so on. The only question in my mind is who to sit with.

I glance around the lunchroom, gnawing on my lip as I think. The popular girls' table is out. I did that back in North Carolina, and I don't have the patience for the petty infighting and jealousy that comes along with that group. I don't play an instrument, so the band geeks are out, and I can't fit in with the regular geeks. Besides, they would see through me in record time. Smart people tend to realize there is something calculated about my responses. It's one of the downsides of being possessed by vengeful, mythological monsters.

There has to be a group high enough on the social ladder to give me a life but low enough that I can still be mostly invisible within the student body. I give myself a mental kick. I should have researched the student body before enrolling. The answer to every problem is on the Internet.

Just as I'm beginning to feel hopeless, while They debate killing a nearby janitor just for a distraction (he cheats on his wife with the neighbor), I spot a table of guys and girls laughing back against the far wall. For the most part they look like they walked out of an ad for jeans, one of those "we're casual and yet so stylish" setups. Their clothes are nice but not new enough to be cutting edge. There is none of the piercings and colored hair I associate with the druggie crowd, although one girl does have a minuscule nose stud. Her eyes meet mine across the cafeteria, and a flash of something flits across her face. Sorrow undercut with hope, excitement, and yearning. She smiles at me, a sign of welcome.

Bingo.

Anticipation swells in my chest as I hip swivel around a jock holding a freshman in a headlock and move toward the back of the room. Kids at other tables watch me as I go. I ignore them, and I'm relieved when I don't even feel the need to injure anyone. The Furies have finally settled down, and Their silence is a welcome relief. With Them quiet I can try to make some friends, try to fit in. I want to belong.

I'm surprisingly good at it.

"Hi. Y'all mind if I sit here?" I ask softly when I get to the table. All eyes turn toward me, and the guys scoot over so that I can sit down, right across from Nose Stud Girl.

"Hey," she says with a smile. She's a mousy little thing. Her bangs are on the long side, and her straight brown hair partially obscures her face. "You're in my chemistry class. Corinne, right? I'm Mindi, with an i." It's an awful name, like her parents wanted her to be a porn star. Still, she seems really nice. I like nice.

I smile widely. "Nice to meet you. It is Corinne, but y'all can call me Cory, with a y." Mindi's face flushes, but I give her a friendly grin. She smiles back, shyly.

Everyone around the table introduces themselves. Tom, Adam, Jocelyn. There are two boys and three girls, counting Mindi. They all seem pretty nice, and I mentally pat myself on the back. Maybe I'm finally getting good at this making-friends thing.

One of the girls, a blonde with frazzled hair, doesn't introduce herself but instead just ignores me. I beam at everyone anyway, ignoring the blonde in return. "Wow, it's so nice to meet y'all. And they say Yankees aren't friendly."

Mindi grins. "'Y'all'? 'Yankees'? Lemme guess, you're from the South."

I nod enthusiastically. "Savannah. Prettiest city in the entire U.S. In fact, they say that when Sherman came through with his army, he found the city and her squares so beautiful, he didn't have the heart to destroy it. This was after he'd burned Atlanta, y'know. During the War of Northern Aggression." It's overkill, but I can't help it. It's something my grandma would have said, and the words slip out of their own accord. The memory of her makes me a little sad.

Bleached Blonde makes a rude sound, but when I glance at her, she isn't even looking in my direction.

One of the boys shoots me a sheepish grin. I can't remember if it's Tom or Adam. Either way, that little bit of friendliness makes me feel better. "Hey," he says, "maybe you can help me with my report for history. I'm doing an essay on the causes of the Civil War. You know, from each side's perspective." I note absently that he's pretty cute. Brown hair on the longish side, freckles across the bridge of his nose, wide brown eyes that remind me of a puppy dog. I bet most girls would love to go out with Puppy Boy.

Me, I couldn't care less. With Them in my head boys are off the menu. It's hard to think about kissing someone with Their constant noise.

Still, I have to be nice. "Sure, I'd love to help." I shoot him my megawatt smile, and he flushes. Even if I wanted to, I can't return his interest. The last time I kissed a boy, he ended up in intensive care. Kevin Eames. He had eyes the color of honey, and sweet lips to match. He lived next door to my grandma, and always smiled at me like I'd hung the moon. The night after I handed down my first-ever justice, he caught me sneaking back into her yard. He thought I was sneaking out to meet him like he'd asked me to. Kevin was two years older, and I thought I was in love every time he looked in my direction.

Unfortunately, They didn't feel the same way, and all it took was a single kiss for Them to burst forth in a hail of rage and heat. My control wasn't so great back then, and by the time I reined Them in, he was unconscious and my grandmother's azaleas were charred to a crisp.

Still, it shouldn't hurt anything to help a guy with his homework. Nothing screams "Not a psychotic killer" like a little tutoring.

Bleached Blonde turns her glare on Puppy Boy. I wait for her to strike, for her to let loose with an angry barrage of words, but she says nothing. She reminds me of a hyena. I can even imagine her large nose replaced by a spotted snout. I file that fact away for later. Hyenas are sneaky and unpredictable.

"Hey, what'd I miss?"

Mindi squeaks and jumps up from the bench. She scurries around the table and throws her arms around a tall boy with midnight hair who appears from out of nowhere. He stiffens and pats her back awkwardly before extricating himself. Everyone at the table shifts uncomfortably, like a distant uncle from prison has just crashed family dinner. Mindi turns around, and he adds another few inches of space between the two of them. She doesn't see his look of panic, and her face glows with joy. "Cory, this is Nikolas. Niko, this is Cory. She's new, all the way from Savannah."

I wait, expecting more from her. She says his name the way someone would say "my boyfriend" or "the love of my life, who I absolutely cannot live without, ohmigod, isn't he wonderful." But there's no other label attached to his introduction. I glance around the table, studying everyone's reactions. They all look anywhere but at Mindi, who's grinning like she just won a reality show competition. Even Nikolas looks a little uncomfortable that she's so glad to see him.

I ignore the tension and stand, holding my hand out to shake. Nikolas looks at it a long moment before wrapping his fingers around mine. His hand is large and warm, and my much smaller one disappears. "Nice to meet you, Cory. Sorry you've been exiled to the boondocks."

A warm blanket of calm settles over me, and my mind is silent. Completely and utterly silent. Not even a hint of Their whispers. I take a deep breath. I haven't felt this way since I was in Saint Dymphna's. Then, I was heavily medicated. Now I'm just holding a hand. A guy's hand. I clear my throat. "Yeah, thanks. It's nice to meet you, Niko-Nikolas." I say it as much as a joke as to give myself a moment. Holding his hand is doing upsetting things to my internal organs. My heart beats rapidly, and if I didn't know that I was in perfect health, I might be worried.

He smiles, but the expression is pained. I wonder if he knows what I'm feeling, even though I'm not sure myself. I want to follow up my earlier comment with something witty, but his eyes hold me captive. They're blue, but completely different from mine. They're a shade that reminds me of how the ocean looks right after a hurricane blows through, wind tossed and angry. A slate gray shot through with darker shades of navy and flecks of cornflower brightness. Clichéd but true. His stormy eyes stop my heart for a second. "Call me Niko."

I blink, and reluctantly pull my hand from his. I smile, unsure what else I can do. I am unsettled by those cobalt eyes that see too much. Niko watches me intently, so I tilt my head to the side. "You look familiar . . ." I murmur, stalling for time. He doesn't, though. There would be no mistaking those eyes, or that unruly hair. Never in a million years could I forget the sadness that swirls so hypnotically around him, etched subtly into his expression. Or the way my chest feels light and constricted at the same time.

He's not for you.

No, no, no! He is wrong, wrong, wrong!

I swallow dryly and try to ignore Their grumblings. I have the feeling that Niko is assessing me, waiting to see what I'll do next. It's not a feeling I like. Part of me panics, thinking that the moment has gone on too long, has stretched into something awkward. I snap my fingers and smirk, breaking the mood. "Charlie, on Hope's Forge. You look just like the guy who plays Charlie on Hope's Forge." I have no clue if that show's even popular here, but it was back in Virginia. I cross my fingers that no one noticed the tremor in my voice.

Mindi twists around and tilts her head back to inspect Niko's face. It's amazing that I forgot she's here, standing between us. She squeaks again in excitement. "Ohmigod, she's right. Of course, Charlie's eyes are brown, but around the chin, and the hair . . ." Mindi nods, reaffirming my assessment. "You totally look like Charlie!" she yelps, and everyone at the table laughs nervously and looks away. Whatever the joke is, I'm not in on it.

The crisis averted, I sit back down in my spot and shovel a couple of bites of chocolate cake into my mouth, hoping the sugar will shut Them up. They yammer nonstop, hissing warnings about the danger of boys. I take a few deep breaths and try to calm my pounding heart. I have to forget about Niko. I have just made my first friends in forever, and I have to find my way around a new school. That's plenty for a first day. It's not like I can afford to lose my head over a cute boy.

The Furies can't read my thoughts unless They've manifested, but if They notice my distraction, They'll try to take advantage of my weakness. I have to be strong. It's like They have Their own little space in my head, right between the childhood memories and my most embarrassing habits. I'm thankful for that bit of privacy, although I think They can sense my vital signs. An increased heartbeat or a bit of fear makes Them appear more quickly than if I summon Them. Keeping calm is key to controlling Them.

There is definitely something symbiotic about our relationship.

Mindi sits back down across from me, Niko next to her. I can feel him watching me, but I avoid his gaze and keep eating. I can't afford another incident so soon, another lapse in self-control. It's bad enough that I let a little thing like a handshake scramble my brain in the first place. I can't spend the rest of lunch making puppy eyes at him. Even if it takes everything I have not to look at him.

Puppy Boy slides down so that he's right next to me. "Chocolate cake and chocolate milk, huh? Not a very nutritional lunch."

I blink and start to stammer out an excuse, until I realize he's teasing. I smile. "Oh. Well, it's sort of a bad habit. I always eat dessert first."

He grins back at me, and I'm surprised to realize that we might be flirting. "Oh, yeah?" he asks. "Do you have any other bad habits I should know about?"

I don't have to fake embarrassment at his question. Before I can answer, he starts to ask rapid-fire questions about my last school. He makes me nervous, but his unwanted attention is a nice distraction from the conflicted emotions roiling inside me. I answer his questions patiently, lying as necessary and meeting his eyes as often as possible. Like Dr. Goodhart once said, eye contact is important to establishing trust.

Out of the corner of my eye, I catch Bleached Blonde looking at Puppy Boy like he should be something on the lunch menu. The only time her gaze shifts is when Mindi leans over to whisper into Niko's ear. The blonde's lips thin in irritation at their closeness. She sees me watching her, and without a word stands up and leaves. No one at the table notices, so I figure this must be a regular occurrence.

The bell rings, signaling the end of the lunch period. I hurriedly drain my chocolate milk, since the sugar rush is silencing Their unwanted advice. Puppy Boy offers to take my tray for me, and I accept. I wait for him near the door, since during our never-ending conversation we've discovered we have history together right after lunch. He has offered to show me where the classroom is, as though I could get lost in the small school. Perhaps Puppy Boy is going to be more trouble than he's worth.

As I breeze out of the double doors of the cafeteria, Niko stares at me, his stormy gaze intent. I wonder what he sees, if he has somehow glimpsed the monster that exists just below the well-maintained surface. I crane my neck, and over my shoulder I see a smile spread across his face. The real thing, not the polite façade he showed at the lunch table. A thrill of excitement runs down my spine, and I wrap my arms around my middle.

Not good, not good at all.

SANCTUARY

I WASTE NO TIME GETTING TO MY CAR AFTER
the final bell. Returning to high school has been more than I bargained
for, and my head pounds from Their constant diatribes and the effort to
restrain Their murderous nature. I am desperate for food and physical
activity—two things that help me control Them. By the time I manage
to get my car into gear, I can see Adam (I discovered Puppy Boy's name
when the teacher called on him during class) on the snow-covered lawn
of the school, turning in a slow circle. He's probably looking for me.
Right now I don't want to be found.

I've gotten pretty good at not being found.

I speed down the school's long drive, barely making the light and turning onto the main road. Driving soothes me. The motions require no thought. I don't have to pretend to like a certain type of music or follow current trends. I can drop the character I've created for myself and just be lovable, murderous me.

It's a bigger relief than it should be. Especially considering how much I want to be around other people.

My mind wanders, and I think about the day They came to me. It seems like forever ago that I was trapped in a dark place, shivering and broken and waiting for death. They came to me then, in the moment when I'd lost all hope. They offered safety and revenge in exchange for my help. They saved me.

But some days it feels like I traded one kind of darkness for another.

A horn honking startles me from my reverie, and I turn onto the side street just as the left turn arrow changes from green to yellow. The person behind me follows too closely, and when I pull down my alley, a gray minivan speeds past, their acceleration an audible middle finger.

I am definitely making friends today.

I put the car in park and head inside. My stomach growls, reminding me that my last meal was all empty calories. I move into the kitchen and pull out several hard-boiled eggs and a cold grilled chicken breast from the fridge. It was supposed to be my lunch. Since it looks like I'll be in lockdown every day at lunchtime, I make a mental note to pack something for tomorrow. I eat the food standing over the sink, since I don't have any dishes. The yolks of the eggs I don't eat; instead I feed them to my cat, Odysseus, who pads into the kitchen as soon as he hears the refrigerator open. Odie, as I call him, is ten years old.

He's the only remnant I have of my old life, a constant reminder of all that I lost.

It was pure luck I found him that night after taking care of Annie's daddy. He was wandering through my old neighborhood, his collar bearing the address of one of the neighbors. They must've adopted him after Grandma died, but I got him back. Heartbreak took me to her boarded-up house, but finding Odie eased a little of that pain.

On my way down the hallway I catch my reflection in the mirror. The mirror came with the apartment. I thought about junking it, since as a rule I dislike mirrors. The face that smirks back at me is nothing more than a cleverly crafted lie, and I hate seeing it. But I loved the mirror's wrought iron frame so much that I kept it. Now I stop and stare like I always do. Not because I'm vain, but because I'm watching, waiting for a sign that I have less time than I think. It was Alekto's first lesson.

Your eyes are the windows to your soul. Use them to see what darkness lurks there.

The hungrier They are, the more They crave justice, the more visible They are within the irises of my eyes. Too much movement in the blue depths and I could lose my hold on Them. If I don't give the Furies what They want, I risk Them trying to possess me completely.

Too little motion from Them? Well, that's never been a problem.

I stare into my eyes, searching the blue irises. My eyes twitch left and right. Seconds pass and nothing happens. Part of me hopes nothing will.

What would I do if I were free of the Furies? Maybe I could go live with relatives. Someone would want me. Not my aunt and uncle. They never really forgave me for the part I played in their daughter's death, an incident I was too young to remember. If they'd wanted me, I never would've ended up a ward of the state of Georgia.

Maybe I could travel the world. I visualize myself lying on a beach, the sand warm under my feet and the sun bright overhead. These mini daydreams make me hopeful.

But hope is deadly, because just as I'm about to turn away, I see it. A shadow flits across my left eye. It's gone before I can track its progress. I wait, and a similar darkness appears in the blue of my right. I hold my breath, and just as I feared, They come swimming back, sharks in the blue pools of my irises, whispers of madness in my mind. The movement could be a trick of the light, but it isn't. The shadows are Tisiphone and Megaera, waiting to be fed.

In that instant I hate Them.

There is too much movement. They are entirely too active. Alders wasn't enough; the entire event was over too quickly to appease Them. I have to go hunting tonight. I can't risk someone at West County High seeing the phantoms that live inside, not if I want a semblance of a normal life. I once trusted Dr. Goodhart to see my shadows. I thought he could help. Turns out, trusting him was a mistake. Not the biggest mistake I've ever made, but a mistake all the same.

I turn away from the mirror with a sigh. If I could cry, I would.

My bedroom is little more than a closet, the space barely big enough to fit a double bed and a beat-up dresser. Despite the small space, I have a closet that is almost as big as the room. That's where I head now. It's my secret sanctuary, that small square space. It's big enough to accommodate my wall trunk, a special antique my grandmother bought me. It was once a magician's trunk, the kind that opens to reveal not only a trunk portion but drawers as well, two small and one large. Stickers from the late nineteenth century decorate the outside, detailing its long history. We saw it in an antiques store a few weeks before my birthday, and I fell in love with it. It was the last thing she ever bought me.

The lid opens to reveal the wooden drawers inside. Nestled in those drawers are a dozen slinky tops and short skirts, outfits that would make a stripper blush. In the little drawer near the top are my fake IDs, more than a dozen different aliases, cousins to the driver's license in my wallet. The other small drawer holds my newspaper articles, clippings of my prey since I left Saint Dymphna's. I place the newest article on top of the stack. There are a couple hundred clippings, and I remember every single one of them. Every bit of justice I've ever handed down stains my soul.

I do an Internet search on Hank Meacham, and within minutes I find everything I need to know about the man. I close the laptop and stretch. There's quite a bit of time before I can do any real work, so I might as well run a little.

I slither out of my school clothes and slip into tight running gear. In the bathroom I see that the bruises on my neck have already faded to a mustard yellow, and I'm glad that I probably won't be stuck with turtlenecks all week. Speedy healing is a side effect of Their possession, and it has come in handy more than once.

I run down the stairs and out the main door, my shoes pounding rhythmically as I find my pace. A pair of boys wearing puffy jackets mark my progress with dark eyes. They don't move, frozen to their spot like leery wild dogs. I grin and round the corner.

Let them try to start some trouble. We would welcome the entertainment.

ABSOLUTION

THE WORLD IS A PIT OF BLACKNESS WHEN I walk out of my house. There are few streetlights where I live, another plus. The local thugs have knocked them out, and the town is too poor to keep up with their replacement. The closest working light is halfway down the block, just far enough away that I can skulk out of my building unnoticed.

I don't need the lights in order to see. My vision is just fine with very little illumination. It's another one of the few benefits of letting Them in. They keep me healthy, and enhance my natural abilities enough so that I'm better than average. It's not much, but it's something.

I climb into my car and put an address into the GPS. It's the location of a bar in the nearby town of Flintlock. Flintlock is a magnet for losers. It's the closest town to the Pequea Valley Correctional Facility, a federal prison. The Pequea Valley Correctional Facility didn't exist ten years ago. With populations on the rise at the other penitentiaries in the state, the government hired a private firm to build a brand-new prison. It's too bad the corporate suits didn't consult with their potential neighbors first, who were less than thrilled about the addition. As awful as West County is, Flintlock is actually worse, a veritable ghost town.

It takes me forty-five minutes to get to the bar, a classy place called Loose Lucy's. A mud-flap-girl cutout outlined in pink neon sits on the roof, the name of the bar scrawled next to her in illuminated purple letters. The place looks like it was once a strip club, but even the dancers have left for greener pastures. Now it's just a bar that advertises cheap beer and a wing special on Thursday nights. The cars in the parking lot are a mixture of rusted pickup trucks and beat-up four-door American family cars, working-class all the way. I park at the edge of the gravel road under a leafless oak. It's darker in this corner of the lot, and I don't want to draw any attention if I can help it.

I get out of the car and strut toward the bar. I'm dressed in all black, a shadow moving across the white snow. The air is frigid, and a stiff breeze cuts through the thin turtleneck sweater and tight jeans I wear. I'm not dressed for the weather, but I can tell from the way They rustle in the back of my mind, I'll be warm shortly.

My plan is simple: Walk in, find Hank Meacham, get him alone, and hand down justice. I'm hoping Hank is a man of habit. Loose Lucy's is where he was picked up on a parole violation a few weeks ago, according to a public records search. Like my grandma used to say, a leopard doesn't change its spots.

I saunter into the bar, which is pretty dead. It's after midnight on a Monday, and I'm the only female in the room. The Furies relay the thoughts of some of the patrons in rapid-fire snippets as I walk past, the descriptions ranging from foul to vomit-worthy. I ignore the play-by-play. The man I'm looking for is here, sitting at the end of the bar. Bald with a week's worth of stubble on his face, Meacham only vaguely resembles the newspaper photo I found. But there's something unmistakable about his eyes, which hold a glint of the malice I've come to recognize in killers. There is something about those who deal in human misery that leaves an indelible mark on them. I wonder if my own tendencies can be so easily seen.

I don't think I really want to know the answer.

Meacham looks in my direction, tracking my progress as I stride to the bar. My heart flutters a little in my chest, and something writhes in my belly. Excitement or guilt, it makes no difference. This is exactly where I need to be. A monster hunting monsters.

I ignore Meacham and perch on a bar stool a couple of feet away. "Excuse me?" I call.

The bartender, a man who has eaten entirely too many buckets of fried chicken, waddles over. The tucked-in flannel shirt he wears takes some of the strain of his large belly, and the spaces between the buttons of his flannel gape to reveal his stained undershirt. His thinning hair is too long and greasy, and he pushes it out of his face with sausage fingers as he walks over. He looks me up and down, leering at me as he licks his lips. "Hey there, sugar. What can I get you?"

The look on his face is enough to send Them into overdrive. My leash on Them is loose, and They eagerly relate his thoughts.

Sweet little thing . . .

. . . such a tight sweater . . .

. . . just a few minutes in the back . . .

It's so disgusting that my smile slips a little. I try to ignore the Furies' howls for blood, hating how They have to relate the foul thoughts of the men we meet. Not every guy we meet is bad, but there's nothing They like more than relating the innermost thoughts of those who are. It's very tiring.

The man watches me with his beady eyes, and I force a wide smile. "My car broke down up the road a bit, and my cell phone's dead. I was wondering if maybe you could call me a tow truck?" I blink and tilt my head at the end, just in case the rest of the act isn't convincing enough. I have to look nonthreatening, even though all I want to do is punch him.

The bartender laughs and leans toward me. Lucky for me there are beer coolers on the other side of the counter. Otherwise he'd be in my personal space. My skin crawls, and I lean back slightly. He doesn't seem to notice. "Honey, I don't have to call you a tow truck. The only driver in town is right there." He gestures toward the man at the end of the bar. "Hank. Hank! You got your truck? This sweet thing right here needs a tow." His words are so close to what They related that I have to take a steadying breath.

Hank blinks at the question. When he realizes the bartender is talking about me, he tosses back his beer and stands. He watches me, and I sense a split second of hesitation. It's the opportunity he's been waiting for, but some part of him, buried deep under the tainted part of his soul, rejects the lust for violence. That part is too small to make any difference, though, and he gives me a grin that sends chills of warning down my spine.

It's disappointing how easy this is.

Hank stretches like an old hound. "I left my truck at the yard. But we can ride there and then go pick up your car. It's sixty-five dollars for the tow. Cash only."

I nod slowly, like I'm mulling it over. In the back of my mind, They gnash Their teeth in excitement. "Okay. Sounds good."

Hank nods, and slaps a ten down on the bar. He slides into a dirty, dark blue mechanic's jacket, his name on a patch on the front. He belches loudly, wipes his nose with the back of his hand, and shoots me a gap-toothed smile. "You comin' or not?"

I follow Hank out to his truck. Excitement makes Them flutter in the back of my mind, and for once I don't try to silence Them. By the time I climb into the passenger side of Hank's truck, I shake, as much from the cold as from anticipation.

This is the part where once upon a time I would have tried to talk myself out of it, to fight the inevitable. Until the last, final, unavoidable act I would try to reason with Them, try to spare the life of the guilty man about to receive his sentence. For a while it worked. I thought I could regain control, return to a normal life without giving in to Their bloody demands.

That was before Dr. Goodhart's betrayal at Brighter Day and the long waking sleep of Saint Dymphna's. I trusted him. I worked hard to follow his suggestions when my parents sent me to him at Brighter Day. And he turned me into a lab rat the first chance he had.

Sometimes when I think back on everything that's happened, I imagine that Dr. Goodhart actually helped or that my parents didn't die in a car accident, that it was them who saved me from Brighter Day and not my grandmother.

But it didn't happen that way. My parents died, I went to live with my grandmother, and I betrayed her by giving in to Their cries for justice. If there hadn't been an eyewitness to a judgment, if I hadn't been covered in the same sooty residue as the dead guy, I never would've been arrested.

But I was. And it broke my poor grandmother's heart.

After I made my escape from Saint Dymphna's, after I listened to Their advice, after They taught me how to survive, I knew They were right. One must be ruthless and unforgiving. That is the way of justice.

And justice is the only thing that matters.

There will be no amnesty for Hank Meacham.

Hank starts up the truck, and classic rock fills the interior. He drives through the parking lot, and before we've gone far, I can tell he is entirely too drunk to be driving. He swerves over the center line several times, and I hope he doesn't drive us off the road into a ditch. That would be inconvenient.

I clear my throat. "So, Hank, are you a religious man?"

Hank gives me a sidelong glance, and chuckles. "I s'pose so. Why?

You about to give me a religious experience?" His hand snakes across the distance of the bench seat, and he grabs for my thigh. I scoot as far away as I can, just out of his reach.

This irritates him, and he suddenly turns wide down a narrow side road. Gravel pings the underside of the vehicle as he guides the truck back from the shoulder onto the paved road. The back end fishtails, the remnants of last night's snowstorm an added challenge for drunken Hank. "You know, if you don't have the money, we could negotiate something else."

I shake my head. "No, I can pay. I just want to get my car and go home." There's a quaver to my voice, a little bit of acting so Hank doesn't get suspicious. The Furies push at the front of my brain, anxious for release. I shush Them. Soon.

Hank chuckles. The sound would make any sane person nervous. "Maybe I don't want your money." He pulls into the parking lot of an ATV repair shop, the truck's headlights reflecting off the airbrushed plywood sign. The only light in the lot comes from a sickly overhead lamp that turns the snow the color of piss. Snow-covered fields surround the lone garage, and beyond there is darkness.

I realize with amusement that I've miscalculated. Again. I thought he would try something once we got to his junkyard, since that was his habit for such a long time. Pick a girl up, do his dark business, stuff the body into the trunk of a car, and crush it. It's one of the reasons the authorities found only four of his victims. How many other girls got turned into scrap metal?

Hank has changed his routine since his stint in prison. It intrigues me that I've overlooked the possibility, and I wonder where he dumps the bodies now. Cornfield? Junkyard? Maybe it's still the trunks of the victims' cars?

While I'm thinking, he grabs for me. I'm already out of the truck and sliding across the snow slush gravel of the parking lot. During our drive it started snowing again, and flakes fly into my eyes as I jog. My muscles are still loose from my earlier run, and my head pounds as They seek their freedom. The frigid night air burns my lungs, and I breathe deeply, enjoying the pain. Hank's footsteps sound behind me. Even from a distance I can hear his labored breathing. He's an old hound, but he's not about to let his bone get away.

I haven't gone far before he catches me. I could have easily outrun him, but that would have defeated my purpose. This show has all been for his benefit. It's so much better when they don't see it coming.

I'm a few steps from the field when he grabs me by my right shoulder and spins me around, holding me upright when I would fall. I swing at him with my left hand, awkward and ineffectual. I could drag this out, savor it and fight him for real, but Hank bores me. With the exception of his choice of location, he's predictable. Plus, he stinks.

He laughs at my weak punch and hauls me up against him, pinning my arms at my side. It doesn't matter. By the time I need my hands, They'll be free.

He says something to me, his breath hot and reeking of alcohol. I am beyond hearing him. All I can think about is how much They're going to enjoy what's about to happen. His hands are roaming over my body now, and I swallow my revulsion at being pressed up against him. With a giddy laugh I release the hold I have on Them.

It's like releasing a long-held breath, the whoosh of air replaced by a rush of wings and the soft sliding of scales. I sigh happily. Hank frowns, confusion overriding his glee. I wonder if he can sense what is happening in his inebriated state. *Hank, buddy, you really shouldn't have had that last drink. You look a little tipsy.* His expression goes flat, and I smile.

"You've been a very bad boy, Hank Meacham." The voice is mine and yet, not. It's deep, throaty, like a stripper who smokes too much. Tisiphone's voice given life by my throat.

Hank releases me and takes a couple stumbling steps back. His eyes are wide with horror. My hair whips around my head, driven by a scalding wind. The night is suddenly hotter than an August day. The snow around me melts and evaporates, and steam shrouds me. My vision splits into three. We see three separate Hanks turn to run. A force blocks him, the serpent reaching out invisible coils to restrain his flight. He shoves at the air, a terrified mime in a box. His stupor is gone, fear wiping away the alcohol-fueled haze. He's screaming now, shouting unintelligible words. Some of them sound like prayers. He blubbers through his panicked tears, pleading with an absent God for mercy.

We shuffle forward and point at Hank, now curled up in a ball on the ground. "Judgment must be passed," Megaera hisses, her voice sibilant and high. It's pretty much pointless to tell him his crimes. He's petrified with fear. I stride toward Hank. The chains that link me to Them rattle as I move, silver links dragging over the gravel parking lot. My fingers wrap around his chin, dragging him into a sitting position. The grip causes him to wince. With a little more pressure I could shatter his jaw. I hesitate, and They urge me to break it, Their voices rising and sliding over each other until the sound is deafening. Their cries echo in the still night. I want to resist, but Their lust for pain is stronger than my will. With a grimace I give in.

The jawbone breaks with an audible crunch, turning my stomach. Hank's screams shatter the night, like an otherworldly choir. We sigh as we savor the sound. The bone crackles as it heals. They could do this all night, breaking and then fixing him, just to do it again. I remind myself that I'm the only thing keeping Them from indulging in Their fun.

I have to be stronger. It's time to stop dragging this out.

Poor Hank begins to sob and call for help, but he knows as well as we do that there will be no rescue, no witnesses. He picked this spot for just that reason.

His whimpering is getting old, so I compel Hank to look into my eyes. He is powerless to resist my will. The Furies crowd close.

In Hank's wild, bloodshot eyes Tisiphone reads the truth of his crimes, and I do as well through our shared vision. Revulsion turns my stomach, and part of me, the part that's still a little bit human, shrinks away from the violence. But I have to know that he is guilty of the crimes They say he is. I will not kill an innocent, which is more than I can say for Hank Meacham. Megaera's sight reveals how much he's hurt people. It's more than I can stomach.

"Guilty," I say, my voice flat.

"Guilty," the serpent whispers.

"Guilty," Tisiphone announces in her husky voice, her verdict dissolving into a manic giggle. I release Hank, and he falls back onto the ground. He sobs loudly. His terror is almost palpable. My three-way vision melts into one, and I alone stand over Hank. I can still sense Them with me, but tonight this last part is my responsibility alone. They have had Their fill of fear this week, and are finally satisfied. I feel a sense of relief, despite the work I still have to do.

I look down at him, and he cries harder. "Please," he moans, his hands covering his face. "Please, just let me go."

"How many of your victims begged you for mercy?" I ask. My voice is hard, and realization slowly dawns in Hank's eyes. He scrabbles backward across the parking lot. The sight fills me with a fierce joy, and I smile. "Justice has no room for mercy, Hank Meacham."

I hold my palm out. Chains hang from my arms, links of metal that surge forward, swirling into my palm. A gleaming silver sword materializes. It shines with an inner light, and the unnatural flash makes Hank sit up. He tries to run away, scampers across the gravel parking lot on his hands and knees, but I plunge the sword through his back. I know the exact moment when it pierces his heart. A shudder passes through me, and my entire being tingles.

It's better than anything else I've ever felt. Joy, love, elation, righteousness, and release all crash through me in a discordant symphony. It's only a fraction of what They feel, but it's enough. There wasn't time to savor it last night, but tonight there is. For a second I let the finality of Hank's death wash over me, and I revel in a job well done.

I can understand why They crave justice so much. There's an addictive quality to the feeling of vengeance. It's more than the pleasure of knowing that a monster like Meacham will never kill again. It's the satisfaction of a job well done coupled with the adrenaline high of jumping off a cliff. I'm more alive when I hand down justice than at any other time in my life.

I would feel worse about handing down Their justice, but I know my way is more humane than Their method. If They could, They would burn away his soul, leaving nothing for the afterlife. I just stop the hearts of the guilty, ending their lives quickly and quietly. I'm not religious, but I like to think there is some kind of final judgment for the men we kill. The fate of their souls is left to the deity who cares. It's not Their way, but we have an agreement. A clean death, and They get to choose the criminals and have my full cooperation. It's better than how things are when They have full rein.

They sigh in relief as They return to Their space in my subconscious. We have completed our justice.

Yet I am the only one still standing in the parking lot.

I slowly withdraw the blade, and Hank falls onto his face. There is no blood or torn clothing, no sign at all of what I have just done. When the newspaper reports his death, if they even bother to report on it, they'll say he died of a massive heart attack. Natural causes. I release my grip on the sword. It and the chains wrapped around my arms dissolve into nothingness.

I bend down and pull Hank's wallet from his back pocket before I step over his body and head to his truck. There is $680 in his wallet. Today must have been payday. I stick the money into the hip pocket of my jeans before wiping my prints off the battered leather, just to be sure. I toss the wallet onto the floor of the passenger side. Rent will be due soon.

Besides, it's not like Hank needs it where he's going.

The keys are in the ignition of the truck, and the engine is still running. I drive back to my car in a fog of lazy satisfaction and park a little ways down the road from Loose Lucy's so no one asks me why I have Hank's truck.

I'm taking a risk, leaving Hank's truck so far from where he died. But it's cold and snowy, and I'm feeling lazy after last night's trek through the snowstorm. The smart thing would've been to leave the truck near the ATV repair shop. But chances are that the cops will just think that Hank was robbed after picking up a hitchhiker, the heart attack the result of his panic. The snow is still blowing around. It should hide my footsteps well enough.

I run to my car. The afterglow wears off during the short sprint. I shake uncontrollably by the time I start up my battered Toyota, the euphoria of justice fading into bone-deep fatigue. The drive home blurs into stops, turns, and starts. By the time I crawl into bed, I'm exhausted and ready for sleep.

Even though I'm tired, I lie in bed staring at the ceiling for a long time. I will my brain to still, to stop thinking about Hank Meacham and the terror in his eyes. It's done. There's no taking it back now.

My breathing finally slows, and as I drift off, my thoughts aren't on what has just happened. Instead I think about going to school in a few hours, and seeing Niko. His blue eyes and mussed hair fill my mind's eye. Deep in my chest there's a tingle of excitement, and my heartbeat picks up just a little. He makes me look forward to school.

I don't know whether that's a good thing or not.

SLUMBER'S END

THE FINAL BELL RINGS. IT FEELS LIKE THE
governor calling with a stay of execution. Thanks to the rotating schedule, my last class of the day is English, and the teacher has droned on
about the tragedy of King Lear for the past hour. It's beyond boring. My
tastes run more to Hamlet.

I dump my books into my backpack and stand up to leave. I want
to run out of the classroom, pushing people aside until the doorway
is clear. It has been a few days since I handed down Hank Meacham's
sentence, and I still feel stable, but I hate waiting for the herd of exiting
students to thin. Too bad the Cory everyone knows here—the one who's
fitting in surprisingly well—would never shove, so I smile and politely

wait for people to file by until I can squeeze out the door.

"Cory. Hey, Cory!" Reluctantly I stop and turn around. Adam hurries down the hallway, not exactly a run but definitely faster than could be considered cool. I give him a smile.

"Hey there, hon. What's up?"

His cheeks pinken at the casual endearment, and he clears his throat. "Uh, nothing. Where're you headed?"

I roll my eyes. "Home. My parents are being totally crazy about unpacking. My mom said it's slovenly to live out of boxes, so it's only school and home until everything's moved in." The lie rolls off my tongue easily. As far as the school knows, I live with my mom and her boyfriend. It's easy to pay someone to register you for school, especially if they're so drunk that they don't remember you a week later.

I head toward my locker, thinking that's the end of the conversation, but Adam trots along beside me. "Well, you can at least come with us to grab some pizza, right? It's right down the road. You could just tell them you had to stay after school or something. It would really make Mindi happy." I've been at West County High for less than a week. Why would she care that much?

I'm about to make another excuse, when Niko heads down the hall toward us. He walks with Mindi, and she's chattering on about something, her hands gesturing wildly. Niko looks like he's mentally counting sheep, his expression detached. They see me looking at them, and Mindi waves in excitement. Niko's gaze is coolly assessing, a degree away from arctic.

I elbow Adam as they approach. "What's the deal with Mindi and Niko? They dating?"

Adam's jaw goes slack at my direct question, and I wonder if I've broken some unspoken rule. Just when I think he won't answer the question, he shrugs. "No, they're just friends. They've known each other since they were little." He studies his shoes, and refuses to meet my gaze, and I know I stepped over some boundary. I squeeze his arm in apology, and he rewards me with a smile.

"Sorry if I'm being too nosy. Don't want to look stupid, you know?"

He nods, and I know we're good again. Crisis averted.

Mindi bounces up. "Cory! Tell me you're coming with us."

Adam nods, his brown curls shaking. He looks a little panicked, his eyes flicking from me to Mindi and back. He glances at her like he's afraid she might start foaming at the mouth. "Come on. You don't want to miss this," Adam says.

I shrug and direct my question to Niko, who has yet to say a word. "It's pizza. What's the big deal?"

Amber, the bleached blonde who basically spends all of her time pointedly ignoring me, walks up. "The big deal is that it's the best pizza in town. They're only open Thursday through Sunday. So every Thursday we go there right after school to eat." She looks at Mindi in disgust before turning back to me. "But I guess you wouldn't know that, would you, Dixie?"

Everyone shifts from foot to foot, waiting for my response. The venom is completely unexpected, since she has spent the last few days pretending I don't even exist. A thirst for violence tears through my earlier tranquility, and I want to rip off Amber's arm and stuff it down her throat. But that's all me, not Them, and I push the urge aside.

Instead I smile and shrug, like the nickname doesn't bother me. "Sounds like fun, but I really shouldn't. All this cold weather makes me want to eat all the time. You saw that chocolate cake the other day, right? I don't want to get fat." I look at Amber as I say it. I'm going for a shared joke, but she flushes scarlet, and I realize Amber took it as an insult instead of a friendly overture.

Before I can stammer out an apology, Mindi giggles nervously. "Cory, you're nowhere near fat," she exclaims, clearly trying to diffuse the suddenly frosty situation. "You can at least have a slice. Come on. It'll be my treat." She sounds a little desperate, like if I don't go, she'll burst into tears. Adam shoves his hands into his pockets and looks away, while Amber's nostrils flare and her jaw tightens. Niko's expression is pained, but he carefully schools his face into a neutral expression when he catches me looking at him.

What is going on here?

I smile and shrug, unsure. I want to go, despite all of the weirdness. I've always loved hanging out with friends. The group I hung out with in Charlotte was the best. They were silly, always going out to do the stupidest things. We even went roller-skating once. It was a lot of fun.

Now I can't even remember their names.

We have the guilty to destroy.

I rub my forehead at Their interruption. I've been doing well the last couple of days, no commentary from the peanut gallery. I can't believe They're back already. I was actually starting to enjoy the silence.

Niko watches me, as though he can hear my mental argument. His open appraisal reminds me of Dr. Goodhart, and a small spike of fear shoots through me. I shush Them. "Okay, sure."

Tom and Jocelyn walk up, holding hands. They date "off and on," and according to Mindi they're currently in one of their "on" phases. I like Tom. He's one of the few guys They're quiet around, so I figure he's really as nice as he seems.

After a quick conversation and another set of concerned looks in Mindi's direction, Tom and Jocelyn decide to come with us as well.

We walk out of the school and figure out rides. Like me, Niko and Jocelyn have their own cars. Mindi quickly volunteers to ride with Niko, and Tom says he'll ride with Jocelyn.

"I'll ride with you, Cory," Adam volunteers. "You know, so you don't get lonely." He gives me one of his puppy smiles, and all I want to do is pat him on the head.

Amber snorts. "It's less than a mile. Like she's really going to get lonely in that distance."

I grin at Adam as his ears redden. "I might get lost, though. I have a terrible sense of direction. It's a good thing I'm great at U-turns. Otherwise I'd be in Antarctica by now."

Adam laughs even though the joke's lame. Amber rolls her eyes. "Antarctica? I wish," she mutters, and I watch her follow Niko and Mindi to Niko's Jeep.

I'm not entirely in love with her attitude, and sooner or later I'll do something about it. But not today. Today I just want to have fun.

Adam and I climb into my car and head over to the pizza shop. He gives me directions, even though it's just a right turn out of the school parking lot and down the road. When we arrive, cars choke the unlined gravel parking lot. I find a small space between two trucks and pull in. There is barely enough room to open our doors, and it's the only space left. Apparently West County High takes pizza very seriously.

Inside, Niko, Mindi, Jocelyn, Tom, and Amber are already at a table, but there's only one extra chair. For a second I think Amber planned it that way, but then I see that there isn't an empty table in the entire place. They were probably lucky to grab the table they did.

Adam looks at the single chair forlornly. I put a comforting hand on his arm. "Don't worry. I'll go find a chair. Go ahead and sit down." He opens his mouth to protest and then closes it. When I turn toward the back of the restaurant, I understand why. The only empty chairs are at a table occupied by several large and intimidating guys. I walk over, adding a little extra swing to my hips. I place my hand on the back of an empty chair and clear my throat. "Excuse me. Can I borrow this?"

All conversation at the table stops, and five sets of eyes turn to me. The nearest guy looks me up and down before shooting me a grin. He's cute, in an arrogant-jock sort of way. Dark hair, dark eyes, pale skin. There's something about him I don't like, though. "Why don't you just ditch the losers and sit down with us? I'm sure we could entertain you." He says the last part in a tone of voice that earns him a chorus of knowing chuckles and high fives.

Ah, that's what it is. He's setting off my internal douche bag alarm.

My face heats, but I manage to keep the smile frozen on my face.

Like a dork I stick out my hand to shake. "I'm sorry. I don't think we've met. I'm Corinne Graff."

He grabs me by the wrist and pulls me forward, turning me around at the last second so that I'm sitting on his lap. Every muscle in my body stiffens. Dear God, he's touching me.

"Dylan. Dylan Larchmont," he whispers into my ear. I try to get away, and his hands snake around my waist. The additional contact sets off more alarms in my head. Slowly They rouse with whispers of what he would like to do to me, and the image makes bile burn the back of my throat. They urge me to cause him pain. I swallow thickly. If I don't maintain control on Them, this fun little outing could turn into a massacre of XY chromosomes.

Dylan laughs, oblivious to my dark thoughts. "See, you don't need to sit with those losers. I have a seat for you right here." He pats my thigh reassuringly.

I try to stand again, but he holds on tight. Dylan is pissing me off. His hands skim places that are definitely off-limits. All I can think of is escape, and I fight to stay calm so They don't fully wake. Panic steals my breath, and I have to forcibly remind myself that I'm not in any real danger. He's just a bully, not a criminal. I squirm around until I can stare into in his muddy brown eyes. "Let me go," I mutter.

He laughs. "Make me." His friends whoop, and a couple offer helpful suggestions as to what Dylan should do with me. I swallow dryly and ignore them. I'm no match for Dylan's strength, but I know who is. I give in to Their sleepy murmurs and relax my hold on Them a little.

The noise of the restaurant fades away as I stare into Dylan's eyes.

JUSTINA IRELAND

His gaze is locked onto mine, and it takes only a couple of seconds before I can feel the shift in his behavior. His smirk fades. A couple of heartbeats more and he jerks in surprise, then squirms in his seat. His breathing quickens and he tenses like a rabbit sensing danger, eyes widening. They can sense his fear, and now They are anxious for release, hungry for a taste of pain. My head pounds and I'm certain he can see Them swirling around in the depths of my eyes. A slight smile curves my lips. There is nothing friendly about it.

"Let. Me. Go." The sound is something more than human.

Dylan releases me so suddenly that I fall backward off his lap. I catch myself and stand, straightening my sweater over my jeans. He's staring at me now like I might sprout another head.

I take a deep breath and force Them back down into the dark part of my consciousness. They aren't happy about being denied Their fun, and I promise to make it up to Them. Dylan's friends groan when I grab the plastic chair. I heft it while shooting the table a dazzling smile. "Thank you, boys." There are a couple of catcalls and lewd suggestions, but Dylan says nothing as I take the chair back to my table. His gaze burns a hole into my back.

I set the chair down next to Adam's and sit down. I still shake a little, so I sit on my hands and lean forward, forcing a grin. Mindi, Jocelyn, Tom, and Adam stare at me in wide-eyed shock, while Amber's lips twist with disgust. The only person I can't read is Niko. His expression is, as usual, indecipherable.

Tom reaches across the table to give me a fist bump. "All right! I can't believe you entered the den of the jock and lived to tell about it."

Adam shakes his head. "Me either." He looks miserable, as though he's just now realizing how weak his hesitation made him look.

I shrug. "No worries. I just had to ask him nicely."

Amber snorts. "Yeah, we saw how nicely you asked him." The glare she sends in my direction makes me push Them further into the back of my mind. They aren't happy, and They do the mental equivalent of snarling and snapping at being denied some fun. They don't even care that she's not male. They just don't like her. I shut Them in the back of my mind, throwing a mental dead bolt on the door that keeps them from ruling me completely. I'm still the one in control.

Mindi makes a choked sound at Amber's comment, but I shoot my would-be tormentor a wide smile. "Oh, that? He was just being neighborly. No big deal."

The corner of Amber's mouth twists down. "You practically gave him a lap dance."

Jocelyn laughs a little too loudly. "Amber, weren't you the one who told me that if you had fifteen minutes alone with Dylan, you'd make him scream your name?"

Amber's eyes shoot daggers at Jocelyn, who isn't even paying attention. Instead she's busy studying the menu. She has the right idea. After relaxing and then tightening my hold on Them, hunger gnaws at my belly. I don't really want to eat, but I hope food will ease some of the ache.

"So, what's good here?" Scooting my chair closer to Adam's, I reach for one of the menus in the middle of the table. It takes everything I have not to scoot away to where no one can reach me, to run back to my apartment and hide out. But I don't. I can't. I have to live in the real world just as much as in Their world, and this is part of that.

I will be normal, no matter what They ask of me.

Relief washes over me when Adam gives me a shy smile. It's hard to believe that I'm actually fitting in. I'm only half-listening as he starts to walk me through the menu. Instead I wonder whether or not Niko would have made me get my own chair.

THE GIRL YOU THINK YOU KNOW

SATURDAY IS A RELIEF, A DAY WITHOUT THE strain of school. The morning dawns cloudy and cold, and the weather forecast calls for six inches of snow. I'm not sure whether that's a lot or not, but it's enough to make me want to stay inside.

I decide to spend the day working out, beginning with a set of plyometrics exercises I find online. It's time for me to change my workout, since I've obviously plateaued. I'd thought I was pretty strong until the run-in with steroid-soaked Dylan Larchmont on Thursday. Now I feel inadequate.

So I pass the morning jumping over my coffee table and doing push-ups that launch my upper body off of the ground. My downstairs neighbor yells at me through the ceiling, but I ignore his complaints. Eventually he settles down. After an hour I'm soaked with sweat, and I decide it's time for a break.

I bound into the kitchen and grab a bottle of water. My cell phone is on the counter, and the screen blinks at me, indicating that I have a message.

It's from Mindi, who is surprisingly clingy. She came over last night and we hung out, watching bad TV and eating junk food. I think she wanted me to ask her to spend the night, but instead I made some excuse about my mom not liking me having company. Mindi probably thinks my imaginary mom is some kind of trashy barfly. She saw a couple of the slinky tops I use for hunting, and I said they were my mom's. Her expression was relieved. I could almost read her thoughts: *Cory is a good girl. No way she'd wear such an outfit.*

Reluctantly Mindi called her dad and went home. By that time it was almost midnight. Even though she left, my evening was spoiled. I'd planned on looking for Dr. Goodhart like I do every Friday, but Mindi's presence completely ruined that. I could have asked her to go home earlier, but every time I say something she doesn't like, she gets this scared little mouse face. The look crumbles my resolve like stale crackers.

So I ended up hanging out with her until way later than I wanted. Still, it was kind of fun. I like her, even if she does seem awfully fragile.

But now I need to comb through the Internet to see if Dr. Goodhart has turned up somewhere. He left shortly after Annie and I escaped, most likely for fear that we'd tell everyone what kind of monster he was. The Furies can't find him, and I wonder if it's because we had our chance with him once before and blew it. I'm not worried, though. The Internet is a powerful tool. He can't hide forever. And when he pops up, we'll be there to end his evil once and for all.

I push my anger aside and flip through screens to Mindi's text. It's from only a few minutes ago. What are u doing 2nite? The text asks. Why? I text back. I hope she doesn't want to go to the mall or something. Malls sort of terrify me. Crowds make Them go crazy, and it can be hard to rein Them in.

Mindi's message comes back within seconds. Party? 9ish? She must have been watching her phone for my answer. Before I can reply, she sends another text. Amber wont be there, shes at her dads. I don't want to admit it, but that text fills me with relief. I'm not sure why Amber doesn't like me, but the way she watches me makes me nervous. It's easier to avoid her than do anything else.

I hesitate before answering. A gathering of people in a small house fills me with unease. But there's no way I can not go. My social standing in the group is shaky, since I'm the new kid. Going to a party is the perfect way to show everyone that I'm cool, even though my palms are sweaty with fears of doing something completely inappropriate.

I quickly squash my doubts. It's a chance to hang out with people who like me. Actual, real friends, not the murderous voices that live in my head. Hell, with my fake IDs I can even buy liquor.

I send Mindi a text that I'll be there and that I'll call her later to talk.

I set the phone back on the counter and feed Odie, who comes running as soon as he hears the food hit the bowl. I scratch him while he eats, and mull over how quickly I've found friends. I don't always end up fitting in so well.

It reminds me of Dr. Goodhart, and the way he was so certain I'd never be able to form meaningful relationships as long as I was beset by Their presence. Shows what he knows. I can control Them and lead a normal life.

Find him. We need to find him and end his evil.

I sigh and head to my computer.

There's nothing new on the Internet, not even on government sites. This makes me unhappy, but I tamp down the emotion. There is a bright side to not knowing where he's hiding. The longer I can put off that particular justice, the more I can pretend that Brighter Day and Saint Dymphna's never happened.

And the more I can enjoy my new life.

After a long run—despite the snowflakes—and a shower, I get dressed. It's a little after noon, and I decide to eat lunch before heading to the library.

It's a little old-fashioned of me, but everywhere I end up, I go to see if the library has anything different on the Furies. I know what the Internet has, and it's not what I'm looking for. But libraries are different wherever you go, and I can't help but hope that one of them will hold the missing piece to give me back my life. For a long time I was convinced that if I just learned enough, I could get rid of Them, beat

Them at Their own game. But in all the places I've looked, I've never been able to find much more on Them than a couple of ancient poems and hints about Their nature. It's almost like people are afraid to even mention Them.

The idea of going to the library fills me with excitement and a little fear. If They knew what I was searching for, They'd be angry. But if I don't look for a cure for Their possession, then I'm giving up, and I hate to think that the answer could be out there just waiting for me. So I keep searching, and keep coming up empty.

But I'm still hopeful.

I grab a sandwich and settle onto the couch, feet propped up on the coffee table. I spend the next hour watching MTV. The people on the endless buffet of reality drama are confident and self-assured, and that fascinates me. I feel that way only when I'm handing down justice.

I eat my food without thinking, and when the program goes to its sixth commercial break, I head into the kitchen to get water.

On the refrigerator a news clipping flutters in a nonexistent breeze, Their way of getting my attention. I pull it off the door with a sigh. My blood chills as I read the headline.

WEST CHESTER GIRL, 12, MISSING; POLICE HAVE NO LEADS

I swallow thickly, my hands shaking. The article is several years old, but I know it by heart. They manifest it whenever They feel I need a reminder of how much I owe Them.

I blink back tears, and crumple the news article in my hand. "I haven't forgotten why I'm here," I whisper out loud. This is a gentle reminder from Them, Their way of telling me They know something is up. A warning not to betray Them. I still owe Them so much.

I start to throw the article into the trash can, but instead I put it on a living room shelf under a figurine of a dark-haired girl reading the Bible. The memory is fuzzy, like all of my memories before They came to me, but I think my dad and I bought my mom the little statue for her birthday. When I went back to my grandma's house after escaping Saint Dymphna's, I found the figurine in my untouched room along with my trunk. Now it's one of the only mementos I have.

I check my reflection in the mirror, studying my eyes for any telltale movement. The blue iris is calm and undisturbed, despite my emotional state. It's surprising, but a good thing. I have enough to worry about right now.

It takes me only a second to grab my schoolbag and make my way out of the apartment and to the library. "Schoolwork," I say aloud as I head to my car. "I need to do some schoolwork."

They may not believe me, but as long as They haven't manifested, I can lie to Them. It seems so silly, but the tiny shred of hope that one day I can be normal again is all I have.

I won't let Them have the satisfaction of squashing it.

VENDING MACHINE ROMEO

THE LIBRARY IS A RELIEF. NO MATTER HOW many places I go, no matter how many times I start over again, the library is always a familiar landscape. Books, computers, tables. The layout may be different and the librarians will range from friendly to downright evil, but there's something reassuring about the musty scent of old books.

I am sitting at one of the study tables in the back of the library with a reference book when I sense someone's approach. I'm assaulted by cologne, a scent somewhere between cat musk and a pine tree. It's so strong that it almost knocks me over. I swallow my nausea.

When I look up, my breath catches in my throat. "Dylan."

Dylan Larchmont grins at me in a way that leaves no doubt that he's mentally undressing me. "Cory. Good to see you again."

My smile freezes in place. Funny, I was thinking just the opposite. I close the book I was leafing through and stand, grabbing for my bag. Dylan moves around the table, incredibly fast, and jerks my bag out of my hand. His smile is playful. "Hey, where are you going?"

"Away," I snap, taking back my bag and slinging it over my shoulder. I don't like him, and all I want to do right now is punch him in his grinning face. I'm not sure why he doesn't get the point. Especially since he had to have seen Them at the pizza place. Does he think it was just a trick of the light?

"Why don't you come over here and help me study. You look like a smart girl, and if you help me, I might be willing to help you." He sits down in the seat I just vacated, and I pause in surprise at his offer.

"Help me? How could you help me?"

He laughs softly and flips through the book I was looking at, *The Library of Greek Mythology*. "Well, you're obviously new and have no idea that you could do better when it comes to friends." He pauses on some picture that captures his interest, and I cross my arms. His cologne is making my eyes water, but I want to know what he's talking about.

"Better, huh? Like you and your muscle-head buddies?"

He isn't fazed by the insult. Instead he smiles even wider. "I saw you hanging around with the mental patient and her white trash entourage, and it seems to me I could introduce you to a better class of people."

I tense at the way he says "mental patient," like it's something dirty. But I am curious. Who in my new group of friends could have needed professional help? Amber, with her narrowed eyes and assessing glares? Or maybe Jocelyn, who always has a bit of gossip to pass on?

But then I remember Mindi's expression when I asked her if she needed a ride home last night. Ah, Mindi. How did I not realize that she might've once been broken? She's so fragile, it wouldn't be a surprise that she may have needed a little extra help.

But it's nothing to be ashamed of, and Dylan's comment just makes me despise him even more. He still watches me with an arrogant smirk, and I'm suddenly not interested in anything else he has to say. More importantly, if I spend another few minutes in his presence I'm going to lose it, and flipping out in a library is probably not a good idea.

I turn around and leave without another word, heading toward the nearest exit, which spits me out onto a staircase. In the back of my mind I can feel Them beginning to stir, which is something I don't need. They're groggy and slow but definitely waking. If They wake fully, I'll have to hunt. That means I won't be able to go to the party with Mindi tonight. The longer They slumber, the more I can live my life.

I really want Them to keep sleeping.

The library, like my apartment, is in a remodeled mansion. Each floor is another section—children's, nonfiction, reference. At some point I realize that the staircase I'm on isn't leading outside, especially when I hit the bottom floor and the double doors have a sign that reads RESTROOMS AND VENDING. I look upstairs, wondering if I should back-track. Up above, a door opens, and I have a flash of fear that it might be Dylan following me. Losing control would be very bad, so hiding is the best thing to do right now. I duck through the double doors and down a short side hall into the ladies' restroom.

I camp out in the handicapped stall for what feels like forever. My stomach is tied up in anxious knots, but part of me wonders how poor Mindi ended up in a clinic. It's not really that hard to end up getting committed. The first place I went to, Brighter Day, had different kinds of patients: eating disorders, attempted suicides, and everything in between. So I'm not that worried that she has a past. We all have secrets that we'd like to keep hidden.

I just wonder if it's something I can help her with. It wouldn't be the first time They took care of a friend's relative who crossed the line. And it's nice when I feel like I'm helping someone.

I wash my hands and study my reflection in the mirror, noting the stillness of my irises. Good. It doesn't look like my irritation with Dylan woke Them fully. That gives me a little time before I have to go hunting again.

I push out of the bathroom doors, heading left instead of back, the way I came in. I'm still hoping to find an exit down here. I end up in a vending area, soda machines and a snack machine lining one wall. I'm pulled to the candy machine, even though I don't really need anything. It's hard to resist the siren song of chocolate and caramel.

"Took you long enough." Dylan sits at a table in a back corner, still wearing that same arrogant smile, and I tense. A flash of memory assaults me, making my heart race. His face is momentarily replaced by an older man's with sandy hair, blue eyes twinkling like they knew every secret the universe had to offer.

I push the mental image away and take a deep breath.

"What are you doing here?"

"Waiting for you. I wanted to apologize." This isn't something I expect from a guy like Dylan. Deep down I know I should run, but I can't help but think maybe I was wrong about him. Maybe my snap judgment was a mistake. So I wait, a doe in the crosshairs of a hunter's rifle.

"Oh?"

"Yeah. I think we got off on the wrong foot." He stands and moves toward me. I try to back up, but after only a couple of steps, I'm up against the vending machine.

"Okay," I say uncertainly. A breath of heated air warms me suddenly. I look up for the source, expecting to see a vent overhead. But there's nothing. Dylan's words are blotted out by a rasping sound, scales sliding through the grass. There's the briefest sensation of feathers tickling my cheek before I realize what's happening.

The Furies are waking.

I have the mental image of my hand whipping out to crush Dylan's windpipe. I see the way he'll gurgle as he breathes out his last few breaths. I swallow dryly, because the thought isn't my own. I try to calm down, to quiet the fear making my palms slick and my stomach sour, but They're waking so quickly that it's just making me more afraid.

Dylan is saying something about friendship and getting to know people, but I can't focus on a single word he says. My heart pounds, and all I can think of is how he isn't the first guy not to take no for an answer. I remember how Kevin Eames looked lying on the ornamental pavers of my grandmother's garden. All because he decided to kiss me. The police thought he had run into our yard chasing a prowler, who'd ended up getting the better of him. Kevin couldn't remember anything when he regained consciousness a month later.

Even as the guilt from Kevin's assault floods through me, I'm thinking how much fun it would be to hurt Dylan, to punch him in the mouth, maybe claw at his face. Behind my eyes They writhe with glee. I take several deep breaths and focus, pushing Them back to where Their bloodthirsty whispers are quieter. My vision hasn't split into three, the sure sign that They've manifested, but I'm hanging on by a thread.

We don't have to kill him. How about a little pain, hmm? We can just break his arm. Megaera's voice is so matter-of-fact that she could be talking about what she had for lunch.

Come on, Amelie. We'll fix him up as good as new after we've had a little fun. Tisiphone's whisper trails off into a high-pitched giggle.

I focus on my breathing, mentally steering Them back into the cage of my mind with the force of my will. While I'm doing that, I turn around and pretend to peruse the selections in the vending machine. The Furies strain and fight, not ready to so easily take up residence back in my subconscious. I count backward from twenty, pushing them back with concentration and some serious mental effort. After a few seconds of resistance, They retreat back into my subconscious, and I slam shut the barrier that keeps Them away. They howl in frustration, and I sweat from the effort.

"So, what do you think?"

I turn around. Dylan is even closer than before. I blink and try to put his question into some sort of context. "Think?"

Dylan smiles slowly and looks at me through lowered lashes. He has me trapped, back against the vending machine. Only a few scant inches separate us, and cold dread uncoils in my belly.

"Yes, think. What do you think about letting me take you out some-time? Like, say, tonight."

I put my shaking hands to my heated face, and blink rapidly. "I don't think that's such a hot idea."

"I think you're just not understanding your options." Dylan's cologne wraps around me like a winter scarf too tightly wound, heavy and suffo-cating. The way he stares at me turns my stomach. The Furies helpfully supply a mental image of the way he hopes this will play out, a scenario so far-fetched, it belongs in a porno. I'm nauseous, and my back presses up against the glass of the candy machine. No escape.

He moves in for a kiss. I stiffen and turn away at the last second, so that his lips land awkwardly on the side of my mouth. Panic swells in my chest, and I swallow it down. "Stop it." It comes out as something closer to a plea than a real threat.

"Don't worry. No one ever comes down here," he murmurs. Dylan has no idea of the danger he's in. He doesn't take the hint and instead leaves a trail of kisses across my cheek, moving toward my mouth. Inside I'm screaming in fear and disgust. I'm sure it's supposed to be sexy, but all it does is fill me with dark emotions. I don't like being touched, and right now all sorts of alarms are going off in my head.

It looks like Dylan is about to be a victim of his own overconfidence.

My fingers curl into fists, and I'm about to pummel him into hamburger, when someone clears their throat loudly from across the room. Dylan slowly steps back. Niko stands in the doorway. I can't believe my luck. Does everyone in this town hang out at the library?

As he takes in the scene before him, Niko's expression changes from surprise to distaste. "Sorry to interrupt."

I take a deep, shuddering breath and release it. My relief is so strong that I'm light-headed.

"You aren't interrupting anything." I duck under Dylan's arm and move toward Niko, my legs weak from the rush of adrenaline. The Furies beat at the barrier in my brain, sensing that They just lost out on some fun. I close my eyes and take a moment to steady myself before continuing. "Dylan doesn't seem to understand the meaning of the word 'no,'" I mutter.

Niko stares at Dylan, a muscle in his jaw twitching. "So I've heard," he murmurs.

Dylan, sensing a shift in the atmosphere, raises his hands in surrender and backs past us toward the door. "Hey, I just came down here for a soda. Calculus makes me thirsty." We step out of the way so he can leave, and before he goes through the door, he gives me a wink.

"I can't believe that guy," I whisper when Dylan's gone. I can't believe I fell for his nice-guy act, especially since I know what kind of jerk he is. I should've let him have it as soon as I realized he'd followed me down here. Why did I even bother giving him the benefit of the doubt?

Niko pats me awkwardly on the shoulder. "Yeah, well, be careful.

Especially where he's concerned." Niko goes to the soda machine, puts in a few coins, and pulls out a can. He pops it open and looks at me over the rim of the can. "Did you need something?"

I'm staring. I flush in embarrassment and shake my head. "Uh, no, just . . . thanks. You saved me from a really bad situation there."

Niko leans against the machine and drinks his soda. "You really should watch yourself around him. He has a reputation. And it's not one a girl like you would like to experience firsthand."

"What do you mean by that?" I tilt my head to the side and study him. Now that he knows I'm watching him, I might as well enjoy the view. He wears a sweater and jeans with a pair of scuffed work boots, and looks good enough to eat. The knit material clings to his chest and arms, revealing that he makes his share of visits to the school gym. For a desperate moment I wish it had been him who'd followed me down here, and not Dylan. I don't think I would push him away if he tried to kiss me with those perfect lips.

Niko grins at me, and my heart does a little kick drumbeat. In the back of my mind They are curiously silent. "You think I don't know your type? You're a good girl. You study on a Saturday afternoon, you say 'please' and 'thank you' and 'pardon me,' and you have no idea what to do when a guy like Dylan doesn't take 'no' for an answer."

I laugh out loud. The statement is so ridiculous that I don't even know what to say. I walk toward him, each footstep slow and deliberate. He pauses with his soda halfway to his mouth when I stop, mere inches away. "Is that actually how you see me?" I say, my voice low.

"Yes. Isn't that what you want people to see?"

His statement cuts me to the quick, because he's right. That is the image I'm trying to project. But it hurts, because I thought Niko was different. For some reason I thought he knew the real me, not the show I put on for everyone.

But now that I think about it, why would he be any different from everybody else? There's nothing all that special about him, no matter how much I may be obsessing over those gray-blue eyes.

Still, I want him to know me. The real me. I think I could drop the charade for him.

I take a step back, shaking my head to clear away the silly thoughts. Nothing will ever happen between me and Niko. Nothing can happen. It's too dangerous.

Still, I can't help but tempt fate a little. "Miss Perfect, huh? If that's how you see me, then you don't really see me at all," I say. My voice is heavy with regret. He'll never know the real me.

A flash of something flickers across his expression, and I freeze. It's too much. I've revealed more of myself than I should.

Before he can respond, I flee.

I'm out the door and up the stairs before I make a bigger fool of myself. Maybe it's because I'm feeling grateful for his timely intervention, or maybe it's the way he makes me feel more alive, but I want to tell him my deepest, darkest secrets. And that can't be a good thing.

I find my way out of the library and to my car, and drive home in a daze. There's too much on my mind. First there's my fascination with Niko, which is starting to feel like something a little more. He's no better-looking than boys I've met at other schools. So why do I feel like there's something between us, some connection that I have to explore?

But my reaction to Niko isn't half as worrisome as Their increasingly violent behavior. There's no way I should've been so close to losing control in the library, and that potential lapse frightens me more than Dylan's unwanted kisses and my response to Niko. My control is so thin these days that I have no idea what'll happen if I lose it on an innocent.

Today's lapse makes me wonder if one day They'll have full control of me, and not just the little bit I allow Them now and then. They need me to exist in the mortal world. That's what They get out of the possession. I'm Their tie to the guilty They crave. Without me They would be trapped in the other realm like Alekto, in the land that's the final resting place of the long-dead god who created Them.

But now I wonder if They'll somehow take me over completely, instead of just killing me by inches. I push the thought away. Now is not the time to worry about it. I have to believe that as long as I let Them have what They want every now and then, I can still have a life, or at least some semblance of one.

But I still can't help but worry that something of Their personalities is seeping into mine, like french fry grease leaking through a fast-food bag. Are They slowly remaking me into Their image, the way They changed my hair and eyes to be more like Alekto's? And if so, what happens when They decide They're finished?

I don't want to think about becoming any more like Them than I already am. So I don't. I shove the thought aside more easily than I pushed Them back into the dark reaches of my brain. Instead of dwelling on my fears, I think about what I'm going to wear to the party tonight.

PARTY MONSTER

I AM MORE POPULAR THAN I EVER COULD have hoped.

From the minute Mindi and I set foot in Tina Faber's house, we are bombarded with people coming over to say hi. Part of my popularity is because of the four bottles of liquor I bring. Mindi called me in a panic right as I was putting the finishing touches on my makeup, saying she needed liquor and a ride. I happily provided both. I went into the state-run liquor store, flashed my fake ID, and grabbed a few of the biggest, most expensive bottles, none of which meant anything to me but just looked cool. Thanks to Hank Meacham, a good portion of West County High will be drunk tonight.

When we walk in, the sight of the booze elicits a kind of awed hush.

One pimply-faced guy wearing a creative interpretation of a beard rushes over. The facial hair barely covers his chin, it's so sparse. "Holy shit. Is that a bottle of Grey Goose? And Patrón? You brought Patrón?"

"Here," I say, thrusting the bottles at him. "They're yours."

"Not so fast," Adam interrupts. He appears from the crowd and gives me a smile before he takes the bottle of tequila from me and hands the enormous bottle of vodka to the guy. "Now get lost, Werner."

The guy gives Adam a dirty look before grinning at me. "Thanks, Dixie." He disappears into the crowd before I have a chance to correct the nickname.

A girl with short dark hair and wide eyes appears. "Mindi, you made it."

Mindi smiles shyly and hugs the girl. "Do you know Cory?"

The girl nods at me without smiling. "Yeah. We have English together, and I heard Amber talking shit about you during Life Skills. Welcome to the club."

I smile. This must be Tina, the hostess. "Thanks. Here, I brought these." I take the two remaining bottles from Mindi and hand them to Tina.

She smiles at me for the first time. "Whoa, you brought Jäger. Nice. I'll take these and put them in the kitchen. Dylan should be here shortly. His brother is supposed to buy me a keg. But there's other stuff to drink until it gets here."

"Dylan?" I have a flash of anger at the mention of Dylan. I'm still pissed at myself for letting him get away with touching me earlier. After I got home, I started to wish I'd let him have it, even if retreat was the best course of action at the time. Guys like Dylan need to be taught a lesson.

Tina tilts her head slightly and studies me. "Yeah. Funny, he doesn't seem like your type."

"He's not. I'm just surprised. From the way he talks, this doesn't seem like his scene."

Tina rolls her eyes. "He's a douche. But West County is so small that we all end up at the same parties. Hell, half of the people here graduated last year. In case you haven't noticed, there's not much to do around here."

Mindi cranes her neck and searches the room, an odd little half smile on her face. "Where's Niko?"

Good question.

Tina gives Mindi a look before shrugging. "He said he might be by later. You know how he likes to hang around outside, anyway. He's not real big on parties. Unless you like freezing your ass off, you probably won't even see him." Tina looks long and hard at Mindi. An unspoken dialogue passes between them. "Are you sure you're okay?"

Mindi beams and nods. "Of course. We're just going to hang out for a while."

Tina gives Mindi one more inscrutable look before moving away to talk to someone else in the crowd. I glance at Mindi. She looks anxious, her eyes darting around the crowd as though she doesn't believe Tina. I turn a questioning look toward Adam, but he is very deliberately not making eye contact. He grabs my hand and pulls me along, and I give up trying to read the subtext of what just happened.

It's pretty obvious that Dylan was talking about Mindi earlier today with his "mental patient" comment. Did her problems stem from Niko? I'm suddenly imagining a total stalker situation, with Mindi hiding in the bushes of Niko's house as she draws hearts around his name in a journal.

I push the image away. Mindi might be delicate, but she's not crazy. She's just a normal girl.

Mindi, Adam, and I move deeper into the house. Most of the people at the party are girls. They eye me with a kind of predatory curiosity, like they're wondering which of the few guys present I'm going to try to take. I don't want any of them. What I want is to lose the guy with a death grip on my hand.

My luck with guys today is nonexistent.

Mindi takes me on a tour of Tina's house. As she's pointing out the bathroom, I smile and tilt my head to the side. "You really know your way around here." Evidently she's been here before, but I want to know in what context and how it may or may not connect to her stint in a mental facility. It bugs me that there's apparently some secret everyone knows but me. It makes me feel like a kid again, but not in a good way.

Mindi flushes a little and nods. "Tina is Niko's cousin." At my blank expression she elaborates. "Niko and I have been best friends since we were little. Our parents were always really close." Her tone clearly states that she would like more, but she doesn't elaborate.

I want her to keep talking, and the silence hangs, heavy and awkward, until I clear my throat. "Wow, so you're almost like family."

Mindi's hands flutter around her head, and she nervously adjusts her ponytail. "Oh, no, um, not exactly." Brotherly love is not what she's looking for. "But Niko's really been there for me through some tough times, you know?" There's something she's leaving out, and I want to pry.

Unfortunately, I'm too polite to ask the questions on the tip of my tongue.

I nod. "It's important to have friends by your side." I drop the subject, and follow Mindi down the hall.

She leads us into the basement, where a bunch of people are playing a video game. As she greets a group of guys, Adam squeezes my hand and smiles. "I'm glad you're here."

"Uh, thanks?" I'm not sure what he means by that, but he seems disappointed by my answer. He lets go of my hand, and I sigh in relief, wiping the sweat off on my jeans. Adam takes the place of a guy playing fake drums. I watch him play for a few minutes before I decide that I'm bored.

Mindi tugs on my sleeve. "Let's go get a drink." I follow her back up the stairs and into the kitchen. Everyone in the house seems to be there, since a keg now sits in a giant red plastic bucket of ice between the stove and the fridge. People are attacking the thing like a pride of lions who've just taken down a wildebeest. I stand slightly outside the doorway while Mindi pushes her way in. People ignore her as she wedges through, pushing a couple of girls to the side. She is determined to get us beer. I couldn't care less.

The only thing I want to know is where I can find Niko. After the scene at the library, I have to see him. It's like itching a bug bite. The more you know you should ignore it, the harder it is to think about anything else.

"Do you think she'll make a scene like last time?" a horse-faced girl next to me whispers to an equally unfortunate girl whose hair looks like it lost a fight with a weed whacker. Ugly Hair Girl shrugs, and leans down to stage-whisper back to her friend.

"I heard she tried to commit suicide last time, you know, because her mom was killed and all."

Horse Face scrunches up her nose. "Really? I thought it was because she saw Niko kissing that Kristen girl. Either way, I kind of hope she loses it. This party is pretty lame so far."

I give the two girls a bitchy look, and they wisely decide to disappear into the crowd. I gnaw on my bottom lip and watch Mindi make her way toward the keg. People give her dirty looks as she pushes through, but no one stops her progress. She ignores them all. She's tougher than she seems.

I think about the conversation I just overheard. I hate that the answers I was looking for came from a couple of gossiping girls. If Mindi's the mental patient Dylan was talking about, then those two girls were telling the truth. At some point Mindi tried to take her own life.

For some reason that I don't understand, sadness weighs me down at the realization. Mindi is such a sweet person, it doesn't seem fair that she would endure something terrible enough to drive her to such a desperate decision.

Mindi fills two red plastic cups with beer and makes her way back.

She hands one to me with a wan smile. "People here are complete asshats."

I shrug. "People are asshats everywhere." Mindi drains her cup and goes back for more. I pour most of mine into a potted palm when I'm sure no one is looking. She returns with a full cup, and we walk into the living room. Jocelyn and Tom sit on the couch, and Jocelyn jumps up with a shriek when she sees us. "It's so great to see you guys!" She hugs us like she hasn't seen us in years, even though we saw her at school yesterday.

Mindi and Jocelyn and a few other girls in the room start talking about people I don't know. "Hey, I'm going to go pee," I tell Mindi, who is entranced by the gossip Jocelyn shares. I wonder how she would feel if she knew a few minutes ago she had been the topic of discussion. Either way, Mindi's occupied, so I wander off.

My instinct is to escape the crush of bodies that seem to press in on me from every direction. I just need some air. Okay, so I don't like crowds. It bothers me that Dr. Goodhart was right about that.

I squeeze past a couple making out in the doorway between the living room and the hall, and I frown, thinking of the doctor. As much as I don't want it to, it bothers me that I haven't been able to find a single mention of him. He's not the kind of guy to fall off the map. Dr. Goodhart likes the spotlight too much.

The worst thing is that we almost had him a second time in Charlotte, but They got sloppy. This was about eight months ago. A wife killer named Delbert Fitzhugh was Their target. I was so anxious to satisfy Their cries for blood that I gave him his judgment as soon as I found him, right in the gated community where he lived. When I was done, a security guard was waiting for me in Fitzhugh's driveway, sporting a smug grin and a gun pointed at my chest. I'd tripped a silent alarm in Fitzhugh's house, and there was no way to get away without severely injuring the security guard. I didn't kill the guard, but my description ended up on the evening news, along with a really bad sketch that made my nose look huge.

By the time we went after Dr. Goodhart, he'd fled once again, and the clinic where he'd been working had no forwarding address for him.

This is why I can't rush. Not again. Because now Goodhart knows I'm after him. And this time, I'm going to end it for good.

I continue retracing the steps from Mindi's earlier tour. The house is small and hot, despite the frigid weather outside. There isn't much to see, especially a second time, and from behind one of the closed bedroom doors come the distinct sounds of people having sex. Classy. The sound infuriates me for some reason, especially the overblown moans of the girl. Is that what guys really want? I turn around in disgust and make my way back to the living room. There are more people here than there were a few minutes ago, and I'm suffocating. Looking around for an escape, I spot a sliding glass door. I crack it open just far enough so I can squeak through and flee outside.

I slide the door closed as I look around the wooden deck. Snow covers it in thick drifts, but there are footprints where somebody else walked out this way. I'm not the only one who got tired of all the "fun."

Awareness prickles along my scalp, and there's movement out among the trees. Is that Niko? Tina said he doesn't like parties either, that he spends most of his time outside. For some reason I want to find him. I'm not sure why. He's off-limits, whether Mindi likes him or not. I don't want to put another innocent guy in the ICU. Still, the thought of him pulls me in the direction of the footprints.

Tall evergreen bushes hide the view beyond the deck, but there are wooden stairs leading off the back and down into the unfenced yard. The possibility that Niko is out there somewhere drives me toward the stairs. I don't think about the logic of my actions. I just go. I follow the footprints down and find myself in a snow-covered field. The sight stirs up a few memories better left buried. We had a similar field behind Brighter Day.

I'm not the enemy here, Amelie. I'm here to help.

Dr. Goodhart's voice comes to me across the years, as clear as it was the first time I heard it. I shake off the memory and continue to walk, the cold air prickling my skin and raising goose bumps under the sleeves of my sweater. The night is quiet, and the darkness relaxing. I learned to love the dark long ago, and now it's as soothing as a warm bath.

It's the light you have to fear.

"I knew you'd change your mind."

I turn around. Dylan wears something between a grin and a leer, his arms folded across his massive chest. If he isn't on steroids, then he has the best training plan in the world. I should ask him for some tips.

He moves closer, his feet sinking deep into the snow. I notice that the footsteps I followed curved around the house a ways back. In my distraction I must have walked right past them.

I haven't spoken, and Dylan has none of the wariness I would have expected after our last encounter. He moves closer. "Hello again. You weren't looking for me, were you?"

"No. I just wanted some fresh air."

Dylan smirks, and I desperately want to wipe the smile from his face. "Fresh air? Really? I don't buy it. I saw you looking for me as soon as I walked into the house."

For a moment I'm confused, and then it dawns on me. He mistook my interest in Niko's whereabouts as interest in him. Dylan's breath reeks of alcohol, and he sways a little on his feet. He's drunk, and I'm pretty sure, after this afternoon, that it's not safe to be around him. He's used to getting his way, no matter what.

The Furies begin to stir in the back of my mind, hissing warnings and portents. "Leave me alone," I mutter. Dylan's response is laughter. The laugh is what sets me off. I heard a laugh like that, full and self-assured, once before. And then my life ended.

Hi, sweetie. Need a ride?

I turn around and dash away from the house. Dylan curses and follows me. My legs sink into the snow, and make the normally easy strides difficult.

Suddenly I'm a kid again, running for my life, my heart pounding. Don't look back. Keep running! He won't catch me if I keep running.

The memory comes back to me, and the fear that gripped me then settles back into my stomach, cold and familiar. I pump my arms, but slogging through the snow makes me slow. Dylan has the advantage of height, and, just like Hank Meacham a few nights ago, just like Roland Thomas so long ago, he catches me with a laugh.

"Where do you think you're going?" Dylan asks. He spins me around in the snow, and then his hands close around my upper arms, hard enough to bruise. The fear is overwhelming now. It steals my breath and leaves my chest tight. I don't know what to do. The expression on his face shreds my ability to think clearly, the terror stunting my thought processes. My control is already thin because of his contact earlier today. It's all too much for me to bear. Before I can second-guess myself, I release my hold on Them.

Anticipation burns through me, and a wild joy follows in its wake. Their excitement is almost scarier than the glint in Dylan's eyes.

A laugh bubbles up from deep within my chest. Dylan has a split second to look confused before I clutch his forearms and jam my knee up into his crotch. He lets loose a whimper and releases his grip on me. I'm free, but it's not enough. He has to pay.

All of them have to pay.

Too late I realize that my vision has split into three. I try, but I can't reclaim my control over Them.

I fight to mentally restrain them, but it's like trying to catch fish with bare hands. They slip through my barriers, and we kick Dylan in the side, meeting muscle and eliciting a satisfying groan. He tries to get up, and when he is on all fours, we bring an elbow down onto his spine, like a professional wrestler. He groans, and Megaera punches him before we dance away, giving him a chance to get to his feet. Tisiphone jumps up and down in the rapidly melting snow, clapping in delight.

Stay down, I mentally beg as I struggle for control. It's a halfhearted plea. I'm enjoying this almost as much as They are.

Dylan gets up, a big dumb bear lumbering back for more punishment.

He squints, so he misses the way They grin at him. He's pissed now. "You stupid bitch. Now I'm gonna kick your ass."

We laugh, the sound deep and throaty. "Promises, promises," Tisiphone sings, her voice deeper, huskier than my normal speaking voice. We give Dylan an uppercut, and his head snaps back with the force of the contact. He has yet to throw a single punch. We follow with a jab that shatters his nose and paints the snow crimson. Dylan screams into the silent night. Tisiphone mocks his shriek with one of her own. The sound echoes off the nearby trees, and brings me back to myself.

Enough! I roar mentally.

Megaera has grabbed him by the hair, ready to slam his face into the ground. The sight of the blood on the snow gives me the strength to shove Them into the back of my mind and shut the door. They shimmer in the night air before fading away. Once back in my mind, They howl with frustration and claw at my mental barriers. Dylan may be an asshole, but killing people at parties will not make me popular.

I'll deal with you later, I hiss at Them, even though the threat is empty. There isn't much I can do but restrain Them in the back of my mind. Correction. There isn't much I want to do.

I go down on a knee next to Dylan. The pain of his beating has finally cut through his rage, and he writhes on the ground. I reach out a hand to him, and he shies away. I sigh. "Are you okay?"

"You broke my fucking nose!" He's blowing bloody snot bubbles and making these little moaning sounds like a wounded animal. I feel a little bit sorry for him.

But not that sorry.

"Look, in a few minutes people are going to come out to see what just happened. You have two choices. You can tell them I kicked your ass, or we can pretend it was someone else." Dylan doesn't seem to realize that I had some help, and I'm not going to enlighten him. I'm already shaking from my loss of control. The threat of discovery is the last thing I need.

Dylan calls me a word I would never repeat. I sigh again and grab him, my fingers sinking into the soft spots behind his jaw. He tries to pull away, and I force him to look at me. He swears again, and I tighten my grip until he stills.

"Listen. You can spend the rest of your high school career being the guy who got beat up by the tiny little blond girl, or you can be the guy who got jumped at a party. I suggest you think long and hard about which one you want to be."

Dylan doesn't answer. There's some commotion from the direction of the house, and I release him. He flops backward into the snow. "Think fast," I hiss. I clean my hands with snow and fight the queasiness that rises up at the sight of the blood. My secret shame, my inability to stomach the sight of blood. I can hand down justice to a herd of guilty men, but one little bloody nose and I swoon like a Southern belle.

People run up, exclaiming over the blood on the ground. I take a few steps back and let them get to Dylan's side. I recognize a few of the guys from his table in the pizza shop. They speak with Dylan in low tones. Mindi runs up next to me, her hair messed up and eyelids drooping. I frown at her appearance. She's trashed. "What happened?" she asks, the words heavy with alcohol.

I shrug, feeling the eyes of the other partygoers on me. "I dunno. I just found him like that. I think he said something about some guy jumping him."

Dylan curses, blinking. "My contacts are all fucked up, and I can't see shit. Help me up." One of his friends takes his outstretched hand, and Dylan uses it to lurch to his feet. I can't believe my luck. Thank God for corrective lenses.

A huge Asian guy steps forward from the jock huddle. "The assholes from the beer store did this. Who can give D a ride to the emergency room?"

Dylan fishes his contacts from the back of his eyes while the crowd watches in sick fascination. His face is a mess of blood, and in the moonlight he looks like a refugee from a UFC match. He's going to need to see a professional about that nose. He flicks the offending lenses onto the ground and spits out a stream of bloody saliva. "No way, dude," he says. "I'm coming with you to kick their ass." A few people clap and cheer, while a murmur goes up, wondering at these mysterious guys who drove out in the middle of the night to fight Dylan.

No one noticed the melted patches of snow. Now the ground is churned from people trying to figure out what is going on, the mud mixing with the drifted snow into a brown mush. I am once again anonymous.

I move back toward the house while Mindi talks to a redhead I don't know. The two girls I overheard gossiping in the kitchen talk animatedly, wide grins on their faces. I'm glad I could liven up the party for them.

There's movement near the bushes on the far side of the deck. I watch openmouthed as Niko walks over. My heart pounds. How long was he standing there?

He walks toward me, a knowing smile on his face. I wait for him to say something to me, but as he opens his mouth, Mindi squeals and runs up, wrapping him in a hug. Whatever he was about to say falls away in the wake of her overzealous greeting. But the appraising look in his eyes makes one thing clear.

He saw something.

The question is, how much? Because if he saw too much, Niko may be the next person on my list.

COMMITTED TO MEMORY

BY THE TIME WE LEAVE THE PARTY A FEW hours later, the snow is falling hard enough to make driving difficult, and it's way past Mindi's curfew. I reluctantly let her spend the night on my couch so she won't end up grounded until the end of time. She's too drunk to notice that she still has yet to meet my imaginary mother. When her dad comes to pick her up early the next morning for church, she hugs me hard enough to bruise my ribs.

"You're, like, the best friend I've ever had," she says, and I'm sure she's kidding, until she pulls away and I see the tears glimmering in her eyes. The show of emotion makes things awkward, but deep down it makes me feel kind of glad. I think Mindi could use a friend, and I'm happy to help.

The snow continues through Sunday, and West County Township gets more than two feet, breaking a twenty-five-year-old record. By Sunday night everything is covered in white, and school on Monday is canceled. Newscasters stand knee-deep in the drifts and declare the county in the middle of a snow emergency. No one goes anywhere.

The snow keeps even me housebound. The plows are slow in removing the snow, and my car is not really equipped to deal with the weather. The cable goes out sometime on Sunday, leaving me without Internet or television. Instead I'm stuck with nothing to do but think.

My mind inevitably turns back to one of my first sessions with Dr. Goodhart. I liked him immediately. He was only a few months out of school, an earnest sandy-haired guy in his midtwenties who really wanted to help. He wasn't like some of the other doctors, who had long since given up on saving anyone and just prescribed meds so they could collect a check, their eyes all but rolling as they pretended to listen. I felt like Dr. Goodhart lived up to his name. He listened to me when I told him about Them, about the ways They made me feel—or not feel. He asked me questions and laughed at my jokes. He gave me calming exercises I could do to maintain control, even though they never really worked. Still, I thought he tried. He made those first few months at Brighter Day tolerable.

The Furies didn't like him, but that was pretty much expected.

Despite being unable to find fault with him at the time, there was always something about him that put me a little on edge. He always seemed a little too eager to talk about my hallucinations, like the only thing that was important was making sure They were quiet.

Like the day he saw me in the hallway. He approached me with a smile, his face seemingly open and friendly. Behind him followed a woman with a clipboard. She wasn't a nurse and I didn't recognize her, so I figured she was one of the clinical trials people. I'd been told during my intake interview that Brighter Day participated in a number of pharmaceutical trials so that they could offer patients the most cutting-edge treatment. It wasn't until later that I found out that the trials were mostly so the doctors could supplement their incomes. In my mind They were uneasy at his approach. "And how is my favorite patient doing today?" he asked.

He is dangerous! We do not like him.

He seeks money and fame, not your health.

I shrugged. "Fine."

"Are you still having trouble sleeping? Still hearing voices in your head?"

I nodded, afraid to say anything more. If he knew what They were saying about him, he wouldn't be happy. And for some reason I thought it was important to keep Dr. Goodhart happy. Because he was my ticket out of Brighter Day. One day he would have to sign my discharge paperwork. I needed him on my side.

Dr. Goodhart frowned. "Amelie, the dosage you're on is very high. Are you sure you're still experiencing audio-sensory hallucinations?"

I shrugged again, not looking him in the eyes. He leaned in close, grabbing my upper arm and squeezing until I flinched. "You aren't lying to me, are you?" he growled, his voice so low, I almost thought I imagined it. I shook my head, afraid of the hard set of his mouth. But all he did was release my arm and make some comment to the lady taking notes on a clipboard. She hadn't reacted at all during our conversation, so I figured I'd imagined the whole thing. After all, there was a very good chance that I was crazy.

That was when I realized that Dr. Goodhart didn't care about me or my problems. He cared only about himself.

That night there were two extra pills in my cup after dinner, one blue, one orange. I took them, and spent the next few days in a woozy haze. By the time my body adjusted to the dosage, They were oddly silent, the bruise on my upper arm had faded to a mustard color, and my parents were dead. While I was out of it, they'd skidded into an oncoming tractor-trailer. I didn't even get to go to their funeral.

I want my sword in Dr. Goodhart's chest so bad, I can taste it.

I blink away the sudden anger and take a deep breath. The last thing I need is Them waking up, anxious to hunt.

Once the Internet comes back on, I spend the rest of the day reading articles. I have no problem dealing with kidnappers, murderers, and rapists. What I really want to know is what guys like. You know, like if beating up a football player is considered hot.

Niko. Lately my thoughts always come back to him.

At the party he said hello to everyone and then made some excuse about getting to work and disappeared. Disappointment welled up inside me, and I felt like a kid robbed of Christmas. Before he left, he gave me one last, long look. That look seared my skin and turned my bones to jelly. It was a look that seemed to say, We'll talk later.

Or that's what I want it to have said. It could just as easily have been a look that said, You are a psycho. I'm not very good at deciphering long, meaningful looks.

Mostly I wonder how much he saw. Did he see Tisiphone and Megaera? I kind of doubt it. If he'd seen the Furies, he definitely wouldn't still be talking to me. More than likely he would've run the other way when he saw me.

The silly thing is that I'm relieved, not because it means my secret's safe but because I might still have a chance with him.

So I spend all of Sunday and most of Monday reading articles with titles like "Ten Surefire Signs That He's into You" and "How to Wow Him Without Trying." They give me absolutely no insight into what to do about Niko, but I do get some ideas about how to get rid of Adam from an article entitled "Just Friends: Drawing Clear Boundaries with Guys."

By Tuesday I'm even more confused about guys than I was before. I'm almost glad for the distraction of school.

ADMIT IT

WHEN I OPEN MY LOCKER ON MY WAY TO LUNCH,
a yellowed newspaper clipping falls out. I pick it up with excitement.
I'm not looking forward to killing a man, but the return to a familiar
ritual is comforting. Especially since I have a new BFF that I have no
idea what to do with.

All day Sunday and Monday, Mindi kept texting me, wanting to
rehash what a great party it was on Saturday. This morning she cor-
nered me in the hallway to ask if I wanted to go shopping or something
this weekend. Trapped, I stammered out something that I think was a
yes. The thought of going to a mall, with all those people pressing into
one another, makes me sick to my stomach.

Being normal is much harder than I thought it would be. Handing down justice to the guilty is so much easier.

It's been a week since I tried Hank Meacham, and I'm amazed at how patient They have been (not counting the lapse with Dylan). I usually can't go more than a week between justices. The exceptions are the years I spent in treatment, especially my stint at Saint Dymphna's. While I was there, They never woke, thanks to the heavy medication I was on. Not a strategy I want to try again.

On the way to the cafeteria, I study the article. The clipping is almost ten years old and discusses a truck driver named Alex Medina. Medina was arrested for the murder of several prostitutes who frequented the truck stops where he parked. He was supposed to go to trial, but he somehow managed to escape court. The article ends with speculation about whether Medina could have left the country, since he had family in Nicaragua. I shove the slip of paper into my jeans pocket with a smile.

Mr. Medina must be somewhere close. Otherwise They never would have brought me the article. They don't bring me just any target, only the ones They know we can punish. I owe Them after ruining their fun on Saturday. If I don't cooperate with Them now, things are only going to get worse.

I push through the double doors of the cafeteria with a smile. Dealing with Medina is just what I need to relieve my rapidly accumulating stress, not to mention Their rising bloodlust. I welcome the relief.

Mindi and the rest of the group are already at our table along the back wall. They look away guiltily when I walk up, except for Niko and

Amber. Niko glances at me with raised eyebrows. Amber wears a smirk. I plop down next to Adam and smile. He looks away, a blush creeping across his cheeks.

"Uh-oh. Were y'all talking about me? I feel like I interrupted something." I open my lunch bag and take out my hard-boiled eggs and a knife. I slice into the eggs a little too roughly.

Adam eyes my lunch and clears his throat. "Uh, it's nothing."

I chew the egg white thoughtfully. They aren't acting like it's nothing. "No, tell me. What's going on?"

"Amber says she saw you." Mindi whispers it so quietly, it takes a moment for me to realize she spoke.

For a moment I'm scared. Where did she see me? At the party, beating the shit out of Dylan? How much did she see? Did she see the Furies? Or just the beat-down? If she saw what I did, my cover's blown.

But then I remember that Amber wasn't at the party, and all of the tension drains away. I shrug. "Oh? Where?"

Amber snorts, and pushes away her slice of pizza. She almost vibrates with glee. "The library. Getting cozy with a special someone."

Everyone looks away, and I know what they think. I laugh. "Oh? Who? Stephen King?" I try to look sheepish. "I admit it. I'm a huge dork. I like to read."

"You weren't exactly reading with Dylan's tongue down your throat. How long did it take for him to get into your pants? A day?"

I level a look at Amber. Now I'm mad. I know what she saw, and that's not the kind of reputation I want for myself. But trying to convince her that what she saw was a prelude to a sexual assault would be useless. "I have no idea what you're talking about." I don't know if my denial of what she's saying will even matter. High school isn't about the truth. It's all about what people want to believe.

Amber leans forward and looks me dead in the eye. Her mouth twists like she just tasted something gross. "So, I just imagined that I saw you making out with Dylan in the vending area of the library?"

I return her unwavering gaze. "Honey, I don't know what you thought you saw. I was at the library on Saturday, but I definitely wasn't there with that meat head. I have standards, you know." If I can make her look stupid, she'll back off. Girls like her are the same everywhere.

"You're lying."

I throw my hands up into the air. "Fine, I'm lying. Don't you think I'd be over at Dylan's table if I was fucking him?" Everyone kind of winces at my tone, and I realize that righteous indignation is the way to play this. They don't want to think a nice girl like me would screw the school man-whore. I can use that to my advantage. "Amber, why would you even make up such a ridiculous story? I mean, really, Dylan Larchmont at the library? He's never even heard of the alphabet."

Niko watches the exchange with interest but doesn't say anything. I can't help but give him a little wink when no one else is looking.

Adam's brows knit together, and he nods. "You know, I can't really see Dylan at the library. Especially on a Saturday."

Tom laughs. "Yeah, I think he'd spend more time in the gym than a library. Books aren't heavy enough to bench-press." Everyone laughs, and in that instant I know I've won.

　　　　　　　　　　　JUSTINA IRELAND

Unless Niko says something. I look across the table at him. He's watching me with an amused look, and he smiles when his gaze meets mine. I don't know if that's a good sign or not.

Amber shakes with rage, her face almost purple with emotion. She looks from me to Adam. "I can't believe you think she's telling the truth. I know what I saw."

I shrug. "Maybe it was someone else."

"It was not someone else! It was you." She glares daggers at me, and I just give her a sweet smile.

"I'm really sorry, Amber, but it wasn't me. I was on the third floor studying all afternoon. I never even saw Dylan."

"You're a liar," she grinds out.

The table goes quiet at the open threat. It's one thing to pass on a rumor, another to openly pick a fight.

Mindi wheels on Amber. "What's wrong with you?"

Amber gapes in surprise at Mindi's tone. Meek, little mousy Mindi crosses her arms and glares at Amber. "And why are you being such a bitch lately? You wanted to dig up some dirt about Cory. Well, you were wrong. Now just drop it."

Amber blinks, and then gets up from the table and storms off. No one says anything for a few long minutes. Mindi's defense makes me feel odd, an emotion I can't identify. Happiness? Relief? I don't know what it is. I only know it warms me inside.

Conversation resumes, and I absentmindedly slice my hard-boiled egg. My mind is pondering what just happened and trying to place it into the context of what I know about interpersonal relationships. The knife slips and slices into the soft part of my palm. Blood wells up, scarlet and bright.

"Shit." I watch the blood slide across my hand. Time seems to stop as a single droplet slides over the edge of my palm and onto the table.

Blood. So much blood.

The memory swells, overtaking me. I'm twelve again, escaping through the kitchen. I slip and go down, flailing in the sticky mess on the floor. I'm covered in his blood. He can't hurt me anymore, but his death seeps into my skin and my memory, a permanent blemish. I get up, but it's too late. I'm stained in red. I know what we did, what I did. I can't undo it.

I can't take back my promise to Them.

"Hey, are you okay? Wow, you really cut yourself." Adam's voice brings me back from the memory, and I stare blankly at the rapidly spreading puddle on the lunch table. Mindi and Jocelyn both gasp in horror. Nausea rises, my aversion to blood making me light-headed. Only Niko is quick thinking enough to press a wad of napkins into my hand.

"Here, put pressure on it," he says in a low voice. I can't tear my gaze away from his hands cradling mine, fingers curled to keep the napkins in place. "Don't let Mr. Hanes find out you had a knife at school. He'll freak out about it."

I nod, struck mute by Niko's nearness. He smells like rain, fresh and sharp. It's so appealing that I find myself unconsciously leaning into him.

"Do you think you'll need stitches?" Mindi asks, crowding close. I shake my head. Already I can feel the heat of Them healing the wound. Injuries are never a problem when They're around.

The bell rings, and everyone except Niko gets up to leave. He still holds my hand, applying even pressure. It's a little bit embarrassing, mostly because Jocelyn and Tom are giving me knowing looks. Luckily, Mindi is oblivious, her worry over me preventing her from seeing that Niko has gone way past the point of friendly.

"Are you going to be okay?" Mindi watches me with brows knit together in concern. It makes me feel like dirt, since all I want is to be alone with Niko.

I toss my hair over my shoulder and grin. "This is nothing. Let me tell you, I have been hurt worse than this." The image of Trenton James, a violent pimp from Charleston, pops into my head, and my mouth goes dry. The last time I was seriously hurt was when I tried to hand down his justice. This was after I'd left Saint Dymphna's and was making my way across the South, looking for the doctor.

I found Trenton James in an alley behind a mini-mart. Only, when it came time to hand down his justice, a junkie appeared from behind a Dumpster, surprising both of us. She took one look at the Furies and screamed, until I knocked her out.

It was all the opportunity James needed. He shot me, and the bullet ripped through my chest. I lost control of Them and fell to the ground. They handed down Their own justice. The alley filled with heat as They burned away the diseased soul of the pimp. James's agonized screams echoed in my ears even after he was gone. Thankfully the addict had remained unconscious. I thought They would kill me and the junkie as well, but They just healed my sucking chest wound and ignored her. Still, it was an utter catastrophe. The alley was filled with a burned sugar smell from James's death and soaked with blood, all of it mine. There was so much, I thought I'd never get it off.

Just like with Roland Thomas.

I blink away the memory and swallow, flashing Mindi a smile. "Don't worry about me."

Mindi nods and gives Niko an awkward hug before leaving the cafeteria. Adam gives me a single dark look, and then follows. Maybe he's finally figuring out I'm not interested.

I pull my hand away from Niko and mop up the blood from the table, ignoring my queasiness. I keep the bloody napkins in my injured hand so that Niko won't see that it has already healed. When I look up from the table, he's standing there, watching me. He doesn't move, and I wonder if he cares whether we're late to class or not. "I think I'll be okay. Thanks."

He grins, and my stomach somersaults. "Anytime."

I stare at Niko as he smiles at me. My chest tightens at his serene expression. This feels like a different Niko from the one who pretty much blew me off in the library. His eyes are the color of the winter sky, and they're so bright, it steals my breath. For a moment the world falls away. I want this moment to last forever.

Niko leans forward with a gleam in his eye, his smile going from friendly to wicked. "By the way, I just want to tell you your secret's safe with me."

I study him for a second, wondering how much he knows and how much he's just guessing at. Either way he probably isn't going to rat me out. He could have done that on Saturday if that was his goal. Shaking my head, I take a deep breath and then let it out.

I can't help myself. I mirror Niko's grin. "What secret?"

He laughs. "You know this is just going to make her even crazier. Amber can't stand it that everyone likes you."

"Oh? Do you like me, Nikolas?" It's supposed to be teasing, but my voice comes out husky and low.

His smile disappears, and he gives me a smoldering look. "Too much. I like you too much." He touches my cheek, and for a moment all rational thought ceases. "You're the most exciting thing that's happened to me in a long time."

My face flushes, and I gather up the remnants of my lunch. I shrug. "Maybe that's just because West County is a boring place?"

Niko grins. "Maybe."

For the first time I realize that They've been awfully quiet while Niko and I have been talking. They can't find one bad thing to say about Niko, and that makes my heart pound. What's so special about him?

He opens his mouth to say something else, but the late bell rings, drowning him out. Niko shrugs, a wistful smile on his face, and leaves the cafeteria. I watch him go. I'm in no hurry to get to class.

So I sit there. Alone, confused, and wondering how I'm going to survive falling for a boy I can't have.

THE GUILTY AND THE DAMNED

MY TARDINESS TO HISTORY RESULTS IN DETENTION
after school. When I finally make it home, I'm exhausted. The thought
of running is about as appealing as poking my eyes out with plastic
forks. Instead I grab Odie and settle in for a reality show marathon on
the old TV in my room.

I awake with a start sometime later. I'm curled up in a ball on the
bed. On the television, celebrities I've never heard of are counting down
the random events of a few years ago, cracking jokes that either I don't
get or just aren't funny. I look at my watch. It's after midnight. While
stretching, I look around for Odie. He usually sleeps curled up on my
stomach like a furry blanket. Not tonight.

"Odie?" He's nowhere to be found, but there's a yowl from the living room. When I get there, Odie paws at the door.

"What is it?" He scratches at the base of the door some more, and I shake my head. "Not here, buddy. This isn't like Grandma's house. Someone's pit bull might get you." In Savannah, Odie had free run of the neighborhood, as much an outside cat as an inside one. Here that is not an option.

I yawn, and as I turn away from the door and back to my bedroom, there's a flash of movement on the fire escape.

I tense, waiting to see more. I'm not disappointed.

A face in my bedroom window stares right back at me.

The features are distorted by the condensation on the window, but I'm certain I saw someone. I run into my room and throw my window open as the person flees down the fire escape. The weighted ladder at the bottom clatters loudly as they ride it to the ground. The person jumps off at the bottom and runs down the alley, but I'm not about to follow them without any shoes.

I slam the window shut, lock it, and yank closed the old, dusty curtain before I storm out into the living room and begin pacing. I should be afraid, but I'm not. I'm pissed. Someone has dared to spy on me, to invade my private sanctuary. I didn't recognize the person. All I saw was a bit of blond hair. It could've been Amber, spying on me, but it could have just as easily been someone looking to break in and steal my television. I don't live in the best neighborhood.

Besides, why would Amber spy on me? Surely she isn't that pissed about what happened at lunch? So I made her look foolish, so what? She'll get over it.

The more I think about someone spying on me, the angrier I get. After a few minutes I've worked myself into a fine rage, and I punch the couch cushions in anger.

I want to find the person who dared spy on me. I'll kill them.

There's a knock on the front door, and I freeze. My blood pounds in my ears. We will rip them apart and feast on their screams. They'll never dare to spy on us again.

"Hey, is something going on?" a female voice calls. It's not one I know, and when I look through the peephole, I recognize the brunette with all of the piercings from down the hall. A strange male voice says something to her, and she answers, "I thought I heard someone screaming."

I swallow and yank open my door with a bright smile. "Hi. Can I help you?"

She takes a step back, a frown on her face. "I thought I heard yelling…"

"Oh, probably just the TV." I continue to grin at her, all teeth. She takes another step backward.

"Yeah, okay. Never mind, then." She heads down the hallway a little too quickly. A guy I don't recognize takes her into his arms before they walk off. I let out the breath I didn't know I was holding, before closing the door.

In my anger, I released my hold on Them, and the conversation with myself that I thought was all in my head wasn't. I stand for a long time in my living room, shaking. How long was the person on the fire escape watching me sleep? What did they see? I don't think They manifest while I sleep, but They could.

What if it was someone who wanted to hurt me? What if someone had come in and attacked me while I was asleep?

Shhh, don't worry. Don't you think we'd protect you?

You're safe, sweet Amelie. We will always keep you safe.

I collapse on the couch and hold my head in my hands, my rage draining away. They're right. They have powers far beyond anything I can do. They would know if I was in danger.

More important, how did They slip my leash so easily? Just like with Dylan in the library, They somehow managed to slip out of my control without my notice. What's happening to me? My hold over Them used to be ironclad. Now the neighbors are stopping by to chat because of Them. That bugs me as much as the person on the fire escape.

It's all just too much. I won't be able to sleep with all of this running through my head. So I focus on something that will calm my nerves.

Alex Medina.

When I was in Brighter Day, I met a boy named Zachary Olmstead. He was there because his parents said he had a sex addiction. Nice guy, even if he was a little high-strung. Besides being a huge fan of naked women, Zach was also kind of a genius. I liked him because he was always willing to help me with my homework. It was because of Zach that I managed to stay ahead even though I missed a ton of school.

Brighter Day was pretty lax, and we had a computer lab, even if there were so many security settings that you were lucky to play solitaire. Late at night Zach would hack through the firewall so he could feed his addiction. I caught him once. I was fuzzy-headed and overmedicated, but I couldn't sleep. I found him in the lab, and he startled when he saw me.

"Jesus, Amelie. How about a little fucking privacy?" he gasped out, face red as he cleared the screen he'd been looking at.

"Teach me how to do that."

He ran his fingers through his brown hair. I had a bit of a crush on him, and I loved the way his hair stuck out all over the place. I like to think that he would've liked me that way too, if I'd been a little older. "Do what?"

"Break through the security system. I want to know how to go where I want."

He studied me for a second, and then nodded. "Okay. But it's not easy."

In two weeks I was better than him, and logging on to hacking sites to expand my skills.

Now my illegal hobby comes in handy. I couldn't hack into the CIA or anything like that, but local government websites are easy pickings. Firewalls set up to keep out nosy citizens fall to me, and my laptop becomes a portal to the world of human misery and those who delight in it.

Which is why it makes me so angry that I can't find Dr. Goodhart. The last hit I got on him was a month ago, when a prominent hospital released a news clipping about opening a new ward for mental disorders. I could've sworn that the man in the grainy picture was Dr. Goodhart, but now I'm not so sure. It was enough to bring me back to Pennsylvania, though.

Eventually he'll turn up. Either They'll find him, or I will. And when we do, I will ruin his life like he ruined mine.

After a quick Internet search I find a few follow-up articles on Medina that were printed after the one that was stuffed into my locker. Then I check the county records where he was arrested. The police still have an open investigation against him. So why haven't they charged Medina? Is it because his victims don't matter? Medina spent his time carving up women who sold their bodies to survive. When he didn't kill them, he left them scarred for life.

A few more articles, and I have the whole story. Seems the local cops didn't do such a hot job processing the evidence, which is how Medina got off on a technicality. I'll do what the police haven't and make him pay for his crimes.

I find Medina quickly. He now works for a long-haul trucking outfit. His name hasn't changed, and I pull up his driver's license to compare the picture to his mug shot. It's the same guy.

I click through a few more screens and find that the company he works for hauls packaged meat to grocery stores and animals to slaughter. I can't help but grin at the irony.

I search through the drivers' logs, handily stored on the website. Skimming through the details, I find that the trucks have embedded tracking devices that update every twenty minutes. No one wants to lose a truckload of filets mignons. I find the location of Medina's truck, and when I put the lat/long into my browser, I get a real-time picture of a nearby truck stop.

A smile creeps across my face, and I feel almost giddy. It's our lucky night.

The Speedy Stop Travel Plaza is lit up like a summer day when I pull in and park at the edge of the lot. The place is twice the size of West County High, the paved lot giving way to a dirt parking area for the tractor-trailers that make their lumbering way in from the interstate. Dirty slush over the hard-packed earth creates an icy hazard for truck drivers who come in for the "Cheap Showers" and "$4.99 Steak and Eggs Special." Carloads of weary travelers stop in every few minutes to fuel up and grab Styrofoam cups of coffee that they sip with grimaces. I watch for a few minutes before getting out of my car and slinking between the trucks, looking for the shamrock logo of Kirkpatrick Trucking.

After making a circuit up and down the rows, I find that of the fifty or so trucks present, there are three Kirkpatrick trucks. I mentally curse myself for not thinking to write down Medina's plates. I'm about to knock on one of the doors, when someone lets out a low chuckle.

"Well, honey, I gotta say I ain't never seen someone so fine trolling the lots before." I turn around, every muscle in my body tensed for action. A hyper-skinny man with jeans and a work jacket stares at me, his eyes lingering rudely on my chest. He's a weasel of a man, and the gleam in his eyes unsettles me. He spits a long stream of tobacco juice onto the icy slush of the lot, barely missing my hiking boots. "So how much you charging? Going rate for the girls here is seventy-five, but I figure a sweet piece like you is probably worth an even hundred." He adjusts his pants in a way that makes it clear he doesn't think I'm selling cookies.

I take a steadying breath and try to give him an indulgent smile. "Actually, I'm already spoken for this evening. I'm looking for Alex. He and I have an . . . arrangement. I'm not sure you can top what he's offering." I toss my hair over my shoulder, and the man lets loose with a low whistle.

"So, you're the reason he always stops in this shit hole. Well, tell you what. It's your lucky night. I ain't gonna take up too much of your time, and I'll still give you your full fee. How's that sound?"

"Sorry. I make it a rule never to engage in business with men I don't know." The excuse sounds lame even to my ears, especially since he thinks I'm a prostitute, but alarm has risen in my chest and slowed my brain. Trucks idle loudly around us, and we're far enough away that no one will hear me scream or call for help. Not that I would. Still, I'm not here for this scrawny waste of protein. Even if he is something you'd find on the bottom of your shoe, I want to give him a chance to carry on with his pathetic existence.

He takes another step and begins undoing his belt. It's somewhere around twenty degrees out, but the man has a one-track mind. "Honey, my name's Chuck, and you can fill in the rest. Now we're friends. Let's do this."

Rage, hot and sharp, surges through me. I snap. I let loose my control on Them, and my vision splits into three.

Before I can think about what I'm doing, our fist whips out and catches Chuck under the chin. His head snaps back, a gurgling sound emanating from his throat. He hasn't even responded to the blow before we give him a roundhouse kick to the middle. Blood and tobacco juice explode all over my shoe, and a tooth lands on the dirty snow. I look down and distantly realize that the shoe is ruined. I'm horrified, but from a distance I can hear myself laughing.

I've completely lost control.

A hot wind whips around me, melting the snow and revealing the gravel lot beneath. We walk forward to finish off the disgusting specimen of humanity, and it's all I can do to stop Them from killing Chuck just for the fun of it. I have to convince Them that it's Medina we need to find.

Their urgings to violence tangle around my thoughts. They want me to hurt Chuck. It would be so easy for us to break his neck, to hear the sweetly satisfying grind and crunch of vertebrae giving way.

I try to shake off Their influence and maintain my sanity. "No, we're here for Medina. He's the one we want."

But *think of the fun* . . . a girlish giggle before wings beat the air and resettle.

The soft susurrus of scales sliding. *Really, it would take only a second.*

Panic swamps me, but I push it back and remain firm. Chains rattle as I cross my arms. "No. We have to find Medina. For all we know he could be leaving soon. Then what will we do? Wait for him to pass back through? We must hand down justice."

They reluctantly leave the unconscious man and follow me through the rows of trucks. I swallow my relief and focus on our task.

"This way. It has to be one of these."

We make our way to the other Kirkpatrick Trucking rigs I noticed earlier. At the first a woman sings country music off-key, and we veer away just in time to see the female driver roll down the window and light a cigarette.

That leaves only one other Kirkpatrick Trucking rig. We make our way between the tractor-trailers, sticking to the shadows as much as possible. Outside Medina's truck we press ourselves to the cold metal of the driver's door, trying the handle first. It's locked, and I'm just about to break the window when we hear a woman's sob.

"Please. Dear God, no. I have kids."

Anger surges through us, and we throw caution to the wind. Tisiphone digs her taloned hands into the door of the cab and rips it off. There's movement inside as she tosses the door away like a gum wrapper. A short man with dark hair and beady eyes is silhouetted momentarily, a bloody knife in his hand, before he scrambles out the passenger door. I want to check on the woman pleading for help, but They are already pursuing Medina across the parking lot, dragging me along between Them.

Medina runs like a jackrabbit, surprisingly fast for his size. My arms pump as we follow him, dodging in between the slumbering giants. Tisiphone flies ahead of Megaera and me, her wings beating the air heavily. I round a corner and skid to a stop, listening for Medina. Someone pants behind me. As I spin around, he slashes downward, carving through my left shoulder and just barely missing my heart.

Pain blinds me, and I go down with a grunt. They howl in anger, the animalistic sound echoing eerily in the cold night. A scorching wind blows across the lot, and before I can move, They are on Medina.

He doesn't even have time to scream before They bombard him with punishing blows. If I don't interfere, They will burn away his soul, leaving nothing for his Maker to judge. I stumble toward the man lying on the ground, and my sword appears just in time to end his life before They do. But pain makes me clumsy. I trip and sprawl across the gravel parking lot, and the sword clatters away before disappearing.

There is a brief moment of silence, and then I hear it. A rushing sound fills my ears, the hot wind of some hell whipping across the lot. I raise my head and watch as Medina claws at his face. Blue flames explode from his eyes and mouth, momentarily illuminating his pain-stretched features before exploding through the pores of his body. For one glorious second he is a fiery blue beacon, and the music of long-dead gods triumphantly fills the night air. But the light quickly fades, and Medina falls to the ground, the thin layer of soot on his skin the only sign of the cause of his death.

They have burned away the man's sin-stained soul.

I swallow past the lump in my throat. There is no justice for Alex Medina, only oblivion.

I climb to my feet and stumble away, back toward the lights of the gas station. There are no trucks in this part of the lot, only a bare gravel expanse. I've made it only a few steps before I fall to my knees and retch, my body spasming until my stomach is completely empty. Once again I'm painfully reminded that They have a very different idea of justice.

Alekto explained it to me once. *Every soul deserves to receive its judgment. My sisters take away any chance for redemption when They burn the soul of the guilty away. Instead there is nothing, only oblivion. It is the absolute worst kind of punishment, and the suffering They inflict makes Them stronger.*

Failure weighs heavily on my shoulders, and I raise my head. They stand before me, and it's a rare chance for me to glimpse Them fully. Usually I have only an impression of Their forms, snatches of wings and scales from the corners of my eyes as We hand down our justice.

My weakness has given Them free rein, and I take this opportunity to study Them.

Tisiphone stands to my left, the wings on her back held close to her body. In the dim light I can faintly make out the talons that take the place of human hands. Her wings are breathtaking, the feathers with the same brown mottling as a hawk's. She stretches them with a grin when she catches me staring at her. Her wingspan is easily ten or twelve feet, and the wings block what little light filters to our corner of the lot from the gas station area. Her face is china-doll fine, the features delicate and perfect, but her eyes are wild, the madness clear even in the dim lighting of the parking lot.

You are injured. Megaera's lips don't move, but her voice echoes in my head. I look down at my shoulder. Blood courses down my arm, soaking my black sweater and dripping off my fingers onto the gravel parking lot. I nod, and the world tilts sideways. It's only when my face crashes into the icy gravel that I realize I fell over.

Well, at least I missed the puddle of puke.

From the ground I look up at the serpent woman. Her hair is made of snakes, and her entire body is covered in scales. She isn't pretty like the winged one, and her mouth has a cruel cast that fills me with fear, even more than the fact that I'm dying. She clutches my shoulder, and my scream of pain trails off into a whimper.

Death is not your fate. You are our servant.

Heat suffuses my body, centering on my shoulder and radiating out. It's not a pleasant warmth but a searing like being tossed into a vat of boiling oil. I moan, but my throat closes off and no sound escapes. I wonder if They are burning away the blackness in my soul as well, and if I'll have anything left. Just when I'm certain I can't take any more, the heat subsides and I return to my senses. The Furies are gone, and I sense Them settling back into the corner of my mind They call Their own. I roll onto my back and look up at the sky, a ragged sob tearing from my chest.

I don't know how much longer I can do this.

After what feels like an eternity, I climb to my feet and stagger back to my car. Nearly dying has taken a lot out of me, and my legs feel like overcooked spaghetti. A couple whispering to each other pause and look in my direction, but quickly dismiss me. I'm pretty sure I look like hell, but luckily not bad enough to attract the attention of the truck stop denizens.

Without another thought I get into my car and drive away.

WOOZY

I'M ABOUT TEN MINUTES FROM HOME WHEN I
drive off the road. The rumble strips on the highway wake me with a
thrumming noise, my car vibrating alarmingly. I straighten the wheel
in time to avoid driving into the ditch alongside the road, and slam to
a stop.

Not good.

My head pounds, and I rest it against the steering wheel. I'm light-
headed and tired and parched. It must be the blood loss from Medina's
attack. This happened after I got shot in Charleston, so I know that
what I need right now is sugar. Lots of sugar.

I slowly guide my car back onto the road and take the first exit. I'm still in West County, but it's a part I've never been to before. The houses look newer, and there's a brightly lit shopping center that boasts a twenty-four-hour drugstore.

I stumble out of the car, catching myself on the door to avoid face-planting into the pavement. Once the dizzy spell passes, I head into the drugstore, making a beeline to the soda coolers at the back. I grab a twenty-ounce bottle of something dark and bubbly, open it, and drink half. I'm just finishing it when I hear a shout behind me.

"Hey!"

"I'm going to pay for it," I snap, reaching for another one. Already the high-fructose corn syrup in my belly is making me feel better. Hooray for science.

"Isn't it a little late for you to be out and about?" I turn around and almost drop the fresh soda in my hand. I sag against the door to the cooler. At the end of the aisle, wearing a red smock and looking as goofy as hell, is Niko.

I'm exhausted, but he looks wonderful. It takes me a moment too long to answer him, and another moment to remember Kevin Eames. It's hard to think about avoiding Niko when he's looking at me like he's been waiting all night to see me.

"Hey," I croak. He pushes off the chip display and saunters toward me, his hands stuck in his pockets.

"What are you doing out at this time of night?"

I smile, because my sluggish brain is having trouble coming up with an excuse. When I got into the car to find Medina, it was after one in the morning. I'm guessing it's somewhere after two or three now. It's easy to lose track of time with Them. "Yeah, my mom's sick. She sent me to get some cough syrup."

Niko nods, and pushes his dark curls out of his face. "Oh. Okay." He seems disappointed, and I wonder if he thought I was here to see him. After the scene in the lunchroom, it might make sense. Anyone watching would've been able to see the sparks between us. Is he as happy to see me as I am to see him?

The thought warms me before I throw a mental bucket of ice water onto the feeling. Why would he be looking for me? Despite the moment in the cafeteria, we've barely spoken. Obviously he's just happy to see a familiar face.

I clear my throat and nod. "Yeah. Um, do you work here?" My brain is already slow, and the fact that he seems as excited to see me as I am to see him throws my thoughts into further chaos. Does he like me? Is there any way I can ask him without sounding desperate?

Probably not.

I need to quit watching so much television. It's rotting my brain. There's no way that Niko is interested in me. It's just wishful thinking. Even if he is interested . . . well, I can't exactly return his feelings. It's wrong. I'm too dangerous.

I can't forget that I'm not just a girl, even though I enjoy playing the part. I'm a monster. My brain shies away from the mental image of Alex Medina's final moments. They weren't exactly kind.

I tear my thoughts away from my inner struggles to what Niko is saying. ". . . so I work here a couple of nights a week. I have insomnia, and I don't like the drugs because they make me a little crazy. Working helps."

He pushes his hand through his hair and gives a little nervous laugh that makes my stomach flip-flop. "I'm not sure why I told you that."

"Because we're friends." I give him what I hope is a reassuring smile.

He grins. "Friends, huh? You want to hang out for a while?"

"Sure." I wonder if I'm making a mistake, answering so quickly. But right now I'm on my own. They're silent, and I probably wouldn't like what They had to say, anyway.

Even though I know better, I follow Niko to the front of the store, grabbing a package of chocolate frosted doughnuts off a display near the register. Niko sits behind the counter and waves away my attempt to pay. "You're a guest in my kingdom." I lean against the other side of the counter and drink my second soda, trying not to grin like a love-struck idiot.

I rip open the doughnuts, stuff one into my mouth, chew it, and swallow it quickly. Very attractive. "Wow, so you are king of all that is the late-night drugstore. You're a pretty lucky guy. Do you get a crown?"

Niko laughs, and snags one of my doughnuts. His fingers brush mine, and a thrill runs down my spine. "Nope, but I do get a nifty scepter. Of course, it looks like a mop."

I look around the place, taking in the soda coolers and shelves crowded with everything from tampons to Hot Wheels. I would go crazy if I had to spend eight hours in such a confined space. Already my skin feels like it's a size too small. That, of course, could be the guilt from staring at Niko's mouth as he talks. *Kevin Eames, Kevin Eames,* I chant mentally. Still, I can't help but wonder if his lips are as soft as they look. "So, what do you do while you're here? Surely you don't get that many customers."

"Naw. Only a few on the late shift. To be honest, this is all still kind of new to me. I've only worked here for about a month, since I turned eighteen. You can't pull the overnight shift if you're a minor, so before that I could only work until midnight." He stretches and yawns, even though he's very much awake. His eyes don't look at all sleepy. I barely notice since I'm watching the way his shirt pulls across his chest and lifts a little, revealing his midriff at the bottom. Dark hair sprinkles across the tan flatness of his belly. My mouth is suddenly dry. He doesn't seem to notice that I'm staring. "I mostly just watch the counter, and read the magazines."

I take a deep breath and reach over. "These?" I pick up a flashy-looking magazine that promises a story entitled "Fifteen Ways to Wow! Your Guy in Bed." My face heats.

Niko waves a hand. "Pshaw. Not even close. Those are actually good compared to the stuff I read. I'm talking the stuff like this." Niko comes around the counter and picks up off a rack what looks like a newspaper. His shoulder brushes against mine as he leans against the counter right next to me, and my heart flutters at the contact. I shove another dough-nut into my mouth to hide my sigh.

Niko is oblivious, and he shakes out the pages of the paper and shows me the cover, bending his head toward mine. GIANT BIRD WOMAN RAINS DOWN JUSTICE is the headline, and for a panicked second I think he knows my secret. Then he laughs and taps the page. "Can you believe this? People actually pay money to read this stuff."

I choke down the doughnut and follow it with a swallow of carbon-ated sugar water. The liquid tingles all the way down, but it gives me time to recover. My heart pounds and I widen my eyes to cover my nervousness. "Oh, my God. People seriously pay money for that?" I sound like an idiot. But Niko doesn't even notice.

He snorts and nods, flipping through the pages before he finds what he's searching for. "Listen to this." He clears his throat and begins speaking in a newscaster-type voice, "'A large birdlike woman was seen killing a man in a small town north of Charlotte last July. A lone witness, eighty-three-year-old Grace Perkins, said the creature looked to her like a Fury, a mythological creature that killed violent offenders in ancient Greece.'" Niko shakes his head and laughs. "How would some old lady in North Carolina know what a Fury looked like? I wonder how much they pay people for these stories."

I laugh hollowly, because when he reads it out loud, it sounds silly. Who would believe that Furies exist? I look down at my ripped sweater sleeve and the newly pink scar underneath. Anxiety pools in my stomach and swirls through my middle, and an awful thought stops me.

Niko turns the page, and stops with a laugh. "This one's even better—"

"Do you like me?" The words tumble out, and at Niko's raised eyebrow I wish I could call them back. But I don't. I plunge on ahead. "You were sort of a jerk in the library, and you never even said hi at Tina's party. But then today, in the lunchroom . . ." I trail off, unsure how to put what I'm feeling into words. "I don't get you."

His expression softens, and he sets down the paper. His gaze meets mine unwaveringly. "I wanted to talk to you at Tina's party." He says it so low, I can barely hear him.

I cross my arms. "Yeah, so why didn't you?" Some inner demon spurs me on. I listen for Their telltale whispers. But They are still silent, still slumbering. This alarm, it's all me.

He shrugs and puts the tabloid away in the display rack. "I don't know. Maybe I was afraid you were out of my league, you know?" He's close enough that his body heat warms my side, and I'm hyperaware of him. I've never felt so alive. Or so afraid.

"No, I don't know. Maybe you should tell me."

His eyes meet mine, a smile crinkling the corners. "I think maybe I was wrong about you. When you first showed up, I thought you were one of those girls who fall for the first douche bag who hits on them, and when I found you with Dylan, I was sure of it. I didn't want to waste my time just to end up dumped for some jock." He shrugs. "But you aren't who you pretend to be. I could tell that when I saw you standing over Dylan on Saturday."

I tense. "You saw that?" My voice is too high and my heart picks up. I feel sick.

He puts a calming hand on my arm. "Not really. I just saw him on the ground and you next to him. Don't worry. I'm not going to tell anyone. With Dylan I can fill in the blanks. It was pretty impressive, though."

Relief washes over me. I don't say anything, just cram the last doughnut into my mouth. He didn't see Them. And he touched me. My skin burns from the contact. He doesn't seem to notice my distress, and keeps talking. "You pretend to be this good girl Southern belle, but you change when you don't think anyone is looking. I want to get to know that girl, the girl who comes out in the middle of the night to buy her mom cough medicine, but could also take down a guy who brags about benching three hundy."

I blink, and my tongue feels too thick. I can't find the words, so I just stare at Niko, wishing I could dive into his ocean eyes and escape the awkwardness of this conversation that I started.

He laughs bitterly, and shakes his head. He's taken my silence to mean something else, disbelief or anger. He pushes his hand through his hair, causing it to stick up in a dozen different directions. "Is it so hard to believe that I might like you and want to get to know who you really are?" It's a ragged plea, and his voice strikes a chord deep within me. Because what he's asking is exactly what I want, someone to know who I really am.

I'm just terrified that if he knows the truth, he'll run for the hills.

Everything is so tangled up together in my mind. I want him, but I can't have him, even though They're quiet and far away. It's Their silence that spurs me on. Maybe They're tired enough that I can have just a little happiness, just a single moment with Niko. I have to believe that he'll be safe.

Because I want to kiss him so badly, I can taste it.

I lean forward, closing the distance between us, and my lips touch his. Niko seems startled at first, but then his arms are wrapping around me, pulling me close. Everything falls away but his lips, his arms around me, and the scent of rain and pine. He tastes like doughnuts, and I press into him. I need more. So much more.

But that single kiss is all I get. Someone clears their throat behind me, and we jump apart. A bedraggled-looking guy stands behind me.

"Diapers?" he asks, exhaustion heavy in his voice.

"Aisle three," Niko answers, and the guy is gone and back before I can say anything to Niko.

"Thank God you guys are open," the guy says, digging out his wallet as Niko rings up the diapers. "I went to the truck stop down the road, but they're closed."

Niko frowns. "That's $25.63. I didn't know they ever closed. I thought they were twenty-four hours just like us."

"They are," the guy says. He slides his card and picks up his purchase. "There were all kinds of cops and stuff there. I guess maybe they got robbed or something. You be careful," the guys says as he leaves. He gives me a pointed look, and embarrassment heats my face.

It's in that moment that I realize I forgot all about the woman in the truck, Medina's near miss. Guilt sours my stomach. How could I have forgotten about her so easily? She could've been seriously hurt, and I was ready to head home without a backward glance.

What's wrong with me?

"I should get home," I say abruptly. It sounds like a blow-off, even though I don't mean it that way. Niko nods, and I walk out of the drugstore with a heavy heart.

"Hey." He runs out as I'm almost to my car. "Don't forget the cough syrup for your mom." He tosses me a red bottle, and I catch it in midair. I was so caught up in the moment that I completely forgot my cover story.

"Oh, thanks."

He wears a small grin. "This isn't over, you know."

I shrug, but the heated look in his eyes coupled with the compliment warms me. I return his smile. "If you say so."

He closes the distance between us, grabs my arms, and pulls me to him for a quick kiss. It melts my middle, and shivers of delight run across my skin. "I say so," he murmurs, voice low. Then he's gone, running back inside.

I head to my car, wondering how I can feel so alive and so scared all at the same time.

THIRD DEGREE

IT'S HARD NOT TO SIGH IN FRUSTRATION WHEN I open my eyes to the red desert of the dreamscape. Mostly because I was in the middle of a delicious dream about Niko. I can't remember the contents of the dream, only that it involved hot cocoa and Niko without a shirt. Really, that's enough for me.

"You are getting careless, Amelie," Alekto says, her voice low and even. She sits cross-legged on a red boulder in the middle of the landscape, her eyes closed as though she's meditating. Her hair and white robes flutter in the breeze. "Twice They have slipped through your leash and people have been injured. My sisters will not be so gentle a third time."

"Yeah, I'm not worried. They didn't hurt anyone important. And I was able to hold Them."

Alekto opens one of her eyes to peer at me before closing it and settling back into position. "Perhaps, but you also lost control over Them during justice. If this keeps happening, They will control you, and you will not be safe. And no man will be safe. Is that what you want?"

Her words send a chill down my spine, despite the hot wind blowing against my face. Kevin Eames's face swims into my mind's eye, and is immediately replaced by Niko, bruised and battered. I think about how awful it would be if anything happened to him. Despair clutches at my chest at the image of Niko hurt, but I don't ponder what that might mean.

I open my mouth to object, to tell her it won't happen again. But she's right. If They'd gotten loose, I wouldn't have been able to stop Them, and it would have been a massacre.

The problem is, beyond keeping Niko safe, I'm not sure why I care.

I shrug at her admonishment and change the subject. "Wow, this is the most I've seen you in probably forever. So, what's the occasion? You know it's still a month and a half until my birthday, right? I do have my eye on a new sweater, if you're interested."

She stretches and stands, a pillar of beautiful golden skin in the ugly landscape. I'm a spindly scrub bush next to her. "Your sarcasm is unnecessary."

"And your visits are a waste of time. What is it you want from me, anyway?"

"The same thing you want. You to regain your freedom. They are bound to you, which gives Them access to your world, making Them stronger. I want you to break those bonds."

I laugh, the sound harsh. "In case you haven't noticed, I'm doing everything I can just to hang on."

She turns away slightly, looking off into the distance. "Here in the other realms the paths in the world of man are sometimes revealed. The time is coming soon when you can be free of Them, but only if you are the one in control. If you keep letting Them kill, They will be too strong and I will not be able to help you."

Bitterness surges through me at her words. She wants to show up every once in a while and chastise me for not controlling Them better, but she was the one who abandoned Them in the first place. Who's she to judge me?

"How have you helped me up to now?" I snap. "I can barely keep Them from driving me insane, even with all of your 'help.' Every day They're in my head, and I'm not sure if the urges I feel are even all Theirs anymore. I like—" The words stick, and I have to force them past the lump in my throat. "I like the way I feel when I'm with Them. Powerful. Unstoppable. And the guilty deserve their fate. They prey on innocents, and if we don't stop them, who will?"

Alekto looks at me sadly and shakes her head. "Is that really how you feel, or is this the result of listening to Them? You used to be disgusted by Their bloodlust."

"Yeah, that was a long time ago. And what I need now are answers, not another lecture."

"If I could tell you how to break your bonds, I would. But I too am bound by a promise made."

I laugh again. "Then I guess we're both screwed."

But Alekto senses my weakness and presses on. "How did you feel tonight when They burned away Alex Medina's soul? Did guilt and disgust not rip through your heart? Remember how you felt the night They killed Roland Thomas." She doesn't mention that I was just a kid when that happened, and I wonder if that's her point. What if the Furies have just been using me this entire time?

Alekto walks away, but stops after only a couple of steps. "Remember how They were in the beginning? Pushing you even when you pleaded with Them to stop. Think of how They murdered heedlessly when you gave Them free rein in Savannah, and how They are unable to find the one man you want to hurt. They are not here for you. They are selfish, and if They have Their chance, They will turn you into Their puppet."

The scorching wind picks up speed and red sand, blowing the grit directly into my face so that I have to blink. Alekto has to yell to be heard over the noise. "This truce you have brokered with Them will not last forever."

When I look again, she's gone, and I'm no closer to understanding how to win my freedom than I was before.

SNOWBLIND

I SWALLOW A YAWN AS I FOLLOW ADAM'S directions to the mountain. After a day of fighting to stay awake in class, the last thing I want to do is hang out and go sledding. But the mountaintop is *the* place to hang out. I take this to mean it's where everyone goes to get drunk and make out. Despite my frequent daydreams about Niko's very kissable lips, it's not really my scene. Rolling around in the snow is not my idea of fun. In fact, I try to beg off with excuses about my mother expecting me, but no one is buying it. After Mindi gives me her scared-mouse look, I know I don't really have a choice. I'm going sledding.

So here I am, sleep-deprived and heading out to play in the snow.

I drive up the narrow road behind Niko's Jeep, the wheels of my car slipping every now and then as they struggle to find purchase. In the backseat Jocelyn and Tom chatter excitedly with Adam in the front. They mostly share gossip. After last night I'd almost forgotten that the whole incident with Amber was just yesterday. It feels like weeks ago. But thanks to her, I am very much at the top of the rumor mill right now.

For the most part I just ignored the looks and whispers, embarrassed and uncomfortable with all of the attention. It was only the thought of Niko that kept me going.

I have never wanted to kill someone as much as I want to kill Amber.

Jocelyn clears her throat and reaches over the seat to poke Adam in the back of the head. "So, where's Amber? Is she avoiding us now?"

Adam flushes and sinks lower in the seat. "How would I know where she is? I'm not her keeper."

Jocelyn leans back, and in the rearview mirror she makes a face at Adam's back. "Sheesh. All right. I just thought you were her BFF now that Mindi's not talking to her. You guys used to be pretty tight."

He shrugs and stares out the window. "Yeah, well, she's mad at me about something, and she told me she's working on some really important project right now and can't be bothered."

I check out Jocelyn's expression in my rearview mirror. She smiles. "Really? Because I heard the project she's working on is hooking up with Dylan Larchmont. Up to her old tricks again." Amber and Dylan? Really? How do I keep missing all of the good gossip?

The car falls into an awkward silence as Adam's jaw clenches. "That's just a rumor. Amber's no worse than"—he looks at me, then pauses and swallows before continuing—"anyone else. You know, you could call her, Jocelyn. You have her number."

I'm angry that Adam gave me that look. He actually believed Amber. Maybe she has more power than I thought.

Jocelyn shrugs and studies her fingernails. "I could, but then I'd have to talk to her. I'd much rather just get the info from you."

Adam stares out the window, but I'm pretty sure I'm not the only one who hears him mutter "Bitch" under his breath.

No one says much after that.

I focus on navigating my car down the narrow road and ignore the weighty silence. The lull in the conversation is finally interrupted by Adam pointing to a stand of spindly trees. "You can park right there. We'll have to hike the rest of the way in."

I nod and park the car. My hundred-dollar boots are going to be ruined after tramping through the snow. I ordered them with part of Hank Meacham's money, a total impulse buy. They arrived yesterday, and I couldn't wait to wear them to school. Now I kind of think I should have paid the rent instead. Forget looking good. I still need somewhere to live.

I wish I could have worn the hiking boots I had on last night, but they're still spattered with Chuck's blood and tobacco juice. I make a mental note to get a pair of snow boots like Jocelyn's, a cross between hiking boots and mukluks. Utilitarian, yet surprisingly stylish. I hope they aren't too expensive. Unless I try to tap into the money from my parents' estate, I'm broke.

From my trunk I pull out the three plastic sleds Mindi stashed there before we left. Adam grabs a bottle of tequila from under one of the sleds. At my raised eyebrow he shrugs. "It's not the good stuff, but we have to keep warm somehow."

We hike through the snow and meet up with Mindi, who is snuggled into Niko's side to keep warm. Rather, she tries to burrow into Niko's side, and he stands stiffly for a few seconds before moving away just enough to put a noticeable distance between them. Niko looks like he just ate something foul, although he does manage a wan smile in my direction.

Neither Mindi nor Niko remarks on Amber's absence, and after the tension in the car, I'm glad. I toss the saucers to the ground.

Niko shakes off Mindi once again and steps forward to pick up one of the sleds. "All right. Who wants to be the first to conquer the mountain?"

Mindi glances away quickly, dashing away tears before anyone can see. Not everything is happy in Mindiland. I want to ask her what's going on, but the way she keeps glancing over at Niko makes it clear it's something to do with him. She's obviously pining for him.

One more reason I should stay far away from him. Going after Niko will not make me a good friend.

To distract my wayward thoughts I look around at the "mountain." It's really just a big hill with an abandoned water tower, a throwback to the days when West County had a couple of struggling coal mining towns and a much larger population. Now the miners have all left, and the water tower is a rusting monolith dusted with snow and graffiti.

Under the shelter of the tower are the remnants of someone's campfire, along with a few places to sit, and I gesture to the makeshift fire pit.

"I'll make a fire, if no one minds," I say, trying not to shiver in the brisk wind blowing across the hill.

They all laugh, and Adam hugs me close. "Still getting used to the cold?"

I smile and wiggle free, duplicating the move Niko used with Mindi. Adam's persistent, I'll give him that. I don't want to have to be blunt with him, but he's clearly not getting the "just friends" vibe I'm sending out.

Niko appears in front of me, blocking my view of Adam and shoving the sled into my hands. "Let Adam make the fire. You have to go first. After all, you're a virgin. At least when it comes to sledding. Am I right?"

My face heats as Tom and Jocelyn hoot at Niko's comment. Adam's eyes narrow, and Mindi's face is inscrutable. She looks like she wants to cry, and I feel terrible.

"All right. I'll go first. Someone has to show you Yankees how it's done," I say, and sniff. Everyone claps and cheers except for Mindi, who seriously looks like someone just killed her puppy. A tendril of worry niggles at the back of my mind. I hope she's okay.

I set the saucer on the ground and sit on it. Look, I know how to sled. I used to go all the time as a kid. The problem is I haven't done it in at least five years. I'm more than a little rusty.

A few feet in front of me the ground slopes downward. I scoot the dish across the ground by rocking back and forth, moving toward the edge a couple of inches at a time. Everyone groans.

Large hands grip my waist, and I tense, resisting the urge to back-hand the offender. "I can tell you're an amateur, so I'm going to give you a little help." Niko's mouth is next to my ear, his voice like honey. I relax into his grip, his touch not at all unwelcome. I'm used to holding myself aloof, but there's something about the way his hands rest on my sides that makes my stomach clench not in anxiety but in delight. His breath tickles my cheek, and my insides flutter. I am entirely too warm.

And They are curiously silent.

"On the count of three I am going to give you a push, okay?" I nod, since I've completely lost the ability to speak. Niko's hands move to grip my shoulders. I can focus only on the pressure of his touch. My heart pounds, not in fear but with a breathless excitement I've never felt before.

"All right. One, two, THREE!" Niko shoves me down the hill, and I have only a second to mourn the loss of contact before I'm flying through the air, hair streaming out behind me. My hat flies off, and a thrill better than the most deserved judgment swells inside my chest. I laugh out loud. I can't remember the last time I laughed honestly and truly rather than as a calculated response to some personal interaction. The cold air stings my cheeks and steals my breath. I want this feeling to last forever. I am flying through the air, a bird skimming the snowy surface, weightless . . . and heading for a tree.

The base of the hill is dotted with pines, most of them spaced far enough apart that I could slide through them. That's assuming I know how to steer the flying saucer hurtling down the hill. I don't. There are handles on either side of my hips to grip, but pulling on them doesn't seem to be doing any good.

"Lean!"

Someone shouts it from the top of the hill, and I throw all of my weight to the left. I start to turn slowly, but the dish catches an edge. The sled flips over, and I go rolling down the hill. I register every single rock under the several inches of snow before I come to a stop on my back, looking up through the branches of a pine tree. There's a whooshing sound, and Niko's face appears above me.

"You alive?"

I groan. "For now."

He grins and holds out the saucer that almost killed me. "You have to go again. You know, whatever doesn't kill you makes you stronger."

Whatever doesn't kill you only makes you stronger.

Suddenly I am back in Saint Dymphna's.

I lay on the tiny twin bed in my room, my limbs made of lead and my head stuffed with cotton. I was too drugged up to do much of anything but drool. In the back of my mind They urged me to wakefulness, but I was completely and utterly helpless.

"Bring her in here. Careful. The sedative should be wearing off soon."

I turned my head to the side, a mountainous effort, and watched a couple of orderlies carry in an unconscious girl I didn't recognize. She was older than most of the other patients in Saint Dymphna's, early twenties or so. I was in the adolescent ward. It was only later that I was able to understand how odd her presence was. At the time my mind was too dull to process much beyond her appearance.

A stream of saliva ran from her slack mouth to the ground, and her bottom lip was puffy and bleeding as though someone had hit her. I watched in muted horror as the orderlies strapped the girl to the bed. Bruises marred her tan arms, and when her head lolled to the side, I saw the beginnings of a black eye.

The orderlies finished up and filed out of the room. As they left, Dr. Goodhart entered the room. He sat on the bed beside the girl and smoothed her long bangs back. The girl didn't move. Her eyes stared off into the distance, not really focused on anything. He bent down and kissed her full on the mouth. And murmured something into her ear. It sounded like "I love you," but I couldn't be sure. I must have made some sound, because he jerked away from the girl and looked at me, the familiar smile slipping into place.

"Hello, Amelie. How are you doing?"

"There's something wrong," I tried to say, but my tongue was too thick to form the words properly. They came out slurred and barely intelligible.

Dr. Goodhart had been through this routine before, and he just patted me on the hand. "Oh, no, sweetheart. There's nothing wrong. This is just your new roommate, Marie. I don't think she'll be here for very long. She's a special case." He shined a penlight into my eyes and smiled. "You're doing well with the new therapy."

"My head," I began, but I couldn't finish the thought. In some part of my mind I knew this was wrong, that things shouldn't be this way, but I was powerless to do anything. I couldn't even wiggle my toes.

I blinked, willing my eyes to focus. Dr. Goodhart got up from the bed, and I saw a familiar rust-colored drop at the bottom of his white lab coat.

"Blood," I whispered.

"Don't worry, Amelie. In no time your body will respond to the increased dosage and you'll feel much better. Much calmer and more stable." He leaned over me, and I could see the blood on his lips from where he'd kissed the girl. His voice lowered to a whisper. "Just remember, whatever doesn't kill you only makes you stronger."

The words echo through my mind from long ago, and I try to sit up too quickly. I'm surprised when my body responds. Niko jumps backward so that we don't bump heads. He gives me a puzzled look.

I smile sheepishly, the memory making my chest tight. "Sorry, but I think I've had enough fun for today." I take the plastic dish and start back up the hill. Niko grabs my arm before I go anywhere.

"Everything okay?"

"Peachy."

His eyes bore into me, giving me the feeling he's reading the sins of my soul. "I want to see you."

I give him what I hope is a carefree smile. "You're seeing me right now," I say. I run off back up the hill, shaking the snow out of my hair as I go. I can't let myself think about how his words make me feel, hopeful and scared and oh-so-alive. It's better just to pretend I feel nothing.

I think I've forgotten why I'm in West County, and the lapse frightens me. I need to be more focused. Dr. Goodhart is my end goal. Not falling in love with a boy with stormy ocean eyes.

I give Tom the saucer once I'm back at the top of the hill. He hands me my hat and winks at me. "Not bad for a first-timer." He runs and dives down the hill, the sled under his belly like a surfboard. Adam frowns when he sees me.

"Hey, what's the matter?" he asks.

I shrug and force a smile. "I don't think sledding is my thing. Too dangerous."

He nods sagely. "I totally understand." He says it like there's no way a girl like me could possibly do anything more strenuous than paint my nails. If only he knew. He holds out the tequila. "Wanna drink?"

I debate whether I should refuse or just pretend to take a drink. Adam's eyes shine, and his cheeks are pink. The bottle is a quarter empty, and I'm not sure who besides Adam is drinking. But the last thing I want is to make a scene. I put the bottle to my lips and tilt it back, but I don't open my mouth. I wipe the tequila from my lips with the back of my glove, and Adam gives me a crooked smile. Unease settles in my belly at his look, and I wonder if he's trying to get me drunk.

I'm starting to think the puppy isn't as innocent as he pretends.

Jocelyn yells for Adam, and as he runs off, a small bag falls from his pocket. I don't have to look too closely to know what it is. The baggie full of green leaves looks like a prop from an antidrug commercial. I kick some snow over it and watch Adam as he sort of flops onto a sled and goes down the hill. I won't waste any more time pretending to be nice to him. After the mistake with Dylan, I've learned my lesson. Adam is obviously a mess, and the last thing I need is any sort of entanglement with a burnout.

I head over to where a fire burns in the ring I noticed earlier. Mindi sits next to it on a large rock, her body hunched over like she's practicing some new form of human origami. It isn't until I'm a couple feet away that I notice she's crying. I stop and stand there awkwardly.

"Uh, do you want to be alone?"

Mindi shakes her head and sniffs, dashing her tears away with her gloved hands. I sit on a nearby rock, the twin to the one Mindi occupies. I clear my throat.

"Do you want to talk about it?"

Mindi shakes her head again, but then stops. "Have you ever wanted something so much that you were convinced that if you just kept hoping and wishing that it would come true?"

I freeze, because her words take me back to a time filled with pain and fear. For a split second I am once again a frightened little girl, praying for someone to come save me. I blink, and the memory is wiped away like condensation on a window. "No," I answer quickly.

Mindi nods and looks away from me, fresh tears tracking down her cheeks. I sigh and prop my chin on my knees, watching the flames as they dance in the fading daylight. They twist and turn, and the images of two women appear in their flickering waltz. One has flowing locks and huge wings. The other is part serpent, her hair made of snakes writhing in time to the crackling of the burning wood. Soon, the two images croon to me, and I get the faintest trickle of Their rage.

It makes me want to flee this outing and plunge my sword into the heart of some murderous bastard.

Maybe I'll never be normal.

GOSSIP

BY THE TIME WE LEAVE THE MOUNTAIN, THE SKY is dark and everyone but me is a little tipsy. Adam is obliterated. He's the only person who can't hold his liquor. It takes Niko and Tom three tries to get him into my car, and once he's belted into the front seat, he immediately lurches toward the door.

"I'm gonna be sick," he slurs. Tom scrambles to undo the seat belt before both he and Niko jump out of the way. Adam falls out of my car to his knees, emptying the contents of his stomach onto the ground. It could be a Jackson Pollock painting, *Vomit on Snow*.

"Well, this is going to be a lovely drive," I mutter. Niko hears me and gives me a grin.

"You're right. Maybe you girls should ride together, and Tom and I will try to sober up Adam before we take him home. If he shows up like this, his mom's gonna be pissed."

I look to Jocelyn and Mindi, who has finally stopped crying and now just pouts, her eyes red rimmed. Jocelyn shrugs. "Sounds good to me. I don't wanna ride with Pukey McVomit anyhow."

Adam stumbles to his feet, barely missing the puddle of throw-up. Tom catches him and sets him on his feet, steering him away from the mess. Niko snags the bottle of tequila from Adam's fingers before it falls to the ground. There's less than a quarter of the bottle remaining. "Why are you always such a bitch?" Adam yells at Jocelyn, only he's facing the trees. He's so drunk that he doesn't even notice the difference.

I look at him in disgust. His lack of control is completely repugnant. The only thing that separates us from animals is our self-discipline. Without it— Adam begins to retch again, interrupting my thoughts. It's time to go.

I open my door. "Are you coming or not?" Mindi turns in surprise at my sharp tone. She wrinkles her nose and nods, and I get into my car without a backward glance at Adam. He can be someone else's problem.

Jocelyn scrambles into the backseat while I start the car. Mindi still stands outside, and I watch her stare at Niko while he helps Adam into the Jeep. She takes a step toward them, and Niko looks up. His brows knit together, and he gives a slight shake of his head. Mindi's shoulders slump, and she walks back to my car and gets in. I put the Toyota into gear and back down the narrow road, barely missing a couple of saplings. Mindi is sniffling again, and I swallow a sigh. This is going to be a long ride.

Jocelyn's car is still at school, and after a short discussion I find out that Mindi lives closer. We head there first. She lives in a modest development near the outskirts of town, and when I pull up in front of her house, she gets out with a mumbled, "I'll give you a call." I nod and smile, even though I'm hoping she doesn't bring up anything touchy later over the phone. Like the subject of Niko.

Jocelyn gets out of the car and says something to Mindi in a low voice before climbing into the passenger seat. I turn the car toward school.

We drive in silence for a little while, the radio the only noise. Finally I clear my throat. "So, uh, what's wrong with Mindi? She looks like she just won fourth place in a three-person race."

Jocelyn gives me an odd look out of the corner of her eye and then shrugs. "I dunno. Same old, same old, I guess. Niko. It's always Niko."

Now I'm interested. I keep my eyes on the road as I ask my next question. "Oh? Are they together?" If anyone knows what's going on, it's Jocelyn.

She lets out a short bark of laughter, and it's almost enough to make me drive off into the ditch. "Who told you that?"

No one. "Oh, you know, it's just something I heard at Tina's the other night."

She shakes her head and stares out the window. "In Mindi's dreams. I wish she would get it through her thick skull that nothing's going to happen. It would make things a lot easier for her."

I blink. Her tone is downright nasty. I thought Jocelyn and Mindi were friends. "So, I guess they aren't together?" I glance at her out of the corner of my eye, and in the glow of the radio I can see her grimace.

"Of course not. Mindi knows that, but she won't accept it. It's getting to the point where it's just sad."

"What do you mean?"

"Niko and Mindi grew up together. He sees her as a sister. Their moms were friends, and Mindi's mom died at the beginning of the school year. She was killed, murdered. It was a really big deal around here. They're still looking for the guy."

I make the appropriate noises of shock, but Jocelyn barely acknowledges me. She's too deep in the spinning of her story. "Anyway, Mindi kind of lost it. She got all depressed and slashed up her wrists at a party at Tina's house. You know the remodeled bathroom? Yeah, blood doesn't come out so well. We had to call an ambulance and everything. In the end it was no big deal, she'd completely missed all of her veins, but we all kind of freaked. That's why we're all so careful around her. No one wants a repeat."

Although I don't necessarily believe everything Jocelyn is saying, this rings true. It fits with what Dylan said in the library and the conversation I overheard at Tina's party.

Jocelyn pauses to stare out the window, and shrugs. "Afterward Niko felt bad, so he kind of started hanging around with Mindi all the time. You know, to keep an eye on her. She began talking like they were dating and everything, and Niko didn't know how to handle it. I guess he figured at some point she'd drop it. Every time she makes some comment about their 'special connection,' he just lets it go. He even tried to date this girl from our school, Kristen. Mindi totally flipped out.

She showed up at his house in the middle of the night and refused to go home until he talked to her and told her it wasn't true. She even punched out his bedroom window."

I stare at Jocelyn, but then I remember I'm driving and look back at the road. Mindi? The Mindi I know is afraid of her own shadow. She's not the kind of girl to go breaking windows to get what she wants. I don't say anything, and Jocelyn fills the silence.

"Niko should have known better. Mindi can't help it. She's always been kind of off, you know? I remember she once cried for the whole day in first grade because our teacher was out and we had a substitute. And then she took a pair of scissors and cut up the substitute's coat, because the woman spelled her name wrong. Who does that?"

I don't say anything, mostly because I'm not sure how much I believe of Jocelyn's story. It must have been horrible for Mindi to lose her mom. Tragedy can change people. I know this better than anyone else.

Jocelyn has confirmed that Mindi has a thing for Niko, but she's also made it clear that it's one-sided. So now I'm torn. Do I let myself pursue Niko and risk hurting Mindi, or do I make the smart decision and ignore the flutter of excitement I feel every time he's around? And if I do start to feel something for Niko, how long will it be until the Furies put a very violent end to things?

I almost miss the school's driveway, I'm so wrapped up in my own thoughts. I turn onto the driveway at the last second and swing into the parking lot near Jocelyn's car.

She gives me a nervous smile. "Thanks for the ride. Sorry today wasn't your thing."

I shrug and force a smile. I'm not quite sure what to say. Rolling around in the snow and watching someone throw up aren't exactly my idea of fun. Unless, of course, justice is being handed down. "It was fun hanging out, anyway," I say, hoping it will erase the uneasy expression on her face.

"Yeah." Jocelyn hesitates and then leans over so that she's in my personal space. She grabs my arm. "Can I ask you for a favor?"

"Uh, okay." I really want her to let go of me.

"Don't tell anyone what I told you about Mindi, okay? We've been friends for, like, forever, and she really is kind of delicate. And she likes you a lot. She used to talk about killing herself all the time, but since you got here, all she talks about is you." There's some bitterness in her voice, but she flashes me a smile. "I don't want her to think . . . you know."

I just nod and smile, and Jocelyn's face sags in relief.

"You're pretty cool, Dixie. Thanks for the ride." She releases my arm, and I pull it back with relief. There is an indentation in my coat from her palm, and I shake my arm, as though I can chase away the personal contact.

After Jocelyn gets out, I turn the car around and head toward my apartment. Throughout the entire drive the only thing I can think about is Niko. It makes my heart trip along happily, and I sing along to the radio the rest of the way home.

It's only after I get home that I realize They've been a little too quiet.

CONFLICTED AND CONFUSED

IT'S AFTER ONE IN THE MORNING WHEN MY phone rings. I've been asleep less than two hours, and I can't imagine who could be calling me, let alone at this time. I fumble in the dark for my phone and hit the ignore button, mercifully silencing the annoying pop song that is my ringtone.

A few seconds later it rings again. I swear into the dark and grab my phone, opening it with my eyes closed. "You have the wrong number."

"Are you sure? Because I'm pretty sure I was told there's a badass Southern belle at this number."

I sit up, suddenly awake. "Who is this?" The voice on the other end chuckles, and chills run across my skin. "Niko." I breathe in relief.

"You're avoiding me."

I think of our last time alone together, and our kiss. I'm suddenly too warm, and I kick off the blankets. "No, I'm not."

"Prove it. Come meet me. I'm a few miles from your place."

"How do you know where I live?"

He gives a low laugh. My heart pounds, and it's not from being awoken in the middle of the night.

"It's a small town. Everyone knows where everyone else lives, princess. Now, are you going to climb down from your castle and rescue me, or are you going to leave me to the dragon?"

I chew on the inside of my cheek, trying to think up an excuse why I can't meet him. And wondering why I desperately want to.

"I can't. My mom will kill me if I go out at this time of night." The lie sits woodenly in my mouth, and part of me hopes he'll buy the lame excuse. I keep forgetting that parents are the biggest obstacle for most other people my age.

Niko sighs. "You know I don't believe you, right? Do you really think I'd believe that you've never snuck out? Especially since I just saw you last night. What was the story? Cough medicine, right?" There's a playful tone in his voice that makes me forget what a very bad idea it would be to meet Niko in the middle of the night.

I immediately silence the thought. Despite what Jocelyn said, I think he and Mindi do have some connection. Dysfunctional, maybe, but I can't buy that a guy would be sensitive enough to go on coddling an unstable girl just to keep her steady. I've met a lot of guys. None of them were ever that nice.

Maybe Jocelyn just had everything wrong. Maybe Niko really does care about Mindi, as more than friends.

So why isn't he calling her?

"Hello, are you still there? Cory?" Niko's voice has an odd edge to it, and I gnaw on my lower lip. I want to know what's behind the emotion in his words. Is it really possible he feels the same compulsion that I do?

"I'm still here. Look, Niko—"

"Ten minutes. That's all I ask. Come and talk to me for ten minutes."

"Why?"

There's a long moment of silence, and then Niko clears his throat loudly. "I need to see you," he confesses. His voice is raw with emotion, and the sound does something to me. It wrecks whatever resolve I had to stay away from him, to just let this thing between us die a slow death.

Because the truth is, I feel exactly the same way.

"I'll be there in a few minutes."

Niko whoops in triumph on the other end of the line. He gives me directions to where he is, a few streets over. "Hurry. I'm freezing my ass off," he says, and then hangs up.

I get out of bed and slip into a pair of jeans and a sweater. I debate putting on makeup before I go out, but I don't want to spend the time. I'll have to count on the darkness to hide the fact that I don't have flawless skin.

Niko's directions are pretty straightforward, and I find him easily. His Jeep is parked in a vacant lot at the edge of town. Dead weeds reach through the snow with sharp branches. Broken beer bottles litter the frozen ground. I get out of my car and grimace, wondering how many bottles are from Niko. He leans against the door of his Jeep, feet crossed at the ankles, a bottle in his hand. Realizing he might be drunk makes me feel silly for being so excited to see him. It's easy to be in love when your judgment is clouded.

"So, you made it. Welcome to my pity party." Niko tosses back the remainder of a beer and hurls the brown bottle into the darkness. It shatters with a musical tinkle.

"Yeah, well, this is pretty lame. You should've at least sprung for a DJ." I notice for the first time that his headlights reflect off a sign advertising luxury town houses, coming soon. Not likely.

Niko laughs. "You know what's funny about you?" Niko twists off the cap on a fresh beer and takes a long drink. "Sometimes I actually think you're exactly who you pretend you are. But other times I think it's all an act. Like, maybe you're a cop pretending to be a high school student or something, you know?" He moves toward me, and he is surprisingly sure-footed, considering how drunk he sounds.

"You watch too much TV. And I'm going home." All of my earlier feelings—the excitement to see him, the way the sound of his voice made my heart race—have disappeared. Niko is exactly like every other boy I've ever met. I was stupid to think he was any different.

I turn around to leave, and Niko blocks my path. He's incredibly quick, and I freeze as he leans in.

"Like right now. And when you first answered your phone."

I sigh and wrap my arms around myself to keep warm. I forgot my jacket in my hurry, and the night air is freezing. "What about it?"

"Your accent. It just disappeared. Poof. Like it's just a prop." Niko takes a deep drink of his beer and moves around me toward his Jeep. He pulls out a notebook and waves it at me. "Like this. Every day I take this to school. I sit through boring lectures given by teachers who barely made it through college, teachers who don't understand what it is they're trying to teach any more than we do. And I write. They think I'm taking notes, but I'm not. It's just a prop so they'll leave me alone."

I watch Niko, unmoving. My curiosity is piqued. "What do you write in there?"

Niko freezes, like it's not the question he expected. "Stock purchase plans."

I blink. I expected him to say "song lyrics" or "poetry" or to show me a set of sketches, preferably of me. After all, isn't that how it goes in the movies? Niko hands me the notebook, and I open it up. In the light from his headlights I can see dates and stock quotes, and at the end of the week a graph charting their progress. I track the lines that move up and down across the page. Underneath, Niko has written his own notes like "should spike after third quarter sales" or "overvalued, wait until after June to purchase."

"Not the kind of thing you'd expect to find in the notebook of the guy who gets a D in math, huh?"

I have no idea what kind of grades Niko gets in math, but the notebook is a surprise. It makes me like him a little more. "How'd you learn all of this?"

"My father was a stockbroker, and when I was younger, he used to talk about that stuff with me. It kind of stuck." The pain on his face is so raw, I can't help myself.

"What happened to him?"

Niko leans heavily against the Jeep. "He was killed by an investor who lost a lot of money when the economy went down the tubes. Guy came into the office and just started shooting people. He wasn't even one of my dad's clients. Afterward my mom married some mechanic she knew from high school."

I don't say anything. I'm not good at consoling people, even though I understand his raw grief. I feel like I should say something, but anything I say will just sound hollow. So I let the silence stretch out for what seems like an eternity.

Niko eyes me, and finishes his beer. "So, enough about my shitty life. What about you?"

"What do you mean? What about me?"

Niko tosses the beer bottle off into the darkness and stalks toward me. "What are your props, Miss Dixie? Hmmm? Lip gloss and designer jeans are a couple. What else?"

I shrug. "I don't have any props. What you see is what you get." His gaze makes me uncomfortable, but I don't feel threatened. I'm excited by the possibility that he's seen through my act. The range of emotions when I'm with him is staggering. It's the first definite crack in the wall I've built. I can't predict what Niko will do next, and I like that. He is the first person in a long time who has surprised me. At least, in a good way.

"Somehow, I don't believe that." Niko moves closer. He's now close enough for me to see the irises of his eyes. The low light makes them shine, the blue the same pale shade as the sky right before dawn. I stand still as his eyes search my face. "You have freckles. And you look a lot different without makeup."

His comment alarms me, and I move to take a step back. His hands snake around my waist, and before I can respond, he lowers his mouth to mine.

The shock of the kiss reverberates throughout my entire body. Niko's lips are as warm and soft as I remember, and the pressure of the contact heats me from the inside. Kissing him is like diving headfirst into a wave, shocking and exhilarating. There's none of the anxiety I usually feel when people touch me. Instead I'm relaxed and fluid, like I'm made of molten metal. For a split second I think of Kevin Eames, but Niko nibbles at my bottom lip, and thoughts of the only other boy I've ever kissed melt away. Just like in the drugstore, my mind is silent. The Furies aren't here to ruin this moment, and that makes the kiss all that much better. I sigh in delight.

Right now I want Niko more than I've ever wanted anything else.

I break off the kiss and notice with some surprise that Niko's arms are pulling me even closer. Our bodies are pressed together, and I'm no longer cold. He nuzzles my neck, trailing little kisses down to the space where it meets my shoulder. I lean into his touch, wrapping my arms around him to steady myself, since my legs have gone weak. He kisses the hollow near my ear. "What's your secret?" he whispers, before nibbling my earlobe. I sigh, since I've lost the ability to speak coherently, and he laughs before kissing me again. "How does a girl as gorgeous as you learn to beat down a guy twice her size?"

His words send a chill of warning down my spine. I start to pull away, but heated, insistent kisses at the base of my throat quickly douse my alarm. I slip my hands under his shirt, and the play of muscles under his skin makes my head feel like it will float away.

Niko kisses a path back up to my ear and laughs softly. "There's something about you that makes me think crazy thoughts. It makes me wonder if the universe sent you just for me."

I know how he feels. He's the most perfect guy I've ever met and a guy They've never found fault with. Maybe They secretly approve of him? Is that why They're so quiet when he's around? Or is it just a coincidence?

I really want it to be some sort of sign that it's safe to feel this way about him.

I don't resist as his hands reach up under my sweater. His fingers are surprisingly warm splayed against the small of my back. He kisses me again, mouth slightly open, and his tongue darts out to meet mine. I tilt my head to the side, slanting my mouth across his so I can taste him. The flavor of root beer in his mouth mingles with the toothpaste lingering in mine.

Wait, root beer?

I break off the kiss and lean back, sniffing his breath. There's no hint of any alcohol. Instead he smells like soda.

"Are you drunk?" I demand, and Niko laughs. He rubs his cheek against mine, and the stubble on his jaw scratches my skin. It shouldn't feel as good as it does. I almost forget my alarm as I breathe in the fresh scent of rain and ocean.

"No. What would make you think that?"

I'm afraid again, and I push him away, backpedaling until there are a few feet separating us. An icy breeze cuts through my thin sweater, stealing away Niko's warmth. I'm freezing now, and I wrap my arms around my middle to try to keep some of the remaining heat. I don't like being manipulated. "They way you were talking, the things you were saying . . . You called me in the middle of the night. I thought you were drunk."

"I thought we already covered this. I called because I wanted to see you. And just now? I was being honest. You're the one who wanted to know how I felt about you last night. I was trying to tell you."

I watch Niko, looking for some insight into how his mind works. There's none. I just can't figure him out. But I think I like that about him.

I take a deep breath. This is my opportunity to figure out the situation between him and Mindi. "Since we're being honest, I have a question for you."

He grins, his good mood back. "Ask away."

"Earlier today Jocelyn told me that you and Mindi are just friends. Is that true?"

Niko blinks at the sudden change in subject. "Yeah." His voice is flat. "What does Mindi have to do with this?"

"Does she like you? Does she maybe think you guys are more than friends?"

He exhales sharply and pushes his fingers through his hair. "Why would you think that?"

I'm starting to shake, but I don't know if it's because of the cold or because I'm afraid of his answer. "Because she acts like you're her Prince Charming. Does she know you only like her as a friend?"

His expression gives me pause, and I know Jocelyn was telling the truth in my car. Or at least a reasonable copy of the truth.

Niko sighs and holds out his hands. "It's complicated . . ."

I turn and stomp away toward my car, anger and disappointment and the odd urge to cry welling up inside. I spin around before I get inside. "Look, let me know when it gets less complicated. I don't know what kind of girl you think I am, but I'm not one who'll mess around with a guy who leads her friend on, no matter what the reason." I pause. "She's my friend, Niko. I don't want to trade her for you." I get into my car, start up the engine, and peel out of the lot before Niko even moves.

The drive back to my apartment passes in a whirlwind of conflicted emotions. I pull onto my street and turn the car off, not moving as I replay the scene in my head. I lightly touch my lips. My mouth still tingles from my contact with him, and when I lick my lips, I can still taste his root beer. With a sinking feeling I realize I want more. I don't care about Mindi's feelings enough to feel guilty.

And that makes me the world's worst friend.

EARLY MORNING REVELATIONS

MY FEET POUND ON THE SIDEWALK, THE BEAT soothing after a night spent tossing and turning. I haven't slept well for the past week, thanks to Niko. The memory of his kisses has haunted me. Those few minutes together are more disturbing than the few memories I have of my past. For some reason I can't get the softness of Niko's lips out of my head, or the way he talked to me so openly, so candidly. If I had a chance to do it again, I would, even though I know that it might jeopardize my friendship with Mindi.

But I haven't had the opportunity. Niko hasn't called me since that night.

He isn't the only thing keeping me up. I'm having trouble finding someone besides Dr. Goodhart. In the pocket of my fleece is a brand-new clipping, and the sight of it in my locker two days ago sent chills down my spine. After Medina's botched justice my confidence is shot, and I'm not really looking forward to carrying out any more judgments. But I don't have a choice. The Furies won't stay quiet forever.

I stared at the clipping while waiting for everyone to show up for lunch on Monday. The headline was missing, but I gleaned everything I needed to know from the remainder of the article.

It was from a Montana newspaper. A man by the name of Jefferson Halsey was arrested after he was accused of touching a couple of little girls at a birthday party. Mr. Halsey spent his weekends working as a birthday clown by the name of Tickles, and he used that opportunity to find his victims.

The article went on to detail how, since the story first broke, four other parents had come forward, all accusing Halsey of the same atrocities. The case against Halsey was airtight, until the district attorney falsified evidence in an attempt to build a landmark case just in time for his reelection. As of the date of the article, a judge had declared a mistrial and local parents were calling for the DA's head on a platter.

The article gave me a weird sort of relief. I hate criminals who prey on children, more than anyone else. That's why They brought me the article. The sooner I can get back on the metaphorical horse, the better. Justice will be a great distraction from Niko and his memory-searing kisses.

Each night since getting the snippet of paper, I've spent several hours looking for Halsey, before finally giving up and going to bed. I've followed so many dead ends that I'm frustrated. I've made myself scarce around my new group of friends, for fear that I'll take my bad temper out on them. I'm not good with failure.

Of course, none of this has anything to do with Niko. I am not throwing myself into finding a criminal just to avoid the fact that I am preoccupied by his rain and ocean scent.

I'm not the only one in my neighborhood having a rough week. A screaming argument next door woke me around midnight, and I stared at the ceiling for the next couple of hours. When I finally did nod off, dreams filled with snow and blood and Niko woke me. At about three thirty I finally gave up trying to sleep and decided to run until I had to get ready for school. My head was a mess when I set out into the darkness.

My mind returns to those moments with Niko. At the drugstore, sledding, in the vacant lot. I turn over his words in my mind, wearing them down into something completely different, like an ocean-tossed piece of glass. I want to find some hint of his feelings about me. I can't believe kisses mean all that much. I've handed down justice to quite a few men who kissed their victims.

For the first time in my life I am obsessed with a boy. The trouble I'm having finding my target is not helping my turmoil.

I turn the corner and complete my loop, heading back to my apartment. My foot slides on a patch of ice, and my arms windmill until I can steady myself. The cold scours my face, and I pick up my pace.

The only good thing about my travels through the Internet last night was finally breaking into the intranet for West County High. I've been trying to break through since I moved here, but their firewall was surprisingly good. I was still able to crack it, but it has taken me a little longer than usual.

It was totally worth the effort.

One of the announcements gave me an idea, and I'm excited to put it into motion this morning. I'm going to take my revenge on Amber.

Over the past week she has gone out of her way to try to destroy me. It may sound lame, but I've never had anyone hate me the way she does. At my other schools it's been nothing more than a little trash-talking behind my back, not too harsh. Amber is taking rivalry to a whole new level.

Someone scrawled S-L-U-T in red lipstick on my locker in gym, let out all of the air in my car tires, and sent me dozens of nasty text messages from a private number, several of which were indecent pictures of women, or as the message read: *sluts like u*. When I see Amber at lunch, she wears a permanent smirk, like she knows a secret that I don't. Each injustice sends my heart racing with rage, which whips Them into a frenzy in the back of my mind. I've probably eaten more chocolate in the past week than in the last five years.

I am so over high school. I don't even know why I'm still here. I should just take my GED and leave town. There's only a month and a half until my birthday and the freedom of being eighteen. Once I'm an adult, I won't have to worry that the state will send me back to the mental hospital. There's really no concrete reason to stay in West County.

Who am I kidding? I know why I'm here. Niko.

I pick up the pace and do a hurdler's jump over a pile of dirty snow. My lungs start to burn, and I push myself even harder, relishing the pain.

Amber's lucky I haven't broken every bone in her ugly face. Without the release of handing down justice to Jefferson Halsey, I'm a time bomb waiting to go off. She can be certain that if I let Them have their way, it won't be anonymous texts and whispered rumors. Female or not, Amber will be dead. Unfortunately, I can't let that happen.

But I'm not putting up with her shit anymore.

I smile as I round the corner back to my apartment, the first rays of dawn beginning to lighten the icy night sky.

I'm going to teach Amber a very valuable lesson: Hell hath no Fury like me.

CONTROL, LAPSE OF

AT WEST COUNTY HIGH THERE ARE TWO BELLS.
The first is a warning bell that sends all of the students into the building like a herd of cattle. The second is the late bell. The goal of most well-behaved students is to socialize until the first bell, grab the necessary books from one's locker, and make it to class before the late bell. Normally that is also my goal. Not today.

I discovered a lot while poking through the school's intranet. The school stores student files on a central server, which meant that I could view grades as well as progress reports and small things like personal histories. I should have done it earlier. I really could have saved myself some effort by picking my friends beforehand.

Through those folders I learned quite a few interesting facts. Adam has several disciplinary actions for alcohol and drugs. Mindi is failing her math class and "cries at inappropriate times." Jocelyn has gotten into several fights over her gossiping, and Tom has regular appointments with the school shrink because his mother finds him "alternating between manic and depressed states since his father left last year." Amber was caught performing oral sex (not a surprise) in a janitor's closet on an unidentified male, and Niko's folder has so many progress reports and warning letters that I'm impressed. The student files read like tabloid articles. According to what I found in the student folders, the only person without major issues is me.

This made me laugh. But at least I now know why Niko keeps calling me a good girl.

The student folders also have the locker assignments, which is how I know that Amber's locker is number 253, right near the side door. My plan is simple: Wait until the late bell rings, go get my books from my locker, and do what I need to do before I head to class. I won't have to tell Amber it was my handiwork. She'll know.

The first bell rings, and I watch the kids file in. Even as much as I hate high school, I still want to be one of them.

Niko saunters into the school, one of the last to go inside. My stomach drops as I watch him enter. There have been no repeats of that night in the vacant lot, and no phone calls or texts, either. I'm not sure if I'm avoiding him or he's avoiding me, but either way it hurts. I want him to feel the same yearning for me that I feel for him.

I don't understand why I'm drawn to him like a bug to an electric zapper. I've convinced myself that there is something seriously wrong with him. It's the only explanation for the way his face pops into my mind every few minutes.

And really, any sort of entanglement with Niko is the last thing I need. He's probably unstable, and crazy, and maybe a little psychotic.

He's also an incredible kisser.

I can't even pretend to care that he might be a sociopath. After all, we'd be a perfect match.

Thinking about him is not helping.

Seconds after Niko walks through the double doors, the late bell rings. I heft my backpack out of my passenger seat. I lied to him that night in the vacant lot, about not having a pretense to fit in. He was right, my lip gloss and designer jeans are props. The problem is that everything I own and do is a tool to further the illusion that I'm normal. My car, my face, even my good-girl act. Everything is carefully constructed to pander to the expectations others will have of me.

I grab my backpack, climb out of the car, and walk across the snow-covered lawn to the front doors. The snow is frozen solid, and I carefully slide along the icy top layer. I'm almost to my goal when someone shouts.

"Hey. Hey! Wait right there, young lady."

I stop and turn. The obese school guard jogs toward me. He wears a thick coat and carries a walkie-talkie in one hand. I am thankfully spared the sight of watching his body bounce up and down as he runs. It's less than a hundred feet between me and him, but by the time he reaches me, he's huffing and puffing. He gasps for breath, and I wait patiently until he can speak.

"Where . . . do . . . you . . . think . . . you're . . . going?" he pants.

My brain has trouble processing the fact that a man so grossly out of shape is responsible for the safety of the entire student population. I smile and point at the double doors. "I'm going inside to my locker. I'm late."

"I have to escort you to the main office. Once you miss the late bell, you can't get into class without a tardy slip."

My smile freezes in place. With lard-ass walking me to the office, I'll never get the chance to exact my revenge. And I'm not exactly in love with the way he's staring at my chest.

I shrug, pushing my frustration aside. "Okay." He leads the way, and I follow closely behind.

"You know," he huffs over his shoulder, "you kids should make an effort to get here on time. You'll never make it in the world if you don't learn the value of punctuality."

I stop. How dare he lecture me? What does he know about success? Rage rises up from deep in my belly, blurring my vision. My heart pounds and I'm overly warm, my breathing rapid. I've just realized what's about to happen when I snap.

My vision splits in three as I step forward and grab him in a headlock, my arm ratcheting down around his throat. He gurgles and flails, but he wasn't prepared for the attack. It's been too long since I've handed down a judgment, and my control over Them is frayed. They rise up quickly, melting the snow around us in Their haste to find release.

I'm not sure who has control of my body.

I release his neck, Tisiphone kicking him in the small of his back when he stumbles forward. He drops his walkie-talkie and falls to his knees with a groan. Megaera gives him a quick kidney punch before I lift my leg up and bring it around, catching him in the side of the head. Blood trickles from his temple, and I come back to myself with a jerk. He collapses into the snow, facedown, and doesn't move.

I moan and mentally push Them back into my subconscious as I regain control of myself. They howl for blood, demanding justice for a dozen imagined crimes. I hold my head as They claw through my mind on the way back to Their prison. My brain is being ripped into pieces. I fall to my knees, biting my tongue until I taste blood, to keep from crying out.

Eventually the pain fades. I shakily get to my feet, brushing off the snow. Whether the school guard has done something wrong or not, I don't know. But I will only punish those They can prove are evil.

Besides, I can't exactly carry out justice on the school's front lawn in broad daylight, can I?

My chest is full of the sting of failure. The guard is splayed face-down in the snow, which has melted to little more than a few inches of slush from Their appearance. I barely even felt Them breaking loose. How did I not sense how close They were to manifesting before Their appearance?

My hands go to my head as I pace. I have just attacked a school employee. Did anyone see? Oh, God, how am I going to explain this?

I shove away the panic and take a deep breath. First things first. I carefully turn his head to the side and check the guard for injuries. He doesn't look like I hurt him too badly. He's lucky he's wearing the thick jacket, otherwise I probably would have broken a couple of his ribs. I scan the snowy ground, but there's no sign of my presence, only the guard's. Of course, the snow is pretty melted here. Maybe no one will notice.

I stomp down the snow around where he lies to make it look trampled. Then I run inside to the office.

There's no time to get my revenge on Amber. I need to save my ass first.

I run to the main office. The secretary looks up in irritation. I'm interrupting her perusal of a tabloid article posing the age-old question, "Will They Get Back Together?" A couple of movie stars I don't know stare at the reader from opposite sides of a broken heart. I can see why the secretary is annoyed at the interruption. This is clearly very important reading.

I breathe heavily, even though I'm not really winded from the run. I need to look as panicked as I feel. "Oh, God. Oh, God. They're killing him! You need to send someone outside to help." I make sure to pour on the Southern twang.

The secretary gives me a slight frown, her gray brows knitting together. "What are you talking about? What's going on? Where's Mr. Carson?"

I assume Mr. Carson is the unconscious school guard. I bury my face in my hands and talk through my fingers. "There were some creepy-looking guys outside. He was walking me in because I was late, when these guys just ran up and jumped him." A sob tears out of me, surprising me and the secretary. It's not fake. The guilt from nearly killing a harmless man sweeps through me, leaving me aching.

I have the secretary's attention now. She's out of the chair and calling for Mr. Hanes, when a burst of static erupts from the radio sitting in a charger on the secretary's desk. Mr. Carson's voice comes across in a groan. "I need someone to get out here to the front lawn. I've been attacked."

The secretary snatches up the walkie-talkie as a whimper echoes through the static. "Bob? Can you hear me? Are you okay?" Another low moan is her answer, and she tries again. "Can you walk?" She gives me a long, appraising look. "Did you see who attacked you?"

There is silence from the other end, and my heart thumps painfully in my chest. If he knows it was me, my time in West County is finished.

And so is any chance I may have had with Niko.

The thought fills me with a wave of self-loathing. I've just injured a man, and all I can think of is a boy I can't have because my closest friend here is unstable and half in love with him. I'm so pathetic.

The secretary eyes me and speaks into the walkie-talkie again. "How many of them were there, Bob? Were they students?"

Bob groans again through a burst of static. "I didn't get a good look at them before they were on me. From the way they came at me, there had to be a couple of them. Maybe three or four. There was a girl . . ."

"She's here. She ran to the office for help." A massive weight lifts off my chest as I'm flooded with relief. He didn't see me. I'm safe from discovery.

The Furies are another matter entirely. I have to hunt. At this rate it's going to be a fight to make it through the day.

The secretary calls for Mr. Hanes again. She looks up at me with a harried look. "Here," she says, slapping the late slip on the counter and scrawling a messy signature on the bottom line. "Fill it out and leave the white copy. You give your teacher the pink copy."

I nod, wide-eyed. "Is Mr. Carson okay?" I ask in a quavering voice. I wish the tremor were an act, but I'm actually worried about him. There are a hundred different ways to kill a man, and They know all of them. Carson is lucky to be alive.

The secretary's expression softens, and she pats my hand. "Don't worry about him. He'll be fine. You need to get to class."

I nod and fill out the slip while the secretary picks up the phone to dial the police. I tear off the white copy of the slip and place it on the counter. Mr. Hanes rushes in from the back. The vice principal is visibly shaken as the secretary talks to him in a low voice. On my way out, he glances up at me, our eyes meeting for the briefest second before his gaze slides away. I slip out of the room before either Mr. Hanes or the secretary can think to ask me what the guys who attacked Carson look like.

I head to class, feeling heavy even though I've once again avoided discovery. I have a feeling that something is happening with Them. I'm afraid that if I don't figure out how to fix it, Alekto's warnings will actually come true.

R.I.P., HOPES AND DREAMS

AT LUNCH, CONVERSATION REVOLVES AROUND two major topics: Mr. Carson getting beat up and the visit of the drug-sniffing dogs.

Like many other schools, West County High has a bit of a drug problem. It's not an obvious problem like in the bigger schools. No cheerleaders are getting coked up in the girls' bathroom, and no one has died from an overdose, like the headlines you see closer to Phila-delphia, but there are enough kids getting high at parties to alarm the well-intentioned parents of the West County school district.

So two years ago the school board decided to hold unannounced inspections at both the high school and middle school. During classes men in dark blue fatigues walk the dogs through, alerting school administration to any lockers that the dogs find especially interesting. The lockers are searched, and the locker owners are suspended if any contraband is found.

The inspections are random, and this morning's visit is a surprise to everyone in the school. Everyone but me. There are few surprises when you have access to Mr. Hanes's personal calendar.

I'm the first one to our table at lunch.

Adam sits down across from me, but he just gives me a mumbled hello and begins eating a slice of pizza. He's been standoffish since I started ignoring him. I hate that I may have hurt his feelings, but it wouldn't have worked out with him anyway. It's kind of hard to spend a lot of time with a person you find pathetic.

I think I know how he feels, though. Niko treats me with the same detached politeness I give to Adam. Which, after the kisses in the vacant lot, sucks. Part of me—the part that still likes watching romantic comedies on television—was hoping he would declare his undying love for me the very next day. But here we are a week later, and he doesn't even show up at lunch anymore.

I wish it didn't sting as much as it does.

Tom and Jocelyn show up a short while later. As soon as she sits down, Jocelyn's eyes gleam and she leans forward. She almost twitches, she's so excited.

"So, did you guys hear?"

I slice off a piece of chicken breast and chew it slowly. "Hear what?"

Tom snorts. "You aren't talking about Carson getting his ass kicked, are you?"

Jocelyn shakes her head, and her sleek dark hair shifts. Conversation in the cafeteria is unusually subdued today, and her hair sliding across her silky blouse sounds like an animal slinking through leaves. "Amber got arrested."

I gasp, and Tom drops an F-bomb. Adam looks miserable, and his shoulders slump. I glance at him, thinking that maybe his behavior has less to do with being mad at me and more to do with Amber's absence.

"I guess she had, like, a whole bag of pot in her locker," Jocelyn says. I'm so surprised, I can't even speak. This makes my plan to humiliate Amber seem childish.

The idea had been that the dogs would have alerted on Amber's locker because of a raw steak I was going smear all over her things. After that I was going to fill her locker with every sort of embarrassing substance known to man. Condoms. Laxatives. Porn. Photoshopped pictures of her and Dylan Larchmont in several compromising positions. Those I was particularly proud of. It took me all night to get the shading just right. The plan was for the rumor mill to churn and for Amber to leave me alone. Childish, yet effective.

But this . . . this is so much bigger.

No one says anything, and Jocelyn continues. "They took her away in handcuffs. Amanda Benson is office assistant fourth period, and she said she didn't even cry, just kept cussing at the cops." Excitement gives Jocelyn's eyes an eerie light, and a shiver runs down my spine.

"That sucks," Tom says, poking at his hamburger. "I wonder if they'll send her to jail."

I pause in my chewing. I don't like Amber, but she doesn't deserve to go to prison.

"Jail?" Adam shakes his head. "No, they don't send first-time offenders to jail for something like a little pot." Everyone gives him a disbelieving look. He flushes. "Do they?" Huh. I wonder if he and Amber are more than just friendly? It would explain a lot of the undercurrent I've sensed between them.

Before anyone can answer Adam's question, Mindi runs up, her cheeks flushed and her eyes shining with unshed tears. "Did you guys hear what happened to Amber?"

I nod somberly. "Jocelyn just told us."

Mindi collapses onto the bench next to me, and I scoot down a bit to give her room. "This is just awful," she moans.

Adam pats her hand. "Hey, don't worry about Amber. I'm sure she won't get any real jail time. It's her first offense." Even he doesn't look like he believes that.

Mindi shakes her head, and tears leak out of the corners of her eyes. I get a flash of irritation at her waterworks. I swear she cries more than a soap opera star.

Mindi swipes at her eyes and continues. "I know, but this week has just really sucked. Last night Niko called and told me he wanted me to stay away. He said he 'couldn't pretend anymore.' Pretend what?" No one looks at her, because we all know what Niko meant. It's hard to be just friends with someone who's obsessed with you.

Mindi is oblivious to everyone at the table. "I just need to see him, to explain that it's not a big deal if he needs some space." She hiccups and begins to sob. She shakes her head. "I'm sorry," she says, jumping up to run out of the lunchroom. I glance around the table. Everyone ducks their head to avoid my gaze. No one has any plans to follow her.

I stand with a sigh and leave the cafeteria. My appetite's ruined anyway.

Predictably, Mindi is in the girls' bathroom. Her sobs echo in the tiled room, the porcelain amplifying the sound into something that could be used for psychological torture.

This is what happens when you get involved with a boy.

A flutter of wings. Heartbreak.

I ignore Them and tap on the door of the stall. "Mindi, it's Cory. Do you want to talk, hon?"

Sniffles are my only answer for a few long moments, and then the stall door unlocks. I slip into the cramped space and slide the bolt closed behind me. Mindi sits on the toilet, her legs drawn up so that her arms and head rest on her knees. Her light brown hair cascades around her shoulders like a cape. I lean against the door and wait for her to start.

"I know you must think I'm a train wreck," Mindi begins, "but I have my reasons."

I say nothing, and Mindi continues. "Last October my mom was raped and killed." Mindi sniffs, and turns her head to the side. "That day my dad took me to Philly to go shopping. Things'd been rough for us, but Dad just got a new job so he wanted to celebrate. Mom had to work, so she didn't go. I guess while I was busy trying on jeans some drifter was breaking into our house. He caught my mom coming out of the shower." Mindi swipes at her tears, and my stomach clenches. While Mindi can only imagine what her mother went through, I've seen it firsthand through the memories of the guilty.

Mindi gives a bitter laugh and continues. "It was the best day of my life. I was so happy, until we got home and I walked into the bathroom . . ." Mindi trails off, and the door squeaks as someone walks into the girls' room.

We wait in silence while the person pees and washes her hands. Finally, after forever, the person walks out.

"Ever since that day, I'm afraid to be too happy, like somehow someone will know and ruin it. The last time I felt truly happy was the time I kissed Niko. I felt like I was turning into little pieces of sunshine, you know?" Guilt swells in my chest. I do know. It's the same way I felt when I kissed Niko.

I don't say anything, though. Mindi keeps talking.

"But now I find out that it wasn't real. I mean, we were in the hospital, after I tried to . . . end it all. That's where it happened. I kissed him, and he just let me. Now he says he was afraid to hurt me." She sniffs again, and reaches for a wad of toilet paper to wipe her nose. "I guess I knew somewhere deep down that he was just trying to be nice. He never kissed me, even after I threw myself at him. I just thought he was being polite, that he was afraid to ruin our friendship. But now he tells me he wasn't interested in me like that, was just afraid I might lose it if he said so. It's like finding my mom on the bathroom floor all over again." Mindi looks up for the first time. "I pretended for so long that he could be happy with me that I started to believe it. How could I have been so stupid?"

I sigh. "Guys can be that way, I guess. But he's not the only one in the world."

Mindi shakes her head like she doesn't want to hear my words. "You don't understand. It's not just about Niko. Last night my dad got a call from the detective on my mother's case. They haven't had any leads in a while, so they're kicking it over to the cold case detectives. It's not a 'high priority,' they said. That's as good as them giving up."

I open my mouth to say something encouraging, but when I see the stormy expression on Mindi's face, I clamp my mouth shut. She clenches her fists. "Not only has Niko given up on me, but the police have given up on my family."

Without warning Mindi kicks the plastic toilet paper dispenser. She growls as she attacks it, like a wild animal. I squeeze backward into the opposite corner of the stall to avoid her, shocked at the sudden violence. It must have felt good, because she kicks it three or four more times, cracking the dispenser badly, before she dissolves into angry sobbing. In between heaving sobs she assaults the dispenser again and again, until it lies in pieces on the floor. I stare at the jagged pieces of plastic in shock.

Maybe Jocelyn was telling the truth about Mindi being crazy. Now Dylan's rant about hanging out with a mental patient makes perfect sense.

Still, I can't fault Mindi for going off the deep end over her mother's death. Aren't we all a little unstable at times? Her mom being murdered seems like a pretty good excuse.

The bell rings, signaling the end of lunch. We both look up. All I want is to get the hell out of Crazytown, but I can't. Mindi is my friend. I swallow nervously. "I don't know about you, but I don't think I can bear to sit through sixth and seventh periods. Wanna go to the mall?" I half-expect her to bite me.

Her eyes widen. "You mean cut class?"

Looks like meek, slightly more stable Mindi is back. Crazy as she may be, she's still the best friend I have. "With Carson gone, there's no one to stop us. We should get out while we can. Come on. I'll buy you a pretzel and we can get makeovers."

Mindi gives a hope-filled look. Although she's surrounded by people, she doesn't have any real friends. Not anyone willing to put her first.

"Okay," she says, wiping away her tears with a piece of toilet paper. "But we should wait until the late bell rings before we try to leave. I'm sure someone will see us if we go right now."

"No problem, but I think I'm gonna go wait in my own stall." She giggles, and I give her a wide grin, feeling for the millionth time like a complete fraud. As a smile lights up her face, I know that I can't go near Niko again, no matter how I ache for him.

Once again They are right. Nothing lies down that path but pain and heartbreak. Mindi is proof of that.

Still, I have to wonder if it might not be worth the trip.

CLOSE CALL

THERE'S A COP CAR SITTING IN FRONT OF MY apartment building when I arrive home after dropping off Mindi. It's dark out, and the interior light in the cruiser illuminates the officer bent over paperwork. My breath hitches. The police make me nervous. I'm not exactly a model citizen.

I get out of my car and head up the walk, and the officer does the same. He gives me a friendly smile and calls my name. "Corrine Graff?"

I stop and give him a confused smile. "Yes? Can I help you?"

The officer holds out his hand to shake, and I take it. "Officer Harmon. Jason Harmon. I'm here to ask you a few questions about Mr.

Carson's assault. I understand you're the last person to see him before he was attacked."

I widen my eyes and nod. "Oh, okay. Uh, can we talk inside? I live upstairs."

Harmon nods, and I lead the way into the building and up the stairs. Once inside I take off my shoes, eyeing the closed door to my bedroom. I can't remember if I tucked all of my news clippings away in my trunk before I left this morning. My thoughts were so totally focused on getting back at Amber that I'm pretty sure my past crimes are completely visible.

Only a door separates me from the possibility of a very, very long prison sentence. I should've talked to him out on the sidewalk.

But Officer Harmon isn't here for me, and I have no intention of changing that. "Why don't we go into the kitchen?" I offer. He nods, and I lead the way.

Once we are in the minuscule kitchen, I pull out a chair for the officer. He sits down and declines my offer of tea or water. I grab a bottle of water for myself and sit in the chair across from him. He already has a notebook out, and he levels a gaze at me, his expression serious. "Why don't you call your parents, Miss Graff? I don't want to do this without their permission."

I laugh, and shake my head. "Well, you'd have to hold a séance to get their permission. I'm an orphan, Officer Harmon. This is all mine." No point in lying to a man who can easily look up my past.

Officer Harmon frowns slightly. "This is your apartment?"

I nod, a smile curving my lips. The Furies love keeping the cops off balance. "Yup. At least that's what the lease says." Actually, the lease says Bernadette Allen. But he doesn't need to know that.

Just to make sure he's a little distracted, I stretch and let out a soft sigh, fighting a smile as his eyes lock on the pull of fabric across my breasts.

Gotcha.

Officer Harmon shifts in his seat and studies his notebook closely, pretending he's not checking me out. "Okay, Miss Graff. Why don't you tell me what happened this morning."

I tell him the same story I told the secretary, adding a few hair flips and catlike stretches for his benefit. He interrupts me several times to stutter out a few terse questions. I get the impression that Officer Harmon is not exactly overflowing with personality.

"So you didn't see the boys who attacked Mr. Carson up close?"

I shake my head for the third time. "No. After they ran up to Mr. Carson, I ran to the office. I've never seen anything like that before. I was scared," I say in a small voice. It's the truth. The only problem is that I wasn't afraid of Carson's phantom attackers; I'm afraid of myself.

Officer Harmon nods and stands. "Okay. Thanks for all of your help."

I stand as well. "No problem, Officer. Oh, how is Mr. Carson doing? The rumor at school was that he went to the hospital."

The officer nods. "He's pretty beat up." He catches himself, then looks at me and taps his pen against his lips. "I'm not supposed to discuss that kind of stuff."

I nod, eyes wide, lip trembling. "I understand. I was just so worried, when those boys ran up to him . . ." I shake my head, like I'm trying to clear a bad memory.

Officer Harmon clears his throat and lays an awkward hand on my shoulder. "Umm, yeah, that kind of experience can be pretty upsetting. But Mr. Carson will be fine. He has three broken ribs and a concussion, but nothing life-threatening."

I'm surprised to hear that I broke his ribs after all. There's a moment of perverse pleasure, but I push it down before the officer notices. That's Them, not me. "Do you think it's safe to go back to school? I mean, do you think the people who did this will come back?"

Harmon smiles. "I think it's safe enough."

I see the officer out and lean against the door with a sigh. I'm pretty sure that I'm not a suspect, but I need to think about getting out of town. I'm not sure what the chances are that Harmon will tell the school that I lied on my admission paperwork, but if he does, it won't be good. If I want to stay here, I'm going to have to hack into the student files and update my information.

But why would I do that? This is entirely too close for comfort, and things are getting complicated. My control on Them is thin, and I'm no closer to finding Dr. Goodhart. It is way past time to leave town. We can find the doctor just as well from the road as we can from here. And I can't guarantee that They won't do something violent at school again. There is entirely too much risk in staying.

And yet . . . I don't want to go.

I grab my bottle of water and a bag of carrot sticks and head into my bedroom to look for Jefferson Halsey some more. I pause. Maybe I should take my mind off things for a little while. TV sounds good right about now. I turn toward the oversize sofa, plop down, and flip through the channels until I land on a police drama.

I love those shows where the cops always catch their criminal, and the perps end up in jail for the rest of their lives. The stories are so unrealistic. Half of the guilty that I hand down justice to have never been to a jail. If the cops ever do catch a suspect, the court system is lucky to put the person away for a minimum sentence, let alone the maximum. Still, I like the false hope the shows give me.

On the screen two bleary-eyed detectives in overcoats question a job site foreman. Satisfied with his answers, they walk away. The shorter guy shakes his head. "I wonder if that guy knows his employee of the month has ten aliases," he says, and snickers.

My breath catches. Aliases. Why didn't I think of that? As a girl who has a drawer full of driver's licenses, I should have considered that Jefferson Halsey might be going by a different name.

I should've considered that maybe Dr. Goodhart changed his name. Maybe I haven't been as focused on finding him as I thought.

I run into my work area and pull Halsey's article out of the drawer, ignoring the way the rest of the articles flutter in a warm breeze. It's just Their way of letting me know They like what I'm thinking.

I scan down the article until I find what I'm looking for. Tickles the Clown.

I type the name into the browser, and get millions of results. I narrow the search down to Pennsylvania, and the first page that pops up is a company called Party Solutions out of Downingtown. That's a little more than an hour away.

The website has pictures of the clown at parties. Under one of them is what I'm looking for: Tickles the Clown, played by Mr. Ulysses Halsey.

I've hacked into the DMV's intranet before, and returning is effortless. I pull up Ulysses Halsey's PA license. A smiling Jefferson Halsey stares back at me. The man is so stupid that he took his hometown as his first name.

Of course, it kept me from finding him for a while, so maybe it wasn't such a dumb move.

I drum my fingers on the desk, debating whether I should do a quick search through the government databases to see whether or not Dr. Goodhart changed his name after Charlotte. If he did, I should be able to find something in the Social Security database.

I pause, fingers poised over the keyboard. If I find him, They'll want to carry out his justice. The thought of confronting him twists my stomach into knots. It feels too personal to kill someone from my past.

I shut down the computer before I can analyze the feeling too closely. There will be time for my personal vengeance later, after I've sated Their hunger.

In the back of my mind, They begin to stir. Restless, eager, excited. The screen goes dark, and in the reflection of the glass, They stand on either side of me, grinning and anxious to hand down our delayed justice.

It's a good night for hunting.

THE WRONG GUY

JEFFERSON HALSEY LIVES NOT IN DOWNINGTOWN but in a depressing apartment complex in King of Prussia. While the area is better known for the mall, there are also a number of cheap housing developments, allowing the retail-wage slaves to live nearby. King's Choice is one of these complexes. It looks like it was once a motel. The building is painted the color of dog crap, a brown so repulsive that I wonder if it isn't a worse punishment to make Halsey continue to live in the dump.

Doors open onto a common outdoor landing, and I try to look nonchalant as I walk along, looking for number 23. After passing three doors, I give up the act. There is a party going on, and people are standing on the landing smoking and telling stories about how drunk they got at the last party. Foot traffic moves between apartments, while rock, dance, and rap music mingles in the chilly night air. Halsey's apartment window happens to be the only one that's dark at this time of night. I guess it's not his kind of party.

As I make my way, I try to calm the fluttering in my stomach. After Alex Medina, I'm pretty nervous. If anything goes wrong, a lot of people are going to get hurt.

I don't even consider coming back to do it another time.

"Hey, do I know you?"

I turn around, and a beefy guy wearing a tight, glittery polo shirt walks up. His dark hair is gelled to within an inch of its life, and he actually flexes a little when I look at him. I swallow a grimace and smile.

I shake my head. "Nope. My roommate and I just moved in."

The guy grins. "Well, in that case, welcome to the neighborhood. You should invite me in."

Ick. Like that would ever happen. The Furies don't even have to chime in. I can tell this guy is a loser by his bad midwinter tan.

I shrug. "I would, but she locked the door. I can't even get in." I pout prettily, and Sparkle Shirt moves closer.

"Well, I could probably help you get into the room. Is your window unlocked?"

Halsey's big picture window is right next to the door. I eye it. "I don't know. How do I check?" I shrug again, pretending to be stupider than dirt.

Sparkle Shirt hands me his beer, and I hold it while he pops out the screen and jimmies the window open. Big handprints are left behind as he slides the glass up. Better his fingerprints than mine. He laughs. "Like that. Now, since I helped you get into your apartment, why don't you invite me in?" Translation: "I let you into your apartment; now let me into your pants."

I giggle and hand him back his beer. "Sure. Why not?" But what I really mean is, "Not in a million years, Neanderthal."

I climb inside the opening and land on a couch that reeks of cat urine. I close the window behind me and lock it, settling the blinds back into place. Instead of opening the front door, I move deeper into the apartment. It takes the guy on the landing a few minutes to realize I'm not coming back, and he begins to pound on the door.

"At least gimme your number," he shouts from the other side.

I've made my way to the kitchen, and I duck behind the counter when footsteps come from the back hallway. I peer around the corner and see a middle-aged man in a ragged bathrobe crack open the front door just a bit. The meathead outside pauses midpound.

"Hey, bro. Uh, is there a really hot blond girl in there?"

Halsey sighs and rubs his balding head. "No, I'm afraid there isn't. Could you please stop knocking on my door?" His voice is soft and meek. It's hard to believe someone so polite could do the things he's accused of.

Sparkle Shirt looks uncertain for a moment. He turns his head at a shout from down the way and holds up his hand. "All right. I'm coming." He turns back to Halsey. "Sorry, man. I'm really, really drunk."

"Of course you are," Halsey mutters, but Sparkle Shirt has already stumbled off. Halsey closes and locks the door, and when he shuffles back to his bedroom, I move from behind the counter and fall into step behind him.

"Jefferson Halsey," I say. He spins around, eyes wide with fear, and I release the hold I have on Them. He tries to push past me but falls back and scoots backward across the floor, his bathrobe falling open to reveal the stained boxers and undershirt he wears beneath. My vision splits into three, and a scorching wind swirls around the tiny apartment, melting the cheap carpet.

"What—what's going on?" he stammers, trying to get away. I move forward and grab him by his robe. Silver chains hang from my arms.

"You have been accused of preying on children. How do you plead?" I ask.

"I didn't do anything!" Halsey's eyes dart back and forth, taking in the Furies. He's trying to process what he sees, but fear is quickly shutting down his brain.

"Guilty or not guilty?" I prod.

"Uh, uh, uh," is all that comes out of his mouth.

I pull him close. Bracing myself for the worst, I look at him through Tisiphone's vision. I see Halsey at dozens of parties, but I see none of the crimes he's accused of. The man is innocent. He's not a child molester after all, just the victim of circumstance. Wrong place, wrong time. I probe his mind for the real culprit, the person who did hurt those little girls. Even he doesn't know the answer to that, and the memory of his persecution fills me with sadness. This man has suffered enough.

"Not guilty," I spit.

There is a slight hesitation, and They still. Through our link I sense something like annoyance, and maybe disgust.

"Guilty," the hawk chirps.

Megaera is the last to speak. "Guilty."

I release Halsey and turn my head slightly. "He is innocent. He didn't hurt those little girls."

Tisiphone grins widely, madness glittering in her eyes. "He's guilty enough."

The serpent grabs Halsey's throat and squeezes. "I agree. No man can be innocent."

"No," I whisper, but I make no move to stop Them. What if They are right? What if there's some crime that I missed? I search the images I saw, but I can't find anything more wrong than him stealing a few cookies when he was a child.

Before I can stop Them, Megaera speaks. "Jefferson Halsey, we have a special treat for you." The change from our normal script surprises me, and I glance in the serpent's direction. I catch a glimpse of scales and hair made of writhing snakes before my gaze is drawn back to Halsey. "Death would be too quick for you," she says. His eyes bulge.

Dread creeps into the pit of my stomach. I want to let Halsey go and then run from the room, but I am rooted to the spot. A buzzing begins in my chest, a pressure so intense it makes me want to cry out. I have the urge to vomit, and from the corners of my eyes I can see Them grinning in delight at Halsey's fear. I open my mouth, expecting to throw up on the apartment's melted carpet. A cloud of tiny black buzzing shadows flies out of my mouth. It looks like a bunch of gnats, only the swarm eats up what little light is in the room as it swirls overhead. The serpent drops Halsey, and as he scoots backward across the floor, the tiny creatures enter his ears, nose, and mouth. He begins to scream soundlessly, clawing at his throat and face, the tendons in his neck standing out from the strain.

It is too much like Medina's truck stop justice.

"The pain, fear, and shame of a hundred victims," Tisiphone says softly, before breaking out into a giggling fit.

"He wasn't guilty." I try to yell the words, but they come out as little more than a croak. The chains hang from my arms, heavy and restrictive. There is no sword in my hand this time. I didn't need it. They have decided on his punishment without me.

They have just hurt an innocent man.

I have just hurt an innocent man. My stomach sours and my head pounds, one awful thought echoing through my mind: I didn't stop Them. I could have, but I didn't. Instead I stood by and let Them do it.

I have become too much like Them.

Halsey writhes on the carpet. There is no sound coming from him, but his face is contorted with pain. Slowly the color leaches from his hair and skin, leaving him as white as a marble statue. He's mewing like a wounded animal, and I turn, trying to find Them.

"I won't do this anymore," I say, my throat thick with regret. Regret that I didn't stop Them; regret that I've been Their willing servant for so long. Alekto was right. I wish I had listened to her sooner. "I won't do it anymore! I'm done." I turn this way and that, but I can't see Them. I catch sight of a feather on the melted carpet, scales shimmering out of the corner of my eye, but there is no way to confront Them. They are too much a part of me.

They go, Their mocking laughter echoing in my brain even after They are once again sequestered in my subconscious. "I said I'm not doing this anymore." But there's no response from Them, only an eerie silence that is somehow deafening.

They know that I really don't have a choice.

I check on Halsey. He's still alive, his breathing shallow, but his mind is gone. He stares sightlessly at the ceiling, his lips forming words he never speaks.

I swallow around the lump in my throat. "I'm sorry," I whisper, but he is beyond my voice.

I pick up the phone on the wall in the kitchen and dial 911, leaving the phone off the hook so that the ambulance will respond. Slowly, like a shell-shocked victim of a disaster, I back away and out of the apartment.

I get into my car, still too numb to think. I want to cry, but I don't. No surprise. I haven't been able to cry since I called Them so long ago.

There is no satisfaction in what I've done. Not this time. Maybe there never was. The deadening effect of my shock gives me a moment of clarity, and I can't help but hate myself. I'm disgusted. After all of the hours searching for Halsey, my victory is hollow.

All of a sudden I'm afraid that killing Dr. Goodhart will feel the same way.

SICK

I SPEND THE DAY AFTER HALSEY'S JUDGMENT AT home in bed. I sleep through my alarm, and when I finally manage to wake, every muscle in my body screams in objection, and my head pounds like a marching band is practicing inside. I try to get out of bed, but my legs turn to mush and I fall on my face. I lie on the floor, half out of it, for what feels like an eternity. It is only when I finally roll over to get up that I see the alarm clock. I've lost an hour. I'm not sure whether I've blacked out or They tried to take me over. Either way it's not a good sign.

I manage to crawl back into bed, but by the time I pull the covers up, I'm shaking from the effort. I'm exhausted but afraid to sleep.

This happened once before, back in Savannah. It was after the incident with Kevin Eames. Because of him, I refused to give in to Their demands anymore. They made me sick until I gave in, and in my hurry to get Them a judgment, I got sloppy. That was how I ended up in Saint Dymphna's.

When I came back to myself in Saint Dymphna's, I made Them a promise: We would hunt down the bad men if They let me live a normal existence again. No more indiscriminate killing. We would be deliberate and cautious in our hunting. They balked at first. But then we were trapped in Saint Dymphna's with Dr. Goodhart, and there was no way They could hand down any justice unless I got us out of there. So They conceded. I thought it was because They needed me to stay in this world.

Now I'm not so sure. Maybe They were just biding Their time.

I remember Jefferson Halsey, guilt and fear hollowing my middle. I can't imagine spending the rest of my life as Their puppet. And now that seems like a very real and very terrifying possibility.

At some point I fall asleep. I'm awakened by my phone a few hours later. I answer it with my eyes closed.

"Hello?"

"Where are you?" It's Niko. I'm surprised to hear his voice, but not upset that he's calling. I can't let him know that, though. I have to stay as far away from him as possible. He's trouble.

More important, I'm trouble.

"This is getting to be a habit, you calling and waking me up," I grumble.

"You didn't answer my question. Where are you?"

I roll over and look at the clock. It's after four on a Thursday. Niko should be at the pizza place. "I'm at home, sick. Why?"

"I'm outside. Let me in."

I sit up in bed too quickly, and immediately lie back down. My head spins, and I'm pretty sure I might throw up. I take deep breaths until the nausea passes. "Why are you here?"

"You have to ask?" There is a moment of thoughtful silence. "I have to see you." His voice is heavy with unsaid things. The moment in the vacant lot affected him as much as it did me.

My mind stops processing as his words sink in.

"Cory, are you still there?"

I sigh. "Yeah. I'm trying to not throw up."

"Gee, thanks."

"No, not about seeing you. Seriously, I am really, really sick."

He makes a noise of irritation. "Then let me come in and take care of you."

It's the strangest offer I've ever gotten, and probably the nicest. Of course, it's also creepy, but in a sweet way that makes me feel squishy inside. He has to repeat the statement before I answer. "You want to take care of me?"

"Yeah." He hesitates, and I wonder if he's just realized what an odd suggestion it is. "I mean, I can at least keep you company." There is another pause. "Did you talk to Mindi?"

"Yeah, we went to the mall yesterday after she broke down at lunch-time."

He's quiet, and then, "Oh."

"Yeah."

The call has just gone from odd to awkward. I want to save the conversation, say something witty, but my mind is blank. The Furies probe at the wall I use to keep Them in my subconscious. Not good. Still, I really want to see Niko. "I'll be there in just a minute."

"Okay."

It takes me what feels like an eternity to get to the front door. I still wear pajamas, an oversize sleep shirt and a pair of fluffy socks. I debate changing. I really don't want Niko to see me this way. Then I decide that if I really want to chase him away, letting him see me sick and in my pajamas is the best way to do it.

I open the door. Niko leans against the door frame. My heart skips a beat when he glances up. He looks amazing. Snowflakes are trapped in his dark curls, like stars in a night sky. I'm surprised they lasted long enough to make it to my hallway.

Then I realize it's freezing. Not just in the hallway but in my apartment. I can even see my breath.

"I think the heat's out," I say to Niko.

He grins, because somehow that's funny, but the expression fades when he looks at me. "Whoa, you really are sick."

My face flushes in embarrassment. I must look absolutely awful for Niko to say such a thing. I'm wishing I had just told him it wasn't a good time and hid out until I didn't feel like seven shades of dead.

But it's too late for that, and I just give him a curt nod. "Yeah," I mutter. Another wave of nausea hits me, and I turn and lurch to the bathroom on shaky legs. I make it just in time to throw up in the sink, the door still partially open. What appears doesn't look like anything I've eaten in the past few days, or ever. The sink bowl is covered in putrid green slime that smells like it came from a sewer. The sight is enough to set me heaving again. It reminds me of the time I watched The Exorcist with my dad, hiding under a blanket so I wouldn't see the scary parts—pretty much the entire movie. Distantly They laugh, and begin to pound against my mental barriers. A whimper escapes me.

I need help.

There's a knock on the bathroom door. Niko has followed me down the hall. He stands in the doorway, a sympathetic expression on his face. I'm horrified, but at the same time I'm having trouble even standing up.

I wash the glop down the sink before he can see it, and rinse out my mouth. The water is icy and refreshing, and I take a couple of seconds to drink it straight from the faucet. When I finally turn toward him, Niko looks at me with concern.

"Are you okay?"

"No, but you should go. It's really not a good idea for you to stay." I can feel Them rustling in the back of my mind, and I fear for Niko's safety. The image of Jefferson Halsey's soundless screaming fills me with despair. What happens if I black out again while Niko's here? I don't want to put him in any danger, but at the same time I'm afraid to be alone. I don't know what's happening to me.

Niko doesn't say anything, just wraps me in the throw from the back of the couch. I look up at him as an idea flits through my mind. "Will you do me a favor?"

"Sure." I'm a little shocked by his ready acceptance. No questions, just immediate concern. It warms me from the inside.

"I need you to tie me up."

Niko's eyebrows shoot up, and a grin quirks one side of his mouth. "As much as I would love to, don't you think you're a little sick for that?"

I shake my head, but the movement compromises what little balance I have, and Niko has to catch me. "No, you don't understand. I have these . . . attacks. I'm supposed to take medicine for them, but I don't. So I need you to tie me to my bed until it passes." My voice is strained. Thinking of lies to cover what's wrong with me isn't easy, but I need his help. It's hard for me to ask him, to trust him. The request is so far away from normal that there is a good chance he will turn around and leave, thinking I'm batshit crazy.

But maybe he really does care about me and wants to know the me that's beneath all of the trappings. Since the first day I saw him, I've felt like there's something important between us. The worry in his eyes makes a bittersweet hope well up in my chest.

He walks me to my bed, half-carrying me when my legs give out. He catches me with a grunt, and I can't even be embarrassed that he's probably wondering why I'm so heavy. I think I'm dying. The thought doesn't scare me as much as it should. At least if I'm dead, I can be sure They won't hurt anyone else.

After resting against the side of the bed for a moment, I go to the closet on legs that surprisingly support my weight, and grab the rope at the bottom. I'm not sure why I bought it. Maybe deep down I knew this day was coming. "You'll have to tie my hands and ankles to the headboard and footboard. Make sure the knots are tight."

He grins, even though his eyes shine with worry. "No problem. I was a Boy Scout."

I laugh. "Somehow I can't picture you wearing that little neck scarf."

"It was usually hanging out of my back pocket."

"Rebel." I lie on my bed and close my eyes, resting them for a moment. When I open them, Niko stands by my side. There's a blanket over me, and my arms and feet are secured to the bedposts. He looks around and sticks his hands into his pockets. I want to close my eyes and sink into unconsciousness, but from this angle I can study Niko's jawline. It's strong and soothing, as elegant as a Michelangelo sculpture. Beautiful in its simplicity, perfect and striking. If I am dying, I want his face to be the last thing I see.

Niko places the back of his hand against my forehead. "You feel like you have a fever. Seriously, you're, like, a thousand degrees. Maybe you should go to the emergency room. When does your mom get home?"

I shake my head, but the motion just makes me want to moan. "They won't be. I'll be fine. Just go. You can come back and check on me in the morning, if that's cool."

Niko disappears, and disappointment washes over me. I'm glad he won't be in any danger if They take control, but a large part of me wanted him to stay by my side until I'm feeling better. My selfishness knows no bounds.

I close my eyes, and open them when the cold plastic of a bottled water presses against my lips. Niko supports my head while I drink, and

I drain the bottle in several gulps. Niko takes it away when it's empty, a shy smile on his face.

"I thought you should have something to drink." He climbs in next to me in the bed, my bound hands and feet causing him to curl around me awkwardly so he doesn't lie on my arm or leg. He pulls the blanket over both of us, and I shiver at the feel of him pressed against me.

"What are you doing?" I whisper. It's getting harder and harder to stay lucid.

"It's freezing in here, in case you haven't noticed. I'm just trying to keep warm. You're hotter than any furnace." There is none of the smarminess in his voice that I would expect from a guy. It deepens my feelings for him slightly, making my chest ache.

I shake my head, but a wave of unconsciousness pushes away rational thoughts. I doze off, and then jerk awake. "No, you can't stay here. I don't know what They'll do."

Niko chuckles low in his chest. "What who'll do? Your mom? Don't worry about her. I can deal with parents." The curve of his smile flattens into a hard line. "Although it's pretty shitty that she left you when you were sick."

"It's not her fault. She didn't want to go . . ." I trail off, memories momentarily distracting me. My stomach roils, and I groan. The tide of darkness pulls me under, but I can't go until I tell Niko something. . . .

I jerk awake again, and Niko looks down at me expectantly. His eyes are the color of the sky in a Monet painting I saw once when I was younger, a gray-blue so perfect that it fills me with a longing sharp enough to cut stone. "Thank you. For staying." He shouldn't be here. I shouldn't ask this of him. But I'm too selfish to ask him to leave again. "If anything weird starts to happen, and you can't get out, there's a tranquilizer gun in the closet, okay?" Another random purchase that may come in handy.

Niko laughs softly and lays his head next to mine on the pillow. "That's a bit extreme. What are you, possessed?" he asks.

"You have no idea," I mutter, and my mind spins toward the darkness. The last thing I feel before I pass out is Niko's cool fingers smoothing my hair back from my forehead.

MOMENTARY TRUTH

I OPEN MY EYES AND THE FIRST THING I NOTICE is the smell. The bedsheets I lie in are completely soaked with sweat. It smells like the stink of a thousand locker rooms. Gross.

I move to get up, but my hands and feet are still secured to the bed. I adjust slightly, inhaling sharply as the muscles of my back and shoulders protest. In the faint light coming from the window I can see the purple of the bruises under the ropes. I register a dozen other aches and complaints as my body slowly comes back online.

Despite the reek of the bed, it's what I don't smell that fills me with relief. The sickly sweet smell of burning sugar. If I'd completely lost control, the room would have been filled with the scorched smell of

Their justice. They would have torn Niko to pieces just for the fun of it, and then burned away his soul to satisfy Their appetite. I'm relieved and saddened that Niko isn't here.

Because I am still tied to the bed.

I look toward the window, trying to judge what time it is. A gray, watery light filters through the dirty curtain. It could be anytime between dawn and early evening. The sunlight isn't very strong in Pennsylvania in the winter, and there is no real way to tell from which direction the light leaks in. I try to get more comfortable, but that disturbs the blanket enough so that I get a whiff of my BO. I reek.

I am burning these sheets.

I lift my head as much as I can to look around the room, and that's when I spot him. He dozes in the desk chair in my closet, the one that pulls up to my laptop. I'm not worried that he's seen anything on the laptop; that's password protected. I'm more concerned about the drawers of the antique trunk that hang open next to him, spilling out all of my dark secrets.

Panic rises in my throat but is almost immediately chased away by a hysterical laugh. Who am I kidding? Considering my current condition, he has probably seen enough that a drawer full of fake IDs and newspaper clippings is tame by comparison.

My laughter startles Niko, and he bounds out of the chair. He looks around the room, eyes wide. He wields a broom handle like a sword, and despite the silliness of it, he looks amazing. His dark hair sticks up in a dozen different directions, and a couple days' worth of beard covers his cheeks. He stripped off his sweater at some point and now stands in his thermal. The tight material traces the hills and valleys of his biceps. His jeans hang low on his hips. My mouth is dry, and I have trouble swallowing. It may be because of him, or because I've been unconscious for so long.

"Can I get some water?" I croak.

Niko points the broom handle at me. There are shadows under his eyes. He looks exhausted. His voice is so low, I almost don't hear him. "Who are you?"

I pretend to laugh, but I'm not sure what he means. He must have seen the fake IDs after all. "I'm Thirsty." He just stares at me, and I laugh again, this time for real. "That's the part where you say 'Hi, Thirsty. I'm Friday. Let's get together Saturday and we'll have a sundae.'" He just stares at me, and I sigh. "Didn't your parents ever joke around with you like that?" When he continues to stare at me, I clear my throat. "Niko, it's me, Cory."

He sags in relief, and falls backward into the chair. He stiffens as something occurs to him. "What's your name?"

I stare at him, which is hard because of the way I have to hold my head up. I relax back into the pillow. "It's Cory. Could we hurry this up? In case you haven't noticed, I need a shower, bad."

I close my eyes for a moment, and when I open them again, he's right next to the bed. His eyes are a little crazed, and they flit over my face like he's reading words written there. I blink. "What the hell is wrong with you?" I ask. I know what's wrong with him. He's probably seen Them. But I'm hoping that Niko doesn't understand what he saw the past couple of days.

"What's your name?" he asks, his face impassive.

"It's Cory, Niko. It's me, Cory."

He leans a little closer, his eyes boring into mine. "What's your name?"

Tears prick the backs of my eyes. I'm so tired, and I smell like a gym sock. All I want to do is take a shower, drink some water, and leave West County. After this I have definitely worn out my welcome. "Why are you doing this?" I wail.

Niko doesn't move. "It's the rule of three," he says. "You have to tell the truth if I ask you three times."

"I think that only works on fairies or something like that."

Niko shakes his head, his gaze never leaving mine. "No, it works. She told me so while you were gone."

His words hit me like a bus, and I stiffen. "Who?"

"The one that glowed. She looked like you."

I sigh and relax against the pillows. "Alekto." I wonder how she was able to appear in this world. Maybe because I was unconscious? "What else did she tell you?"

"The names of the others. Megaera and Tisiphone." Niko rubs his face. This close I can study the new shadows around his eyes. I thought they were caused by exhaustion, but now I'm not so sure. He sighs. "While you were out, I got to talk to them more than I wanted to. At first I thought you had multiple personalities, like on TV, but then that other one appeared . . ." He trails off, as though he realizes how insane it sounds.

I take this in, nodding slowly, the pillow matting the hair in the back of my head even further. I seriously need a shower, but I'm curious why They talked to Niko. "What did Alekto say?"

He shrugs. "She kind of told me what was going on with you, how the other two . . . things were trying to take over your body and you were fighting Them. She told me about the rule of three so I would know who was in your body at the time. They pretended to be you, but I could tell there was something off about the way They sounded." He pauses, thinking. "Alekto also said I had to help you, that I'm your anchor to this world." Niko rubs his temples and closes his eye. "I didn't know what to think."

"Yeah. I told you I was sick. You should see me when I have the flu. It's way worse," I joke. An uncomfortable silence stretches out between us, and I ask the question that we've both sort of been avoiding. "What did the other two say?"

Niko glances at me with equal parts horror, disbelief, and wonder before looking away. It's the wonder that gives me hope. "They said you were Theirs, and that I couldn't have you."

I close my eyes, and tears leak out of the corners. They know. They know about Niko, that he's the reason I'm changing. They knew it before I did. Yet, now that I think about it, I can recognize the emotion for what it is.

I'm falling in love with Niko. Really, how could that be a surprise? Any guy who can tie a girl to a bed and then stick around when she starts to lose her mind has to be a keeper.

I think back to the drugstore, and the way it felt to kiss him that night in the vacant lot, to feel free. I want to show him that deep down

I'm a normal girl. Heaviness presses down on my chest, because that's not my future. I gave myself to justice. They won't let me go back.

It's not like he'll have me when he knows the whole story, anyway. I'm too much like Them.

But he said Alekto told him he was my anchor. Does that mean he has the ability to save me? Is that the big secret Alekto couldn't tell me? I think I need that from him, because I can't seem to save myself.

"You never answered my question." His eyebrows knit together as he trails a single finger along the bruise marring the skin on either side of the rope around my wrist. The touch is so tender, despite the fact that I stink, that a little tendril of hope flutters in my chest. They try to quash it, but I can sense Their weakness. They put everything They had into attempting a coup, and They failed. They'll try again, though.

But until then I'm going to try to be happy. And that means being with Niko. If he'll have me.

I take a deep breath and blow it out, making my decision. A week, two at most. Just a little happiness. Then I'll leave. A few stolen days with Niko, assuming he doesn't run screaming after the past couple of days, and then I'm back on the run.

I turn my head to meet Niko's eyes. There is only one way I can regain his trust. I have to tell him the truth. "My name is Amelie Ainsworth."

Niko leans back and crosses his arms. The light goes out of his eyes, and he scowls. "Where is Cory?"

I shake my head. "Cory never existed—"

"Where's Cory?"

"Niko, I'm trying to tell you—"

"Where's Cory?"

My temper explodes. "Dammit, Niko. I'm trying to tell you. I was never Corinne Graff. The name was a cover so that no one would find me. My real name is Amelie. Amelie Ainsworth."

Niko tilts his head to the side and studies me. "You changed your name so no one would find you. Why? What do you have to hide?"

Plenty. But that's a conversation that needs to be eased into.

I struggle to lift my head, to look at him as he gets up to pace. The muscles in my neck and upper back scream in protest, and I settle back with a groan. "I'll answer all of the questions you have, I promise. I just need you to do me a couple of favors."

"What?" Niko doesn't slow in his pacing, and as I stare at the ceiling, I can hear his work boots tread on the bare wood floor.

"First, quit doing that rule-of-three shit. It's annoying." I lift my head to gauge his reaction. Niko stops pacing, and when he turns toward me, a slight smile curls his lips.

"Fine. What's the other thing?"

I make a face and flop my head back onto the pillow. "Could you untie me and let me take a shower? In case you haven't noticed, I smell."

There's no answer, but the ropes around my ankles loosen. I sigh as I draw circles in the air with my feet, trying to get the blood flowing. Niko appears near my head, his fingers on the rope around my left wrist. He frowns. "At least tell me why you're here in West County."

I want to lie, to declare my love for him and give him some sappy

Hollywood-worthy story about tracking him to the ends of the earth to find him, my soul mate, my anchor. But Niko is entirely too reasonable to believe bullshit like that, so I tell him the truth.

"I came here to hide from my past. And to kill the man who ruined my life."

TRIPPING DOWN MEMORY LANE

WHILE NIKO RUNS TO GET FOOD, I STAND UNDER the hot spray of the shower, letting the water rinse away the grime. For two days I fought Them, alternately lucid and possessed. Niko won't tell me much more than he already has, but the way his expression shadows when he talks about it makes me think it was very, very bad.

And yet, he's still here. I hope what I'm about to tell him won't be the straw on the metaphorical camel's back.

The water starts to turn cold, and I get out and wrap myself in a towel. I clear away the steam to get a good look at myself in the mirror, and then lose my nerve. The face looking back at me is so awful that I can't bring myself to assess the damage. My wrists and ankles already look like I was part of some violent ritual, the bruises darkened to a horrible plum color. I hate to think of how the rest of me looks.

I pull on some pajama pants and a camisole, covering my bare arms with a hoodie that matches the pants. My old pajamas go into a trash bag, along with the sheets and comforter from the bed. I toss the bag out the bedroom window onto the fire escape. I'll deal with it later. For now it's enough that it's out of my apartment.

I'm too tired to do my makeup or really even care, and once I finish cleaning up the biohazard, I collapse on the couch. I don't even have the strength to turn on the TV.

I'm still surprised that They tried to take me over. I've kept my end of the bargain. So why did They change the script at Halsey's? Why strike now? Surely my weak objections weren't enough to make Them move against me, were they?

After so many years of being powerless, I can't believe a single "no" could send Them into panic mode. But it's not like it matters. I can still feel Them squatting in the back of my mind, unwelcome guests. Even after a failed attempt to take over my body, They still haven't left. I don't think They can.

Despair settles over me like a heavy blanket. I have nothing to live for. I can't spend the rest of my life helping Them kill any man who crosses Their path, and I can't get rid of Them. I've been coasting along for so long that I never thought about what I would do if something like this happened. I really thought They needed me. Knowing that They don't makes me feel like the past five years have been a complete lie.

So what am I going to do about it?

Odie jumps into my lap with a plaintive yowl, startling me from my doze. The front door opens and closes, and I twist around to see Niko. A bag dangles from his hand, and his hair is wet. I sit up, and the scent of him curls around me seductively. He smells like the ocean and fried chicken, and I don't know whether to bite him or kiss him.

Niko sees my expression, and a slow, knowing smile spreads across his face. I blush at being so transparent. He doesn't seem to notice. "I got a whiff of myself on the way to get food, so I swung by my house and took a shower."

I can't help but lick my lips. "I don't know what smells better, you or the chicken."

He moves toward where I sit on the couch, setting the bag on the coffee table before sitting down and snuggling in close. His lips touch mine, and I forget about eating as my fingers graze the stubble left behind on his cheeks. There is something strangely addicting about Niko, a mixture of softness and roughness that blends together perfectly. I want to sink into his arms, to meld myself into him like a second skin, my body against his.

I would, too, if my stomach weren't growling like the engine of a sports car.

Niko pulls away with a laugh. "Let's eat before you waste away to nothing."

We dig into the food, laughing and talking about the reality TV show Niko turns on. I'm polishing off my fourth piece of chicken when Niko sits back with a sigh, muting the television. My eyes meet his, and I stop eating. "What?"

"I hate to miss the end of this"—he gestures toward the TV, sarcasm dripping off every word—"but I want to hear your story. How you ended up . . . possessed."

The memory of my promise saps my appetite, and I set down the mostly naked chicken leg after tearing off the last few pieces of meat and giving them to Odie. I wipe my greasy fingers on a napkin, staring at the cheap paper. "It's not a very interesting story," I say, avoiding his question.

Niko sits up and takes my hands in his. I stare at the strength in his long fingers, at the way his hands are so much larger than mine. He raises my hands to his mouth and kisses the backs of my knuckles. My stomach lurches, but They are still suspiciously silent, and the lack of objection lets me enjoy how endearing the simple act is. My reluctance melts away. I can trust Niko.

I clear my throat. "I grew up not too far from here, outside of Philly in West Chester. My mom worked for a medical firm, testing experimental vaccines. My dad was a trust fund kid. My grandparents were loaded, and Dad was a bit of a Renaissance man. He taught archeology at a nearby college, not for the money but just for something to do."

Every morning he would get up and sing songs from musicals. He would chase me around the house belting out tunes like "Oklahoma!" or "If I Were a Rich Man" while I got dressed for school. Mom would always scold him for making me late, but she would never frown at him. I think she loved his singing as much as I did.

The happy memory makes me ache for my parents.

Niko says nothing, just looks at me with those deep ocean eyes, and

I continue. "Everything sort of fell apart when I was twelve, almost thirteen." I swallow, searching for the words to tell him what happened. I open my mouth, but all I can do is listen to my heart pounding in my ears.

Hi, sweetheart. Do you need a ride?

Niko's hands tighten around mine, and the contact breaks through the spell. His lips thin as he studies me. "What happened?"

I take a deep breath. "I was kidnapped. On the way home from school, my friend Steph and I had a fight. She wanted to go to a friend's house, and I wanted to go home. We split up, and a block later someone pulled me into a car. It was four months before I saw my family again."

Horror transforms Niko's face, and I forge ahead before he can say anything. "I don't remember much of it. The psychologists I went to after I came back said I blocked out most of it. I guess it's a pretty common thing. The truth is, They took the memories away from me when I called for Their help. For the Furies' help." I remember when I first felt them. I lay on the floor of the basement where he kept me, cold and hungry and hurting. I could hear him moving around upstairs, heavy footsteps that echoed throughout the dark. *Please, someone find me,* I prayed, and not for the first time. But this time I wasn't praying out of fear as much as rage. I was angry that I was so powerless. It wasn't fair.

Please, anyone. I'll do anything to hurt him like he hurt me.

From out of the darkness a glimmer of awareness prickled my mind. I could feel Their divine anger, Their rage. It warmed me in the cold dark of my prison. *Anything?* They asked.

I thought I was going crazy, that my mind had finally snapped. What did it matter? I knew Roland Thomas would kill me anyway. "Oh, yes," I sobbed in answer to Their question, hope a painful thing after all I'd been through. "I will do anything."

At the time I didn't know what I was getting into, but desperation robbed me of any real choice. I could live on Their terms, or die, another of Roland Thomas's victims.

"Why you?" Niko asks. He's watching me with a mixture of fascination and pain, and I place a kiss in his palm. His fingers twine with mine, and I search for the words to answer his question. There's nothing to do but answer him truthfully.

"I didn't know at first, but over the past few years I've figured out why. I had an older cousin, and we were at a barbecue when I jumped into the nearby lake. I was really little, not even in school yet. She screamed, and raced after me, my dad and uncle right behind her. She jumped into the water and dove under, but my dad found me first, and gave me CPR. I was okay, and it took a while for everyone to realize that Melissa never surfaced. By the time they found her, she was gone. From the stories I heard, they think she got disoriented under the water and couldn't make it back to the surface. It was a quarry lake, and really deep."

Niko shakes his head. "I don't get it. So what?"

"I killed my cousin, Niko."

"That's stupid. You were a little kid."

"Maybe, but I was still responsible for her death. That stain on my soul is what the Furies needed to enter me."

He nods very slowly, and sinks farther into the cushions of the couch. "So how did you get away from the guy who had you?"

I meet Niko's steady gaze. "The first thing I did once They joined me was kill him. I got to him before he could get to me." The basement door gave way like paper when I slammed my shoulder into it. Later the police would wonder out loud to my parents how a half-starved girl suffering from dehydration and a badly healed broken left arm could have knocked the door down, let alone done the damage that I had to Roland Thomas. I didn't know either. I'm lucky that I don't remember. There was so much blood, I had nightmares about it for months.

"The police found his DNA attached to ten other cases. I wasn't the first girl he'd grabbed, and the police actually found a couple of other bodies in the backyard of the house." My parents discussed the case in agonized whispers when they thought I wasn't listening, the same way they'd discussed me.

It's something I try not to think about.

"I was back home for less than a week before my parents sent me to a psychologist to help me deal with the trauma. The Furies were in my head but mostly quiet. A whisper every now and then, but nothing I couldn't ignore. The first couple of doctors weren't so bad, mostly because they were more interested in getting paid than fixing me. But then . . ." Tears overflow my eyes at the memory, and I dash them away. "They sent me to a new doctor, and he had me committed."

I open my mouth to continue the story, to tell Niko the rest, but a sob tears out of me instead. I cover my face in shame and surprise, and Niko wraps his arms around me. He holds me while I cry. The pain of the memory is as sharp as it was on the day my parents told me.

After a couple of minutes of blubbering, I take a deep breath and calm down enough to finish my story. The tears are unexpected, but I feel better now that they're out. I can't remember the last time I cried. And it's easier to tell the story wrapped in the warm strength of Niko's embrace.

"Living with Them in my head was hard, and I began to lose sleep. The Furies wanted me to do certain things, but I refused. It began to kill me a little inside. My parents saw the toll it was taking on me and thought it was because of the kidnapping. When they found me a new shrink, I was unlucky enough for it to be Dr. Goodhart."

Niko snickers. "Dr. Goodhart? That was seriously the man's name?" I tilt my head back to look at him. He frowns, his dark brows kitting together in an adorable way. My breath catches at the sight, and I want to stop telling my story and kiss him until I can't breathe. But I continue with a sigh.

"Yeah. He worked for a local program that had this state-of-the-art treatment regimen. Brighter Day, it was called. The kind of place where rich people send their teenagers to have them 'fixed.' Drug and alcohol treatment, depression counseling. There was even a special area for kids with eating disorders. Dr. Goodhart had an eighty-eight percent success rate.

"At first it wasn't so bad. Dr. Goodhart was nice, and the other kids were pretty normal compared to me. I learned a lot there, and even made some friends. It was supposed to be for six months. But then I let it slip that the Furies sometimes told me what to do. Pretty soon he had the whole story out of me. He decided to try an experimental treatment. My parents found out and freaked. On the way to have me discharged, they got into a car accident. It took my grandmother a month to get me out, and when she did, I was little more than a vegetable."

I remember the way I would sometimes wake up and not know where I was, or even who I was. Sometimes I would think I was trapped in Roland Thomas's basement again, and start screaming. All the while They would be in my head, whispering to me, urging me to hurt the men in the building. I would dig my nails into my arm, hoping the pain could drive away the fuzziness surrounding my brain. When I drew blood, the orderlies would inject me with something, and Dr. Goodhart's face would swim above mine, his lips twisted with disgust. "I'm here to save you from yourself, Amelie."

I shake my head to clear away the memory. "All of the paperwork that my parents had was in the car, and when Grandma realized they'd basically had me committed, she filed to have me pulled out of the program. I moved with her to Savannah. She was a smart woman, and she didn't trust shrinks. But Dr. Goodhart was obsessed, and eventually followed me to the South."

Niko shakes his head in disbelief. "Why would he do that? I'm sure there are enough messed-up kids that he didn't need you."

"You're right. There were two reasons. While I was at Brighter Day, I used Their abilities to look into his memories. I found out that he was getting money from drug companies to try out experimental treatments on his patients, usually without their knowledge. He used me as one of his lab rats. More important, though, is that he thought I had multiple personality disorder. It's like the Holy Grail of crazy, despite what they show on TV. He thought I was the case that would make his career." Publishing a case study on me would have made him famous, and would've made it easier for him to dope up future patients with experimental drugs.

"Goodhart began contacting my grandmother, trying to convince her that something was off about me. She pretty much thought him a quack until I lost control one weekend. She saw me acting weird, and called him for advice." I bite my tongue as I consider my words.

I won't mention that I was arrested a week later after an eyewitness saw me standing over the body of one of the guilty. I should tell Niko, let him know what kind of monster I am, but I'm a coward.

Funny as it sounds, it's more than fear of what he'll think about me being a killer. I'm still not comfortable with letting him know about my shaky handle on humanity, and I'm afraid of what he'll do if he knows how little of my compassion remains. Maybe I am too much like Them. Maybe They are close to being in control.

I push the notion aside and rub my temples. I'll let Niko in on the ugly truth of my past at some point. Just not now. Later, when the time is right.

I'm very good at lying to myself.

I watch Niko while I gather my thoughts. His gaze is steady, and although his lips have thinned into a grim line, he seems to be taking it all in stride, like I'm telling him what I did over my summer vacation. What did They tell him while I was out? What did he see that makes my story seem tame? I'm afraid to ask.

"My grandmother died from a heart attack shortly after I moved in with her." I leave out the part about my arrest causing the heart attack. "I became a ward of the state, and Dr. Goodhart spoke with my caseworker and convinced her to sign my care over to him. She agreed. I was sent to Saint Dymphna's in Savannah for observation. The next year was pure hell. Once he had me under his care again, he started injecting me with different drugs in the hopes that he could fix me. I was going to make his career. Eventually he found a combination that he thought worked." It wasn't until the night I left that I finally realized. The doctor was crazier than me.

Something in my expression makes Niko pull me closer, adjusting so that I lean back against his chest. He pulls my hair down from its ponytail, burying his face in it and inhaling deeply. I can feel him tremble, and his response to my story causes something vital to shift in my chest.

"So what happened?" he asks, his voice hoarse.

I manage a smile. "The Furies were stronger than he thought. I ran. A few weeks later I went back to Savannah to get some of my stuff. I've been running for the past two years, waiting for the opportunity to hurt Dr. Goodhart for what he did to me."

Niko rubs his cheek against mine, the stubble on his face scratchy and utterly appealing. "Why?" he asks, his mouth next to my ear.

"My parents died on the way to Brighter Day. They were coming because of Dr. Goodhart, because he put me under that experimental therapy. My grandmother had a heart attack because of me. She couldn't handle raising me. But that stress was because my parents were gone. His recklessness took my family from me. And now I'm all alone."

I slump back against the couch, feeling utterly hopeless. Now that

I've actually let myself think about my plans, I realize how pointless it was to tell Niko any of this. Even leaving out a great big chunk of the truth, it's still pretty obvious that I'm a killer. How many girls plan to kill their doctors?

I push the heels of my hands against my eyes until bright spots appear. The apartment is completely silent. The only sounds are Niko's and my breathing.

Neither of us moves, and I finally drop my hands back into my lap. "You can leave if you want. This is the point where you realize I'm bat-shit crazy and head for the hills. Really, I don't mind."

Niko wraps his arms around me, smoothing back a few tendrils of hair. I remain stiff for a few moments, but when he presses a soft kiss to my forehead, my resolve melts away. I curl into him, savoring his strength. I don't deserve his compassion, but I'll take it anyway. His heartbeats are steady and strong under my cheek, and my fear fades away as I listen to his even breathing. "I don't think you're crazy. Maybe I would have if I hadn't spent the past couple of days with you. I don't know. But I saw something while you were ... occupied." I adjust within the safety of Niko's arms, leaning my head back to study his expression. His eyes are closed, his lashes casting dark crescents on his cheekbones. Again I want to ask him what happened while I was unconscious, but there's a tension around his mouth that warns me off. I say nothing, and instead lay my head back against his chest.

I close my eyes with a sigh, and Niko kisses the top of my head. He squeezes me tight, and I squeeze back. "We can figure out how to deal with this. You can just forget about finding this doctor, and we'll do an exorcism or take up voodoo, or whatever we need to do to keep Them away. I won't lose you, not when I've just found you. You make me feel alive, and something else. I don't know. Maybe it's because you're so different from everyone else. You make me want to try, and I'm not willing to give that up."

I want to tell him that it won't work, that I've tried fighting Them before, with disastrous consequences. Even Alekto hasn't been able to help me do more than control Them, delaying the inevitable craving for justice. But I can't find the words. I'm too selfish. The last thing I want to do is burst the bubble of happiness that's surrounding my heart.

So instead I tilt my head back so I can kiss the underside of his chin. He angles his head so his lips can meet mine, and I sink into the kiss with a sigh. I tangle my fingers in the hair at the back of his neck, and swallow the words I should say.

There will be plenty of time for reality later.

MY HAPPINESS

THE NEXT FEW DAYS PASS IN AN AMAZING BLUR.

Niko and I spend every waking moment together. We go to breakfast at the town's diner, and wax poetic over beloved childhood cartoons. We drive to King of Prussia to loiter in the mall. There Niko talks about his life before his father died, and I try to remember the happy times with my parents and grandma.

We drive up to the mountain in the middle of the afternoon and go sledding on the last of the icy snow. It's a lot more fun with just the two of us, and we spend as much time kissing as we do sliding down the hill. Afterward we huddle next to each other in front of a fire, toasting marshmallows on wire hangers. I share anecdotes of the places I stayed during my trek from Savannah, carefully omitting my hunt for Good-hart in Charlotte. Niko talks about the places he wants to go, which is anywhere but West County, PA.

Through it all They are suspiciously quiet.

We even use a couple of days looking for information on Them. Niko finds quite a few Internet articles on the Furies, and he reads them out loud from the screen of my laptop. None of the information we find is helpful. The myths only vaguely resemble the story Alekto told me, and there are no hints about eliminating Them. There is nothing about Them possessing people to carry out justice, only tales of how They are relentless in Their pursuit of the guilty.

Does this mean I am the first person They've actually possessed? I doubt it. I want to ask Them, and I wonder once again why Alekto abandoned Them.

More important, what happens if I let Them have Their way again? What happens to me if They take over my body? At some point I'd really like to have a clear idea of what I'm dealing with.

Not knowing the answers to these questions makes me anxious, but I can't exactly ask Them about it. Not only have I not heard Them in my head, but if my guesses are correct, They don't exactly have a reason to tell me the truth.

So I wait for Their next move. Or for Alekto to visit.

I spend my time with Niko on pins and needles, expecting him to say something about my past, to attempt to pry into my memories of the months in Roland Thomas's basement. He hasn't asked me about the newspaper articles in my room, or the fake IDs and slutty outfits. Is he really that clueless, or is he giving me time to tell him the truth, the whole truth, on my own?

And how long can I avoid what is sure to be a painful conversation?

He doesn't ask me about any of it. Instead he just acts like we're a completely normal couple. The only hint I have that he thinks about it are the moments when he thinks I'm not looking. Then he watches me with a pensive frown, as though he's trying to reconcile my manufactured Barbie exterior with the Internet images of a trio of women tearing people to pieces.

If he knew the parts I haven't told him, it would be easier.

Niko suggests we try to find some books at the library, and he's so excited about finding out something that might help me that I don't mention I've already searched what the local library has to offer. The little we are able to locate is all stuff that we already found on the Internet and stuff I found last time. The librarian is young and seems charmed by the sight of us reading books together, and she recommends that we check out the state library in Harrisburg.

"They have a very large collection, and even though we can get most of their stuff on interlibrary loan, if you have a car, it's faster to drive down there."

Niko thanks her, and she turns to me conspiratorially after he excuses himself to go to the bathroom. "How long have you been dating?"

"Not long." I'm uncomfortable talking about something so personal with a complete stranger. She gives me a small smile and nods.

"You two are such a cute couple. It's so great that you can do research together." I'm not sure what kind of a response to give. I can't exactly tell her we're trying to find a way for me to eliminate the mythological creatures possessing me. So I just smile.

After striking out at the local library, Niko and I follow the librarian's advice and spend a day driving all the way to Harrisburg to do some research in the state library. The holdings list several antique books about Greek mythology, but when we ask the librarian to see them, he glares at us like we're crazy. I guess he doesn't want to trust an expensive collector's item to a couple of teenagers.

Instead we search through the periodical holdings for any stories about murderous bird or serpent women. With the exception of a few vague stories in a Philadelphia paper from the late 1800s, we come up empty.

But on the way back to the car, time seems to stop. A man walks past me, and the sight of him makes my middle clench in agony. His hair is blond sliding into silver, but the line of his jaw and his gait are familiar. I can't breathe, my eyes locked on him. But it's not his face I'm looking at, exactly. It's the four long scars that mar one side.

Dr. Goodhart. For months I've been looking for him, and all this time he's been a few miles down the road.

As I climb into Niko's Jeep, I watch the man walk into a building, my heart thudding loudly in my chest. The gold lettering reveals the building's purpose: Pennsylvania Department of Public Welfare. He's been here, right under my nose. Now I can make him pay.

But why didn't They know he was here? We're so close.

The bubble of happiness deflates in my chest, and it's all I can do to hide my despair from Niko.

Because I know he won't understand. He's made it pretty clear that he thinks I should give up my quest to find the good doctor, but I can't. I want the man dead. The question is, do I want my revenge more than I want to be with Niko?

I can't answer that. I'm almost afraid to try.

I don't let myself dwell on the dark side of things. Being with Niko is great, and I'm so happy, I could sing. It isn't until it all comes crashing down that I appreciate how wonderful it has been.

We slip inside my apartment after an early dinner at a pizza parlor and games of Ms. Pac-Man on an old table-video-game. Niko killed me, but I had so much fun trash-talking that I barely even noticed. If there was any doubt in my mind that I was starting to love him, the past week has erased it. From his curly hair to his battered work boots, Niko is everything that my life was missing.

The best part about spending time with Niko is his total understanding of my reluctance to go any further than a few heated kisses. I want to do more with him, but I'm still very uncomfortable with the idea of it. I don't know what it will do to Them, especially since They've been so quiet. Kevin Eames will always haunt my conscience, and even though They haven't responded to the closeness between us, I still worry that taking things further will unhinge Them.

Despite my worry that Niko will lose his patience, he doesn't seem to mind. Every time his fingers skim across the sensitive skin of my belly, I pull back in alarm, and he pauses and removes his hand. Before I can stammer out an excuse, he kisses me on the nose and smiles. "I'm in no hurry. You shouldn't be either."

With the exception of Their presence in the back of my mind and the guilt over not telling Niko everything, my life is perfect.

So I'm less than thrilled when Niko's phone rings as we settle on the couch.

"Just ignore it," I say. We've both been getting calls all week, not just from our friends but from the school as well. I've missed almost two weeks of school, Niko only a few days less. I'm going to drop out, especially since I need to leave soon if I'm going to stay anonymous. I've waited to bring that up with Niko, along with everything else I'm keeping from him. I'm hoping he'll want to come with me and that he'll overlook the wrongness of my crimes. Right now I don't want to face reality and how unlikely it is that he'll follow me like a lost puppy. I just want to stay in my cocoon of happiness. *One more day*, I keep telling myself. *Then I'll come clean.*

When will I learn that this kind of bliss never lasts?

Niko gives me a sympathetic smile and answers his phone anyway. I can hear the person on the other end yelling, so I move away into the bedroom to give Niko some privacy.

I busy myself by making the bed, putting new sheets and a comforter on it. The purchase ate up the last of Hank Meacham's money, leaving me with nothing but the money I had set aside for food. But the sheets are so soft that I'm pretty sure it was worth it.

Afterward I lie down on the mattress, relishing the luxurious feel. I sigh in delight as Niko walks in. His expression is initially grim, but when he catches sight of me, his eyes light up and a deliciously wicked smile spreads across his face. "Wow."

I roll over so that I can look at him upside down, my head hanging off the side of the bed. "I know. Come lie down. It's crazy comfortable." I pat the mattress, and Niko runs across the room to do a belly flop onto the space next to me. I bounce up into the air, and when I land, I'm laughing like an idiot.

This is what it feels like to be happy.

Niko rolls over and kisses me lightly on the lips. It's a teasing kiss, and before I can get my fill of him, he pulls away. I sigh, and his expression darkens once again. "I have to go home."

His tone is so bleak that I snap upright. "Why? What's wrong?"

Niko rolls over and groans. "Well, besides work calling my mom and telling her I haven't shown up in more than a week, the school has been calling her and threatening to expel me if I'm not in class tomorrow. She's pissed, and a little worried. She thinks I'm on drugs, especially since Amber made the paper. They're talking about charging her as an adult." He sighs and runs his hand through his hair. I trace the same path, winding a silky curl around my finger. He's so preoccupied that he doesn't really notice. "I need to hang out at home for the next couple of days, just until my mom calms down. What really got her worried was Mindi. I guess she called her a couple of times as well, crying."

I stare at him, afraid to say anything, terrified where this conversation is going. Niko puts a warm hand on my knee, and it feels so nice that it's hard to remember he's about to give me the brush-off. "Let me take care of this, get my shit together. I have to at least talk to Mindi. My mom and her dad are still friends, and he's been through a lot, you know? I can't let anything happen to Mindi. Not like last time."

I like that Niko's such a sweet guy, but it's hard to appreciate his sensitivity when his concern for others is directed at another girl, even if she is my friend. Was, I mentally correct. She probably won't want anything to do with me after she finds out about Niko and me.

Still, I don't want Niko to go. I swear inwardly and hide my face in my hands, disappointment settling over my shoulders like a funeral shroud. "I knew this couldn't last."

Niko sits up and gently takes my hands in his. "Hey, this doesn't change anything. Mindi and I still have clear boundaries. And you and I will see each other at school and everything. We still need to figure out how to get rid of the Furies. Nothing's changed."

I nod, but I can't really believe it. As soon as we let reality intrude, things will get complicated. Right now they're simple. I want Niko. Niko wants me. End of story.

But when we go back to school, things will be different. Mindi will be upset, probably inconsolable. Tom and Jocelyn will probably side with Mindi, since they've been friends with her longer. Adam will most likely be hurt, and Amber will hate me.

Okay, so not everything will be different.

"Maybe I shouldn't go back." Now that my time with Niko is creeping to an end, all of my problems come rushing back. Dr. Goodhart. My false enrollment and the school guard's assault. I itch to be on the move, but I don't want to go by myself. I want Niko by my side.

He looks at me and gives me a kiss on my forehead. "Of course you're going back. It's only a few months until graduation, and you have to get your diploma. Even a slacker like me knows that." He grins, and my middle turns to mush.

One of the things I love about Niko is his innate goodness. I like that he's the opposite of me, always willing to look on the bright side, to speak words of encouragement when they're needed most. He's a good person, and he feels obligated to make everything better even if it means shortchanging himself. If I can delay him leaving to "fix" things, I will.

But the opportunity to keep him by my side has already slipped through my grasp. Niko climbs off the bed and gathers his stuff from where it has landed around my apartment over the past few days. Clothes, a couple of movies he brought, his video game system. Watching him clean up his stuff and cram it into his backpack is like seeing him pack up little pieces of our time together.

I'm surprised to find tears pricking my eyes, and I quickly blink them away. I'm being unreasonable, but I can't help it. I slide off the bed and help Niko gather up the rest of his things. It takes less time than I would like, and afterward we stare at each other in the uncomfortable silence. I should say something, but I'm no good at this type of thing.

Niko stands by the door, his backpack over his shoulder and sadness etched on his face. "Are you sure you're going to be okay? I mean, it'll just be you and Them. I know you said They've been quiet and all—"

"I'll be fine," I say, waving away his concern. I force a smile. I won't let him know that I'm terrified of being alone, and of what will happen once They realize he's gone.

He gives me a wistful smile and a peck on the lips before disappearing out the door. He doesn't even say good-bye, and I close the door before I give in to the urge to beg him to stay.

I collapse on the couch and reach for Them, but I find only silence and a curious emptiness. I feel around in the back of my mind, the mental equivalent of probing a back tooth with your tongue. I can sense Them still back there, nestled in tight, but I can't reach Them. I throw my arm over my face and fight the melancholy that threatens to completely overwhelm me.

I always end up alone.

OUTCAST, CAST OUT

RIGHT AWAY I KNOW THAT SOMETHING AT school has changed. Girls give me the evil eye as I walk down the hallway, and guys whisper about me after I pass. I don't see Niko all morning, and Mindi is suspiciously absent from my chemistry class. I'm starting to feel like I imagined the past few weeks, when Niko finally sends me a text midmorning: *Wont be at lunch, wait 4 me after school?*

My stomach sours when I read the text. I came to school only to spend time with Niko, and I'm more than a little afraid of seeing the rest of the group without him. After all, I'm the interloper. Mostly I just don't feel grounded without Niko around. He's like a drug, but my addiction to him clears my mind and helps me function, something Dr. Goodhart's cocktails never truly did.

And secretly I'm afraid what will happen if Niko doesn't reappear. During the time I spent with him, I actually considered finding a way to get rid of Them. Now I can feel the dark urges creeping back in, even though They are still alarmingly silent.

I push all of this aside and send Niko a quick *okay* with a happy face. I can't let him know how messed up my head is, and not just from Their presence. I think I might be genuinely screwed up, and I don't want to scare him off.

I spend the next couple of classes fighting to control the alternating sadness and rage that threatens to swallow me whole. Sadness because I want Niko, and rage because I hate being trapped in the school when I should be planning my escape from West County. I wonder if They have something to do with my roller-coaster emotions, but I haven't heard a peep out of Them. Still, it's strange to feel so much so quickly, especially since I've felt next to nothing for a very long time.

The only bright spot in the day is English. We have an open library period, and I manage to snag a computer and research Dr. Goodhart's position at the Pennsylvania Department of Public Welfare. From the unhelpful website I find out that the Department of Mental Health falls under the Department of Public Welfare. I can't find out anything about the employees without hacking through the back door of the site, and it doesn't seem like the best idea to do it with my English teacher walking around.

It's frustrating, but it also delays the inevitable question of which one I'll pick—revenge or love.

All too soon it's lunchtime.

I bump into Jocelyn in the hall right before lunch. She is breathless and excited, and her eyes dart back and forth. I wonder if she was trying to avoid me. I debate making some excuse, but she talks before I think of anything. "So, is it true that you and Niko are an item now?"

The question catches me off guard, and I shrug. "Not sure."

Jocelyn rolls her eyes and hooks her arm through mine, leading me to the lunchroom. Her overt affection is surprising, since I expected a very different reaction. I am, after all, the crush-stealing whore. I heard the whispers in the hall, most likely started by Jocelyn, queen of gossip. "Don't lie. Niko told Tom that he broke up with Mindi to be with you."

I stare at her. "I thought they weren't dating."

She waves away my statement, and I realize they weren't. Already Jocelyn is twisting the story around in her mind to make it more interesting. Suddenly Mindi's unrequited love becomes a girl betrayed by her friend, which is much more scandalous. Jocelyn seriously needs to get a life.

She keeps talking, oblivious to the look I give her. "Oh, they weren't dating, but it's still harsh, you know? I mean, they've been friends since, like, forever. Anyway, I figured the reason you two haven't been to school is because you guys ran off to get married."

I shake my head, uncomfortable with the conversation. "No, I was sick." Jocelyn keeps talking a mile a minute, going on and on about how she knew Niko and I would end up together. She doesn't mean what she's saying. She's just looking for gossip to pass on. I know that's the case from the shadowed looks she gives me when she thinks I'm not looking.

Why did I even bother coming back to school?

We stand in the lunch line. I should be out planning my escape from West County. I'm not going to see Niko until after school. I can tell him everything then. Why am I standing here staring at a bowl of brown bananas?

Jocelyn and I pick up our food, an orange for me and a slice of pizza for her. My mind is crammed so full of leaving that I'm not paying attention when she seamlessly changes topics.

"Oh, did you hear? Amber is supposed to be coming back to school today."

Jocelyn and I are the first to arrive at the table. "Oh?" It's the most I can get out. The thought of having a confrontation with Amber terrifies me. For the first time I kind of miss Them. Their constant dialogue made it hard to worry about anything more than keeping Them happy, and the only fear I felt was fear of discovery. With Them gone, every emotion bruises.

I peel my orange, only half-paying attention, while Jocelyn keeps talking. I fight down a yawn and rub my eyes. I slept miserably last night; my thoughts kept drifting to Niko, the things left unsaid, and my next steps. I couldn't help but think that his leaving so quickly had more meaning than just trying to placate his mother.

I take a deep breath and set down my orange. I can't turn off my brain, and I have to get out of here. I can't stand to spend another moment in this place.

I'll never be normal. And I think I'm okay with that.

"Ohmigod, there she is. Wow, she looks like hell." At Jocelyn's anxious whisper I turn around to see Amber walking in with Adam. She's hanging all over him, looking at him like he's a celebrity, which he's probably enjoying.

I watch Adam and Amber walk to the lunch line, oddly in step, like they've been together since the beginning of time. Jocelyn looks at them nuzzling up to each other and snickers. "God, she's lucky he bailed her out, but she's just being ridiculous."

I pause, a section of orange halfway to my mouth. "Adam bailed Amber out?"

Jocelyn looks at me in shock. "Haven't you heard a single word I've said? Amber's mom and dad freaked and thought it'd be a good lesson for her to stay in jail until her court date. She called all of us, begging us to see whether we could come up with the money for her bail." She rolls her eyes. "Her bail was, like, five thousand dollars. As if any of us have that kind of money."

"But Adam does?"

She snorts. "I guess. Probably from dealing. He's such a lowlife." Jocelyn sighs. "I should've gone out with him when I had the chance. Tom is always broke."

I'm pretty sure I hate her.

Amber and Adam settle down at the other end of the table from Jocelyn and me, and even though they are within earshot, they ignore us like we aren't sitting there. Jocelyn gives me a worried glance, but I just keep eating my orange, the maelstrom of emotions inside me swelling to epic proportions. I have to get out of here. There's no reason to stay, and I can't handle this. I'm not prepared for the rawness of the emotions battering me, mostly the fear. Niko keeps telling me how it's a small town, and everyone knows where everybody lives. Someone could figure out my secret.

Like Amber. Now that she's out, will she pick back up where she left off, making my life miserable? I need to get out of town.

Tom comes in, takes one look at the split table, and turns to leave. The look on his face is too much for me, and I already can't bear to sit in the lunchroom one more minute. I call out to him as he heads to an empty table.

"Sit here. I was just leaving."

A look of embarrassment flashes across Tom's face before he gives me a relieved smile. I pick up my tray of orange peels and stand. I'm the cause of the schism in the group, and there's no point in pretending otherwise. The only person I want to talk to is Niko, and he's not here.

I dump the peels from my tray and go to leave the lunchroom. I'm almost out the door, when there's a hand on my shoulder. I spin around, ready to drop into a crouch. Amber gives me a twisted smile and crosses her arms.

"Thanks for setting me up, you bitch," she spits. I stare at her, open-mouthed, wide-eyed like a deer in headlights.

"What?"

"You don't think I know it was you? Where'd you get the drugs? You a dealer *and* a whore?"

It takes a long moment for what she's saying to click. She thinks I had something to do with her drug charge. I don't get a chance to defend myself, because she keeps talking. "It doesn't matter how hard you try to fit in. We both know you don't belong here." Her words hit me like a slap, because it's exactly what I've thought more than once.

I turn and push through the double doors, fleeing the cafeteria and the whole damn school.

Amber is right. I don't belong. My throat tightens and I choke back tears.

It's time for me to go. The scary thing is, if Niko won't come with me, I might just lose him forever.

THE SPACE BETWEEN MEEK AND MENTALLY INSANE

I WAIT IN MY CAR, WATCHING FOR NIKO. OTHER than his text message I haven't seen or heard from him, and after Amber's confrontation in the lunchroom, I'm worried. I really thought for a moment she would try to rip my throat out.

I'm not sure why Amber thought I put drugs in her locker, though. Does she think someone set her up? And if someone did set her up, who was it? The Furies? Did They use Their newspaper clipping trick on Amber, exchanging marijuana for the front page?

It doesn't make any sense. They aren't the type to care about high school antics. Unless They knew Amber was getting too close to my secrets. The thought leaves me cold.

I turn on the car and crank the heater up to high. I've been sitting here since lunchtime, turning it on intermittently to keep warm. With Carson still out, it was easy to get out of the building. I should have gone home, packed up my things, and left. I could have called Niko after I was on the road, told him I'd be back in a couple of weeks. But Niko said he would meet me after school, and the possibility of seeing him again is more than I can resist.

The final bell rings, and I watch people stream from the building. Tom and Jocelyn walk along deep in conversation, and Amber exits the building wrapped around Adam like a strangling vine. I hope he doesn't regret it.

People continue to filter out of the building, and eventually the flood slows to a trickle. Just when I've given up hope of seeing Niko, he walks out, head bowed against the blustery wind that has come up. I watch his long strides to his Jeep, wondering if I should go talk to him after all. He said he'd see me after school, but I don't want to seem all stalker-ish, waiting for him in the parking lot. I have to let him know what I'm planning, and that I'm leaving. While waiting, I rehearsed my speech, and I think I can be honest without sounding needy. I'm hoping he'll come with me.

I'm even going to tell him the true nature of Their possession. Maybe. I'm still building up to that mentally.

I laugh softly at myself. I thought I was strong, but it turns out I'm just as weak as the people I hand down justice to. While they crave the violence of hurting others, I crave acceptance. Even if it's based on a lie.

Niko reaches his Jeep, and I've just decided I won't talk to him, when a white blur bounds across the parking lot and slams into him. My heart leaps into my chest, and I'm just about to get out of the car and run to his rescue when the person's hood falls back. Mindi stands in front of Niko, and although I can't see her face, I can tell by the irritation on Niko's that he doesn't want to hear whatever she's saying. My heart pounds in my chest as I imagine her begging him to give her a chance. Niko shakes his head once, twice. The third time he says something to her that causes her shoulders to sag. I watch, mouth dry, and Niko gets into his car and leaves. The whine of the Jeep engine is an angry conclusion to the scene I just saw.

I start to follow him, but stop. Maybe I should give him some space after his confrontation with Mindi. Remorse claws at my chest anew. Why does my happiness have to be tied to Mindi's misery? Why can't we both be happy? What else can I give Mindi to make her whole, something besides Niko? A pony?

I rest my head on the steering wheel, taking deep breaths of the superheated air of the car. I focus on Niko and our future, instead of feeling bad about Mindi's hurt feelings. My inheritance is more than enough to live on, and in a couple of weeks I'll be eighteen. Then it'll all be at my disposal. I think of Niko, and the way his face lit up when he talked about the possibility of traveling around the world. Maybe that's something we could do together?

Would that be enough to convince him to come with me?

I'm startled out of my reverie by a sharp tap. Mindi's angry tear-streaked face is pressed to the glass. I roll down the window, even though it's the dumbest thing I could do. Still, I owe Mindi an explanation.

"You had to have him, didn't you?" she demands, face twisted with a combination of anger and pain.

"It wasn't on purpose," I whisper, her pain affecting me as sharply as if it were my own. Maybe I could have fought my feelings a little more, worked harder to keep my distance. But I didn't, and there's no taking it back now. "I tried to avoid him."

The hurt in her expression melts away, and rage scrunches her face instead. "Right, sure you did. You were just using me to get close to him, weren't you? It was all a lie, even that day in the bathroom. You were never my friend."

I shake my head, but my protests die on my lips. I'm not handling this right, but I don't know what to do. I've never been in a situation like this before. I clear my throat and try again. "Mindi, let's talk about this. Why don't you get in and I'll give you a ride home? I think it's supposed to snow tonight."

Mindi pushes away from my door and gives me the evil eye. "Are you serious? Do you really think I would go anywhere with you?"

I shrug, but it ends on a shiver. "No, but it's freezing out, and the least I can do is give you a ride home." Emotion clogs my throat, and I take a deep breath to talk around it. The disappointment on her face is heartrending, and all my earlier thoughts of Niko go out the window. "I really am sorry about the way things turned out. If it makes you feel any better, I turned in my paperwork to leave school today."

Mindi crosses her arms and shakes her head. "You don't get it, do you? This isn't about how you feel, or what you do now. It's about what you did. I thought you were my friend. I stuck up for you. I even got rid of Amber for you."

The world gets eerily quiet, and I look at Mindi, really look at her for the first time. There is a shine to her eyes that is too familiar, the same glimmer I've seen once or twice in Tisiphone's eyes. "You put the pot in Amber's locker."

"I was trying to give you a break from her. I saw how she messed with your car, the rumors she was spreading about you. You eventually would have gotten tired of it, and you would have left me. So I picked up the baggie the day we went sledding and held on to it until the day the dogs were supposed to show up. Tina's mom coordinates the visits, and she always gives us a heads-up so none of us gets in trouble. But I shouldn't have even bothered. You're evil. You pretended to be my friend, and the moment you saw an opening, you took my boyfriend."

"He wasn't your boyfriend. Mindi, you need help." Hey, pot, this is kettle. How's it going?

Mindi's face goes from angry to pissed, her nostrils flaring and lips pressing into a fine line. "Whatever. You're a fucking joke, and I hope you know there's a special place in hell for people like you." Her words strike me like rocks. She's right.

Thinking the conversation is over, I roll up my window. Suddenly Mindi makes a sound like a wounded animal and lunges for me, sticking her arm through the gap. I lean toward the passenger door in surprise, and she yanks her hand back so the automatic window doesn't crush it. She tries to open my door, but it's locked, so she kicks it a couple of times with a booted foot, then pulls at the door handle again. Bits of foam fleck her lips and land on the window. My brain freezes as it tries to process what I'm seeing.

She wants to kill me.

I stare openmouthed until she tires herself out, planting one last fierce kick before she spins around on her heel and walks away. My hands, gripping the steering wheel, shake with shock. How did I miss how unstable she was? Mindi really does need serious professional help. I should know.

The worst part is, crazy as she might be, she's right. I didn't have any business going after Niko, even if there wasn't anything between them. My first loyalty should've been to Mindi. She was my friend.

But if wanting Niko is so wrong, why do I still ache for him?

HONESTY IS OVERRATED

I DRIVE HOME IN A FUNK, WONDERING WHY They're being so quiet when They could revel in my misery. This prolonged silence isn't like Them, and that only worries me more.

Maybe it's because I don't need Them anymore, or maybe because They realized I'm strong enough that They'll never take control. Either way, I'm hopeful that Their silence is a good sign, that I'm truly free. Maybe loving Niko has given me that strength. All I want to do is spend the rest of my life with him.

I smile as I round the corner toward my house. I've already dismissed the confrontation with Mindi, my thoughts tangling around Niko once again. I'm certain that we can be together. Perhaps we'll go to California, either San Diego or LA. I've never been out West, and it sounds nice. I want to see if the Pacific matches Niko's eyes.

I'm making plans in my head when I pull up to my apartment building. I park the car, and Niko walks down the steps. His head is down, his hands tucked into his pockets. His damp hair curls over his ears haphazardly. He looks like heaven itself.

"Hey!" I call breathlessly as I climb out of the car. He must have gone home and taken a shower and then come directly to see me. Now I'm glad I didn't talk to him at school like some lovesick romance heroine. The afternoon is silent, and Niko's head snaps up at the sound. He waves weakly, tension riding the breadth of his shoulders. I frown, wondering what's wrong.

"We need to talk," Niko says by way of introduction. I nod, dread plunking down into my stomach like heavy coins. I take a deep breath and inhale his ocean-rain scent. I want him to take me in his arms and kiss me until my head spins, but that's not going to happen. His tone and body language are all wrong for this visit to be good.

"Okay. Do you want to come upstairs?"

Fear runs across Niko's face, and he shakes his head. "How about the Greek diner?"

"Okay. Do I have time to check on something?"

Niko looks off into the distance and then gives a halfhearted shrug. "Sure. Why don't you meet me there when you're ready?"

Niko's acting very strangely, but I want to know why, so I just nod and smile brightly. "Sure. Gimme, like, thirty minutes?"

He nods morosely and sets off. I watch him walk to the end of the block before I run upstairs to my apartment.

I throw everything I own into my trunk in record time, my stomach and mind both churning. I can't imagine what would make Niko so sad. Did he talk to Amber? Does he think I put that bag of pot in her locker? I can just tell him that Mindi is more unstable than anyone knows. That actually is the truth, oddly enough.

I stop packing and stand completely still. What if it's something more? What if he knows the parts of my past that I left out, the guilty that I helped Them kill in the name of justice? I told myself I was going to be honest with Niko before I go. So I need to tell him the truth. If he asks me about it, I'll give him the entire story. No more half-truths.

But how would he have found out about that? It's not like I've left a lot of witnesses.

I swallow my worry and shove the last of my clothes into the trunk. Anything that's dirty I'll just have to leave behind. I don't have time for laundry.

I lug my trunk out of the apartment, sidestepping Odie as he meows at me. "I'll come back for you after I talk to Niko," I tell him, but I go back and fill up his food dish anyway. Odie ignores me in favor of the food, and I drag the trunk down the stairs and to the back of my car before walking the couple of blocks to the Greek diner.

Niko sits in a booth, cradling a cup of coffee, when I walk in. The Greek diner is actually called the Arch Street Diner, but at one time it was owned by a Greek family, and the name stuck. It's a stereotypical restaurant with a black-and-white checkered floor and cracked red vinyl booths. The floor looks like it hasn't been replaced in years, and Elvis posters in cheap plastic frames cover the walls, most of them sun-bleached. The place is pretty empty. The only other people in the diner are a frazzled waitress, a sweaty short-order cook watching a basketball game, and a homeless man nursing a cup of coffee at the counter.

I slide in opposite Niko with a wide smile, hoping he doesn't see the worry in my eyes. Overhead, Elvis croons about some girl breaking his heart, and I grit my teeth. The music isn't helping, and if anything, the sound makes me edgy.

"So, what's up?" I ask, my voice entirely too chipper. The waitress appears before Niko can say anything, and I order coffee. She scurries off and comes back with a full mug that sloshes all over the table when she sets it down. I pull some napkins from the dispenser and blot up the extra liquid. Now that I'm sitting here, I can't look Niko in the eyes. I'm afraid of what emotion I might find there. Disgust? Fear? Or maybe disappointment?

I should have just left without saying good-bye. In a couple of weeks I'll probably forget all about him.

I wish I could believe that.

Niko takes the soggy napkins out of my hands and drops them near the salt shaker. He gently wraps his fingers in mine, and I can't resist looking him in the eye any longer. His ocean gaze is filled with pain, and my stomach drops.

"Someone left this for me in my mailbox." He reaches beneath the table and produces a manila folder, the kind you see in doctor's offices. His name is written across the front in bold letters. He slides it across the table at me, and I hesitate before opening it. There's nothing saying where it's from or who left it, and the mystery makes me nauseous.

"What is it?"

"I think you'd better look at it yourself." He says it so low that I have to guess at his words.

I flip open the cover without looking at Niko. A black-and-white photo of a kitchen is the first thing that I see. Roland Thomas's kitchen. The cabinets, floor, and walls are covered with a substance that appears black in the photo. The blood would be more impressive in color.

I move past the photo and quickly skim the rest of the file. News clippings from my kidnapping. The terrible sketch of me that appeared in the newspaper after the incident in Charlotte. Kevin Eames's medical report. Copies of my police record from Savannah, even though I was never brought to trial. And worst of all, my write-up from Brighter Day, where my parents went into explicit detail about why they were having me admitted, and later where Dr. Goodhart wrote up his diagnosis— multiple personality disorder, narcissism, amoral behavior stemming from a childhood assault.

Someone has compiled all of my secrets into one handy file. There's only one person who had access to this much information. The world slips to the side and tilts a little. I hadn't expected this. I flip over the folder and compare the handwriting to the photocopied notes from my medical file. It's just as I thought. I close my eyes and try to push down my panic. "Dr. Goodhart left this for you."

"It doesn't matter who left it. You didn't tell me the truth. The reason you're on the run isn't because of some doctor but because you kill people." Niko squeezes my hands before he continues. "Tell me that it isn't true, that this is all just a coincidence."

Niko's eyes don't meet mine; instead they are focused on our interlocked fingers. I'm surprised he can even touch me if he thinks any of the file is true. His eyebrows are knitted together slightly, like he's not entirely sure he believes what's in there. Maybe there's hope after all.

This is my opportunity to deny it all, to foist the blame on the Furies in my head, to say I'm the victim in all of this. But that would mean I have to lie to him again, and I'm not sure I can. I want to be as good as Niko thinks I am, and to do that I have to be honest with him.

"It's true."

Niko's head snaps back as though he's just been slapped, and he pulls his hands away. I'm cold without his touch, and I wrap my arms around myself. His eyes take a few seconds to focus on me. He seems conflicted. For a moment his mouth twitches, and I think he's going to tell me to forget it, to let's eat some pancakes and then head off on an adventure. But his lips thin, and I know he has made up his mind. "How many?"

"A few," I say.

"Roland Thomas was the first, but he wasn't the last."

I shake my head. "No, he wasn't the last."

Niko's hands have a slight tremor now, and he looks everywhere but at me. I can't blame him. Don't I have trouble looking at my own face in the mirror? "I saw the clippings in your room when you were sick. I wondered—" He breaks off with a strangled sound, as though he can't quite put the thought into words. He closes his eyes for a moment and then reopens them. "Why? I can understand why you killed Thomas, but why the others? Why didn't you fight the Furies?"

"I did. I did the best I could, Niko. That's why my parents sent me to Brighter Day. They're quiet when They get what They want. But it's hard to ignore Them when They're hungry. There are so many bad men in the world who want to hurt women. Like Roland hurt me." A horrible wave of pain crashes toward me, filled with memories that I don't want. I resist it. I won't give in to it.

"Amelie, I love you. But this—" All of the joy I might have felt at his declaration is consumed by the way he fumbles nervously for his coffee cup. I can imagine how it all went down. Niko looking at the grainy crime-scene photos, the articles triggering his suspicions into full-fledged doubts. This moment is my nightmare come to life. Niko now sees me for the fiend that I am.

How can anyone love a monster?

I wrap my hands around my mug and drain the scalding liquid in one gulp. There isn't all that much I can say in my defense, so I don't even bother.

Niko sets his coffee down and scrubs his hand across his face. It doesn't take a genius to see that my affirmation may be too much for him. "The pictures. Did you really do that?" he asks again, like he can't believe my earlier answer.

The waitress appears and refills our coffee cups, giving both of us curious looks before disappearing again. I'm shaking now, with despair, with fear at the direction this conversation is taking. I look down into my coffee cup. "I don't know. I guess, in a way. I wasn't in control then. You saw what I'm up against. Sometimes I have . . . lapses. When They're in control, things get messy."

"Messy." His voice is flat. It was the wrong thing to say. "And what about when you're in control? Do people still die?"

I'm about to say, "Only the guilty," when the memory of Jefferson Halsey stops me. He's right. When I'm around, people die. Guilty or not.

Niko takes the pause as agreement. "This is so much bigger than what you told me. Was any of that true?"

"Yes. It was all true. I just left some parts out."

He laughs bitterly. "You don't say." Niko sits back hard and exhales. "What the fuck, Amelie?"

"Yeah." My voice is little more than a whisper. Inside I'm being torn apart, each one of his words a jagged piece of glass slicing through my heart. "It doesn't change the way I feel about you, though. I love you." It sounds pathetic.

Niko closes his eyes for a moment, and then looks at me. Really looks at me. The pain in his expression gives me an odd sort of hope. "How do you know what you feel, Amelie?" he asks. "How can you even know what love is, or that you love me?"

I blink back tears and resist the urge to reach across the table to touch him. When I speak, it's the honest, unvarnished truth, as ugly as it might be. "Because I never thought about hurting you."

Niko's face twists, his expression landing somewhere between horror and pain. What's left of my heart shatters into a million pieces. I stare down at my lap, and my tears fall unchecked onto my thighs. I'm surprised to see them, but I can't seem to feel anything else. The agony is too great. I deserve this. I should feel like my chest is being ripped open. This is what I get for being a psycho.

Niko leans forward, tipping my chin up so he can look into my eyes. "Don't cry. Please. I still love you. But this thing with the Furies, and you killing people . . . I don't know if I can handle this. It's not like you're skipping class or smoking pot. You kill people. And you lied to me about it. Worst of all, I think you might like it." He pauses, and it's a struggle to hear his next words, his voice is so soft. "You're better than this. I know you are. You have to be." His sorrowful tone is a slap in the face after his calling me a killer, and I can't hide my flinch.

He pulls away and drums his fingers on the tabletop. "I need some space to think, to figure out what to do. Maybe we can talk about this in a couple of days. . . ." He trails off, hands held out beseechingly. I look away for a few long seconds. When I turn back to him, he pushes his hand through his hair and swears under his breath. I don't want to see the emotion on his face, so I quickly look down. "I'll give you a call in a couple of weeks, okay?" he says. It's not a promise. It's a blow-off. Because I couldn't be honest with him and because I'm a killer, I've lost him forever. My anchor.

And now I'm adrift in a sea of despair.

He tosses a five on the table and departs, leaving the manila folder. The reality of what has just happened hits me like a sledgehammer. I clutch at my mug, swallowing my sobs until I hear the door of the diner open and close. Then I release any control I have left.

I cry loudly for a few minutes, a black wave of sorrow causing me to hunch over in pain. The waitress hovers behind the counter nervously. She has probably witnessed this scene before, and she makes no move toward me. It is only when the mug shatters in my hands that she hurries around from behind the counter, worry etched into the fine lines of her face.

"Oh, sweetie, let me get that for you." She pries chunks of broken ceramic out of my hands, and I let her have them. She sweeps them up, and I push the folder holding my guilt toward her as well. She takes it with a curious look, and I'm relieved when she dumps the entire mess into a nearby trash can. I don't want any reminders of this afternoon.

Tears run freely down my face, and I swipe at my snotty nose with the back of my hand. It's only when I pull my hand away that I realize a piece of the mug sliced open my palm. The sight of the blood jars me, and I panic a little. I grab for the napkins from the dispenser, smearing the stainless steel with scarlet. I scrunch the paper in my hands, trying to slow the bleeding. The sight of my hands clutching bloody napkins just reminds me of the moment with Niko in the cafeteria, and I start crying all over again. Sobs shake my body, and I want to lie down on the floor and die.

Did you miss us?

A brush of wings, the soft movement of scales. A hot wind blows my hair back from my face, drying my tears. The Furies fill my brain, murmuring soft assurances, soothing hurt feelings, and blanketing me in concern. The ache in my chest subsides and is replaced by a warm outrage.

How dare he leave a girl like you! Tisiphone's voice is husky and soft, and soothes my fears effortlessly.

Men are only interested in one thing. Filthy creatures. Megaera hisses.

My hands heat painfully, but when I open them, the cuts from the mug are gone. I smile, full of joy. I've missed Them.

I pause. Wait, have I? I could have sworn that I was glad to have Them gone.

Before the thought is completed, a warm wind calms me. I can almost feel the cool touch of the serpent's hand on my cheek. She coos lovingly in my ear.

Let's go hunting, dear.

Yes, let's.

I drop my last twenty onto the table for the waitress's trouble and head out of the diner. I run full tilt to my car, my head bursting with their compliments and suggestions, with their admiration and encouragement. A few people step aside on the sidewalk to avoid me, but I ignore them. This is what I was meant to be, a vessel for Their workings.

By the time I slide behind the wheel and head toward the highway, I've forgotten all about Niko stomping on my heart.

KILLER, HANGOVER

I WAKE WITH A GROAN, DISORIENTED AND SORE. Weak sunlight filters through the boards on the room's lone window, and I sit up.

Wait, boards?

I survey my surroundings, and my heart sinks. I don't know where I am, but I'm pretty sure it's an abandoned building. Wooden slats cover the windows, and the room has the musty smell of disuse. I lie on a dirty mattress, the fabric reeking of piss and dust. I sneeze, probably because there's a thick layer of grime covering the battered wood floor. Something scurries in the pile of crumpled newspapers in the far corner, and I shakily get to my feet. When I stand, I try to flex my fingers, which are stiff from the cold. I watch my fingers curl and uncurl. There is something off about them, and I stare until my tired brain can figure out what it is. I gasp, and it ends on a choked sound.

My hand is covered with soot.

I turn my head to the side and vomit, deep, violent heaves that bring tears to my eyes and make my stomach muscles ache. Nothing comes up but bile, and my throat burns. I collapse back onto the mattress. I want to get up; the smell from the mattress makes my stomach twist again. I'm too weak. Tears leak out of my eyes and down into my ears, and I take a few steadying breaths before leveraging myself up into a standing position once again. Waves of dizziness batter me, and I widen my stance to keep from falling back onto the putrid mattress.

I make my way to the doorway, the spaces between the window boards providing enough light for me to see the gaping holes in the floor. My sweater scratches my neck, the once soft material now stiff and unyielding. It's black, so a visual inspection reveals nothing. I pull at it, and a sickly sweet scent assaults my nose. Bits of black ash, thick and oily, fleck onto my fingertips, and I take a sharp breath. The dark material is saturated with the substance, like grease from a grill, and a deep sense of foreboding settles in for a long stay. This is bad, because it means I wasn't in control of the justice that was handed down. When I carry out justice, there is no blood, no soot, no sign of anything amiss. When They are in control, it's a massacre. I can't remember what happened, but if my current condition is any indicator, it was bad.

I need to get out of here.

The door leads to a hallway and a staircase that doesn't look safe to use. The handrail lists away from the stairs, and there are dark spots where the treads are missing. I'm debating trying to find another way down, when I sneeze and lose my balance. Gravity takes care of the rest.

I topple forward, crying out as I flip over and my spine strikes something sharp. I fall forever and finally come to rest with my head and shoulders on the dirty wood floor and my legs askew on the stairs. I groan. Not exactly the preferred method for descending stairs.

Pain ratchets up my spine and steals my breath when I try to move. I lie there on the floor, waiting for my body to respond. Fear slices through me. What if I'm paralyzed? I try to wiggle my feet, and they respond with sheer agony. I quickly do an inventory of the rest of my body. I'm hurt, and very cold, but I don't think anything is broken.

I spend the next few minutes carefully picking myself up off the floor and making my way toward the front door. I stand and lean heavily on what I hope is a water-stained wall. I can see the front door, but the thick coating of dust on the floor makes me think I didn't come in that way. The cops would have been here long ago if I had just broken the front door down. I turn in a slow circle and see a dark dusting that marks a trail to the back of the house. My stomach roils again. Hansel and Gretel have got nothing on Them.

I follow the shadowy spots down the hallway and back toward what I figure was once the kitchen. The copper pipes and appliances are both long gone, but the window over the sink is broken and unblocked. Even better, the back door hangs drunkenly off its hinges.

I walk out into a small courtyard, and freeze. A light dusting of snow covers the cracked and weed-choked concrete patio, but it's not enough to hide the fine black powder that covers everything, or the bodies piled by the back gate. There are at least three of them, younger guys dressed in puffy jackets and baggy jeans. The one closest to me lies on his stomach. Even in death his face is contorted in fear.

I prop my hands on my knees and heave a little. The cold air helps clear my head, and the endorphins flooding my system block some of my horror. I have to find a way out of the yard, but the bodies of Their victims block the fence's only gate.

Our victims, dear. You were right there with us the entire time.

Pain slices through my head, and the memories of last night overwhelm me. I swallow a moan at the scenes that play out in my mind's eye. From what They show me, the three men here aren't the only ones. The Furies were in control for almost three days, and in that time They cut a deadly swath through several of the rougher neighborhoods in Philadelphia. Drug dealers, pimps, murderers, thugs, and random passersby all fell to Their wrath. Anyone They could get alone for more than a few minutes was fair game. I whimper and hide my face in my hands. I can't keep doing this. It's wrong.

More important, the more I let Them have Their way, the closer I am to completely losing mine. Their price is too high. Despair swells in my chest, and I hug myself as I cry quiet tears.

This must be what rock bottom feels like. I hate what I've become. I don't want to be this person. No matter what They want me to believe, I'm not a cold-blooded killer. I won't be.

A breeze kicks up, slicing through my sweater and ruffling the hair on one of the bodies, an olive-skinned man with dark hair and wide staring blue eyes. In another life he could have been Niko. I shiver, and consider taking one of the jackets off the bodies in front of me.

No, that would be worse than rock bottom. I'll just freeze, thanks.

There's a slat missing in the side of the fence, and I head toward it. Looking at the bodies in front of me makes me feel crazed. I did that. I killed those men, burning away their souls. It wasn't just Them. I gave in to Their demands, and now there are dead bodies littering the streets.

"I have to find a way to get rid of Them," I mutter to myself.

Why? Tisiphone wails in my mind. *You enjoyed it every bit as much as we did.*

Memories threaten to push forward, and I mentally shy away from them. Tisiphone is right, and the knowledge fills me with self-loathing.

I push out through the narrow gap and walk down the alley. It's still very early, and although the sun is up, the streets are deserted. Thank the gods for that. If I had an audience, who knows what would happen.

There are very few cars on the street, and my body is stiff from the cold. I think I might have frostbite, because I can't feel my fingers or my toes, and my feet are heavy and wooden. Now that I'm away from the house of death, my body begins to register a million different aches and pains. It's all too much for my mind to deal with, so I do what I usually do when I'm overloaded.

I run.

I start with an easy jog, going past mini-marts and hollow-eyed street people with shopping carts. My feet pound erratically as I push past the pain in my hip. I'm hoping the dull throb means a bruise and not something worse. After a few blocks my body begins to warm, and

I wiggle my fingers. I pass a church. Sharply dressed black women file inside, their colorful church hats making them look like exotic birds. I ignore their stares and hushed whispers. It's Sunday, and a weekend has passed without me. I increase my pace.

I run through lights, narrowly avoiding cars with thumping sound systems and families headed to breakfast. I'm not counting the blocks, but my mind has finally shut off its agonized wail of shame, when I see it. A stack of blue and white parking tickets are jammed under the windshield wiper, and someone busted out my back window, no doubt to get to my purse. Even the enormous dent in the driver's-side door is beautiful. It's a miracle it hasn't been towed, but that's my car. I almost cry in relief.

I slow and come to a stop, looking around the block to make sure no one watches me. I pull the parking tickets off, and they flutter to the ground like broken butterflies. My frozen fingers delve into my front pocket, searching for my keys. Tears course down my face when I touch the cold metal, and I open the already unlocked driver's-side door with shaking hands. I get in, start up the car, and crank the heater to high. My coat is on the passenger seat, and I slowly pull it on. I shiver as I wait for the air from the vents to warm up. It's all I can do not to break down. I bite my lip until I break the skin, using the pain and the salty tang of blood to help me focus. "I'm not like Them," I whisper, the words swallowed by the roar of the heater and the hum of the engine.

Please let it be true.

GIRL MADE OF MAKE BELIEVE

I'M A WRECK. I CRY THE ENTIRE DRIVE, UNABLE
to stop sobbing long enough to even pay the toll. The booth operator
gives me a bored look as I dig through my wallet for money. Meanwhile
They suggest that I gouge out the man's eyes.

What a lovely shade of blue. That's your favorite, right?

Their mocking laughter echoes through my mind as I throw a
couple of crumpled bills at the booth operator and peel away. It's
amazing I even have any money, but there was a thick roll of twen-

ties in my pants' pocket, most likely from one of my victims. It disturbs me that They were careful enough to take the time to think about money. They are starting to think about the long term, about the possibility of a future. It's unsettling. And They chose locations and victims that wouldn't be readily discovered. They are adapting, becoming smarter about things. That scares me.

They're going to win. And I don't even know how to fight back.

The sun on the highway blinds me, and I flip the visor down to shield my eyes. When I do, a sheet of folded paper falls into my lap. I pick it up in surprise, and almost drive off the road as I try to read it. It's an e-mail, from Dr. Goodhart to someone at an e-mail address I don't recognize. The message is only two lines:

> Marie: parents due tomorrow, early. Black Lexus, plates FVX1393.
>
> The brakes are a good idea. You know I'm counting on you. S.

My mouth goes dry, and I reread the message again. The date makes my chest tight, and I have to pull to the side of the road until I can breathe again.

It's the same week that my parents died. And they owned a black Lexus.

You're welcome.

I study the e-mail, wondering why They kept it from me for so long.

My stomach clenches, and I cover my mouth as I fight more tears. I have to go after Dr. Goodhart, the other monster in the closet of my mind. All I want to do is take a shower and try to wash away the past three days, before I curl up into a ball and cry myself to sleep. But I won't have that luxury. I have to assume the e-mail is one last gift from Them, one last loose end that They will let me tie up before They take control. Forever.

I crumple up the e-mail and pitch it out the window, heedless of the littering laws. I can do this. I will follow through with this. I may be doomed, but I'm taking that son of a bitch with me.

Right after I go back to my apartment and get my cat.

Then what?

I don't care. I'm not going to worry about the future. I don't have one.

But there is some satisfaction in knowing that Goodhart doesn't have one either.

I'm too exhausted to drive the hour and a half back to West County, so I plan to hit up a store and then find a hotel room. Odie will understand. I'll grab him, and then we'll head to Harrisburg to find Goodhart. That's all I can focus on right now.

It hurts to walk through the megastore, grabbing toiletries and food. While walking up and down the aisles, people give me odd looks, but the mothers with screaming toddlers have more pressing issues to worry about than the girl with soot smeared on her neck. I somehow managed to miss the spot, even after scrubbing my face with a wet wipe from the center console of my car. It's surprising no one stopped me on my run to my illegally parked car. Every square inch of exposed skin was streaked with black ash, like I'd just gotten done with my part-time job as a chimney sweep.

I find the world's cheapest room in the scariest motel in America. The bed feels like a rock, but after a hot shower I don't really care. At least it doesn't smell like cat piss.

I wake a few hours later, surprised by how bright the room is. It was midafternoon when I went to sleep, so I expect the room to be dark. When I turn my head toward the source of the light, I have to cover my eyes. Alekto sits in the wingback chair, a beacon in the far corner of the room.

"You have shitty timing. Where were you three days ago?" I ask. The room is hot, hotter than August in Georgia. I kick the covers off and wipe away the sweat that's beading on my forehead. She doesn't answer, so I say, "What are you doing here?"

"I am here to finish the story. I think you are finally ready to listen."

I lean back against the pillows and close my eyes. I still don't like her, but it doesn't hurt to listen to what she has to say.

"After They joined together in the early dawn light, the Furies cut a deadly path through the land of man, killing those with the stain of evil upon their souls. Lifetimes passed, and things settled into a predictable pattern.

"But then everything changed."

I open my eyes and study Alekto, the true Third. She glows brightly, and I look at my hands as she talks. The sight of the soot in my nail beds reminds me how much I actually need her and whatever wisdom she can offer.

"One day They were called to a small town where a priestess was accused of murdering her lover. The woman protested her innocence, and the townspeople were wary of murdering a holy woman. So they prayed that the gods would send the Furies their way. The Furies were known to be impartial, and if the woman had killed her lover, the Furies would take care of the matter in Their own way.

"The Furies arrived and read the woman's soul, finding that she had played an unwitting part in the young man's murder. It was revealed that the husband had poisoned the dish the woman had prepared for her lover, not knowing that the priestess had had no intention of eating the food. The Furies made to punish the husband, but before they could, a young man stepped forward from the crowd.

"He declared himself the beloved of the golden Fury, and told the crowd how he had begged the gods to grant him an endless life so that he could be with the woman he loved. The golden Fury could not remember the man, but as she stared at him, an odd thing began to happen. She began to cry, the tears washing away the sorrow that had blinded her to everything but punishing the guilty. See, her mind could not remember the man standing before her, but her heart did."

As much as I want to hear the end of the story, I can't help but snort. "Let me guess. He swept her up in his arms, and the two lived happily ever after. Meanwhile the other two Furies decided to kill everything in sight because that's what They do."

She smiles sadly and shakes her head. "Not quite, but close. Tisiphone and Megaera need the soul of a human to tie Them to the mortal plane. Without a Third, They will be pulled to the underworld, the final resting place of the slain god. You already know that Their Third must have blood on her soul, even if indirectly. Blood calls to blood."

"Good to know. But what does that have to do with me? I can't exactly get rid of Them."

"But you can. That is what I came to tell you. They are drawn to sorrow, to rage. But They are weakened by love and forgiveness. They seek to tempt you, to make you like Them. But there is still goodness in you. There is love. Do not let Them remake you in Their image."

I rest my head in my hands and sigh. "They didn't remake me in Their image; They remade me in yours."

She gives me a sad smile. "Do not let Them change your heart. They will try to turn you back to your rage, away from your love for Niko. You must hold tight to your true feelings. As long as you are not totally corrupted, you can resist Them."

The weight of the despair crushing my chest makes me moan a little. "Niko's gone. He can't help me." The words are so low, I almost whisper them.

"You do not need him. You need the way you feel about him. The Furies are rage and anger. They do not understand love."

It finally clicks. It's so simple, and yet it took me all this time to finally have the answer. "I invited Them in, but They stayed because I'm just like Them."

"No, you are not. But your anger gives Them strength, as does passing Their judgments. They have a limitless appetite for punishment. It was that hunger that drove me away. There was no room for compromise. I could not rejoin my beloved and help Them. There is nothing but vengeance for Them. I was Their true sister, born of the same blood, and They decided They would rather have the violence than me." A wistful sadness flits across her face. "There is no way you can match Their longing for destruction."

"So what do I do? How do I stop Them?"

Alekto smiles. "I'm still forbidden to tell you that. But I think you know the answer. Your love for Niko will give you the strength to follow through."

I blink. That's less than helpful. "That's it?"

She stands and walks toward the door. "I wish I could give you a clear answer, but you just need to know you have the power to resist Them."

I laugh bitterly. "Great. Thanks for the pep talk."

She turns around and gives me a knowing look. "Focus on your feelings for Niko to help you save yourself. Take strength from your love for him. The only thing separating us from Them is our capacity to love."

She walks through the door and disappears in a flash of light, and when the spots clear, I'm still sitting in bed. I pinch my arm, the pain assuring me it wasn't a dream. This is the first time she has appeared while I'm awake, and that sets off alarm bells. Something has changed.

But what?

I stretch and get out of bed, surprised that I'm refreshed and revived. All of my hurts and aches have disappeared, and even the bruise on my hip, which was the color of concord grapes when I took my shower, has disappeared when I examine the spot.

See? We do have our benefits, dear.

The voice in my head gives me pause. It sounds . . . louder, some-how. I go into the bathroom to relieve the pressure on my bladder, and when I'm done, I examine my reflection in the chipped mirror behind the sink. There are deep shadows under my eyes, and my face looks haunted. My hair is frizzy. On either side of me I can see Their ghostly outlines, and Tisiphone waves at me happily.

"Go away," I say.

Megaera frowns and strokes my hair. Fear trills through me at the tug on my scalp. I shouldn't be able to feel Their touch.

Now, now. Why the long face?

Tisiphone picks up a length of my hair and twists it into a braid along the front of my hairline. She finger combs the snarls from my hair, and the curls magically smooth out into shining coils. I try not to flinch at the caress of her talons.

Someone's been talking to Alekto. Poor dear. Our wretched sister must've unsettled you. Has she been spinning her lies again?

I swallow thickly. "Yeah, something like that." They step away from me. Their smiles are strained, and fear sours my stomach. "So, are we going after Dr. Goodhart, or are we going to hang out here and do makeovers all night?"

They don't move, and instead of giving in to my terror, I drive my fist into the mirror, cracking it. Anger They understand and respect. The pain is bracing, but fades too quickly. I look at my hand, the scrapes on my knuckles already fading away. A faint shimmering hovers above my arms, and I recognize the shape of the silver chains. Something has changed.

Alekto misunderstands. Megaera hisses in my mind. *We don't want control. We want a partnership. Don't you want to belong, to have sisters?*

Ah, so that's the tactic They're trying now. Instead of a hostile takeover, They want cooperation. They hope I'll just give in and let Them turn me into a single-minded killing machine.

Sadly, it doesn't sound like such a bad idea.

I'm so tired. I've lost Niko, and I can't think about anything else right now. My heart is raw, and even thinking about him brings tears to my eyes. I can't struggle against Them and try to get over Niko. I'm just not strong enough.

Plus, I want Goodhart dead. No mercy for the bastard.

"Of course I want sisters. Nothing would make me happier."

They move close to me again, whispering platitudes and flattery, twisting my hair into some complex style of a civilization long gone. I close my eyes to block out the sight of Them, and to hide the frustrated tears that burn behind my eyes.

I'm not even strong enough to fight.

I don't think I ever was.

NOT MUCH LEFT TO ANALYZE

I SPEED ALL THE WAY BACK TO MY APARTMENT, anxious to get Odie and get to Harrisburg to find Goodhart. I can see Them the entire time out of the corners of my eyes, and Their constant presence disturbs me. Somehow They've manifested of Their own accord, and no matter how much I try, I can't grasp Them with my mind, let alone shove Them back into my subconscious.

I'm terrified, but I push my fear aside and just drive. Eventually I feel nothing, my terror numbing me and silencing the thoughts running through my mind. The only thoughts come from Their running dialogue.

The Furies urge me on with fevered whispers, cajoling me to pull over and start a massacre in every small town we pass through. They detail how much fun we could have injuring other motorists, and how many men we will punish once we are finished with Goodhart. There is an almost painful pressure behind my eyes as They blather on nonstop, Megaera in the passenger seat, Tisiphone behind me, her wings taking up the entire backseat. They both wear wide Joker-esque smiles, and I wonder if They are happier about Their freedom or the impending killing.

The only good thing about having Them in the car is that the heat of Their presence completely negates the frigid air coming in through my broken back window.

When did I get so good at looking on the bright side?

It takes me only an hour to get back to my apartment from the roadside motel where I crashed. I trudge upstairs, dragging my feet up each step like it weighs a hundred pounds. Dread has settled on my shoulders like a wet blanket, and I'm not sure how to stop the impending disaster. There is no way this can go well. At some point They will figure out that I'm not exactly overjoyed at the thought of being Their pet.

First my cat, then everything else. One thing at a time or I'll break.

I get to my door and rest my head against the jamb, gathering my thoughts. I'm so tired, exhaustion that goes bone-deep. Is this the physical toll for carting Them around? Will They burn through my life too fast, the price of Their presence my few allotted years on this planet? It might be preferable to the alternative, an eternity spent at Their bloody beck and call.

I push my key into the lock, open the door, slip inside, and close the door behind me. I move into the apartment, calling for Odie. A muted footfall echoes behind me, and I turn. A crawling sensation writhes over my exposed skin, like insects walking across my arms.

Goodhart stands in the doorway to my bedroom, Odie in his arms. "You know, I've never cared for cats. They simply don't have the loyalty that dogs do. Did you know that cats will actually eat their owners after they die? Dogs will starve before they take a single bite of their beloved master."

I will not show my fear. "You know you look like a B-movie villain, right?" Odie jumps down when he sees me and twines around my ankles. I bend down to scoop him up, ignoring the gun that Goodhart points at me. Well, this is new.

"What are you doing here?"

"I saw you and your little boyfriend in Harrisburg. Luckily, the librarian at the state archives is a friend of mine, and he handed over your information when he heard that you were a former patient of mine. Apparently, you seemed a little off to him."

So said the guy who freaked when I asked to look at a book. I don't say that, though. The doctor does have a gun pointed at my chest.

"So, you came here to kill me? Nice. By the way, you look great."

He looks like hell. His eyes are shadowed and a little wild, the scar from Tisiphone's talons making him look sinister. His blond hair has grayed too early, and his clothes are dirty and wrinkled, and the hand pointing the gun at me trembles. He looks as bad as I feel.

"Shut up, you stupid bitch. You've ruined me. Do you know how much money I lost when you escaped? For more than a year I invested in you, and then you ran." He says it like he can't believe a creature he cared for would turn on him. "And then you try to kill me, hunting me like some animal. I saved your life."

"Funny, I don't quite remember it that way. You used me as a guinea pig. And you killed my parents." A flicker of surprise crosses his face, and I laugh. "Ohmigod, you thought I didn't know? Who do you think They are?" I gesture over my shoulders, and he frowns.

"Who are you talking about? I don't see anyone."

I shrug. "My friends. You remember Them? Tisiphone did give you a memento last time we met," I say, tapping my cheek.

His expression darkens. "I don't know what you're talking about. You did this. You're sick, Amelie."

I pause. What if he's right? What if They're all in my head? Fear makes me cold, and I clutch Odie close.

No. They're real. They're just waiting for me to take the offensive.

I adjust my weight, moving forward slightly so I can get in a good kick. Before I can make my move, Goodhart gives me a twisted smile. He levels the gun between my eyes, and a sliver of panic shreds my bravado. Where are They? He waves the gun at me. "It doesn't matter. Soon you'll be dead, and I'll be able to live my life without looking over my shoulder."

I bury my face in Odie's fur, and inhale his kitty scent. A single awful thought crosses my mind, but I don't want to consider it. I shake my head, and beam at Goodhart. "Okay."

He gives me a confused look, and I go to the front door. I don't want to die, not at all, but I have to admit that it probably is best all around if he kills me. If I die, They'll lose Their tie to this world.

Or at least I hope so.

I open the door, Dr. Goodhart a nervous shadow behind me. "What are you doing?" he snaps, the gun waving in my direction.

I drop Odie on the other side of the door. He meows at me once before walking down the stairs. He's finally getting his wish to go outside. I hope he remembers enough to survive until some Good Samaritan finds him.

I close the door softly and turn back to Dr. Goodhart. "I was letting my cat go. Now, we were discussing your killing me. You should probably do it soon, because I'm pretty sure They won't like you taking away Their chance for freedom."

"Who?" he snaps.

"Them." I gesture, and he turns around to where They've manifested behind him. The serpent grabs him by the throat, and he drops his gun, the weapon clattering on the floor. Megaera throws him against the wall. He crashes into the drywall and cracks it. There goes my security deposit.

Dr. Goodhart groans and scrabbles away from Tisiphone, who's advancing on him with deliberate steps. She smiles at him with a mouth full of pointed teeth.

"Don't be afraid. This is only going to hurt a lot." Her throaty voice makes the words an even greater mockery of his fear. She kicks him in the ribs, the whoosh of his exhaled breath audible throughout the room.

Megaera clucks. "Now, now, Sister. Don't take all of the fun for yourself. This is Amelie's vengeance. A deal's a deal."

Tisiphone pouts momentarily and then gives a languid shrug. "I suppose so. The first one didn't really count, did it? After all, you didn't even get a chance to touch him before we tore him apart."

I blink, and something in the back of my mind clicks. There are a lot of memories I don't want, too full of pain and fear for my mind to process. But there's one that I need, and it floats to the top.

For the first time the memory of Roland Thomas's death comes back to me. The hawk is right. Before, all I could remember was all the blood, but as I focus, the events of that day fall into place. I remember it now. The rage that had burned in my chest, propelling me up the stairs. Their voices crowding out all rational thought. Roland Thomas screaming in pain and fear while I stood rooted to my spot by the basement door. And then . . .

Running. Through the woods. Away from the pain, blood, and fear of that awful place. And Their voices calling after me, echoing through my mind.

We are sorry. We lost control. It has been so long . . .

We owe you.

Why couldn't I remember everything before? It comes back to me in bits and pieces, along with the awful memories of Roland Thomas. The truth of it makes my breath hitch.

They altered the memory. They altered all of my thoughts. Because I was supposed to kill Roland Thomas. That was our deal. His death for my cooperation.

But I never killed him. They've been lying to me all this time.

It's almost too much.

Rage at the memories of my mistreatment drives me to Goodhart's side. He lies on the ground, moaning from Their brief assault. I twist his arm, a snap signaling when it breaks. His screams reverberate in the tiny apartment. I look him in the eye, fury boiling under my skin as he endures the pain.

"Why did you kill my parents?" I demand.

He blinks at me through a mask of pain. "They were going to pull you out of the study. I had a grant for an experimental drug, but the study called for a trauma survivor with possible multiple personality disorder. You were the only patient who qualified."

"You killed my parents for a little bit of money?"

He coughs, blood frothing on his lips. "It was five million dollars. That is not a 'little bit of money.'"

"How?" The pain of my parents' loss starts to creep in, and Megaera rests her hand on my shoulder. They stand behind me, looking on proudly. When Goodhart doesn't answer my question quickly enough, I twist his arm, waiting until his cries have subsided to ask again. "How?"

"A patient at Brighter Day. Marie Layton. You met her at Saint Dymphna's."

I remember the dark-haired girl the orderlies carried in, bruised and beaten. She wasn't there very long, maybe a couple of months. When she left, Annie took her place.

The doctor coughs, and continues. "She got out, and cut the brake lines the morning your parents were supposed to come and pull you out of the program. Your father and I had talked about the shortcut they took through Monaghan Gap, and I knew there was a particularly steep hill that would work. It was just dumb luck that it was raining. No one even thought it was anything but an accident."

It all makes sense now. Dumb luck. Just like it was dumb luck that I was in Saint Dymphna's while Dr. Goodhart slowly poisoned the girl who'd killed my parents, my pretty dark-haired roommate with blood on her lips. Dumb luck that Roland Thomas followed me and not my friend Steph. It was dumb luck that had caused a much younger version of myself to waddle into a lake when no one was looking and made my cousin drown. Dumb luck that They were listening when I prayed for help.

There's a lot of dumb fucking luck going around.

I look down at Dr. Goodhart and smile. I can feel Their excitement almost as though it's my own.

But it's not mine. It's Theirs, and I'm tired of being everyone's pawn. I don't want to kill Dr. Goodhart. No matter how much he deserves it. Dumb luck or not.

"I guess it's your lucky night," I say. I still hold on to his arm, and I squeeze it one more time in a futile attempt to cause him as much hurt as he caused me.

I may not want him dead, but I can make sure he suffers.

Their outlines grow stronger on either side of me. He's in too much agony to notice Them. The serpent looks at me and smiles. "Just kill him already."

Megaera's words are enough to break through the haze of my righteous fury. I drop the doctor's arm, and he falls to the ground in a heap, sobbing and cradling the limb. I look at the serpent and at the winged woman, both standing in front of me. Something is wrong. I begin to shake as I realize what it is. The threefold vision is gone. Does that mean I no longer need Their help? Are we now equals?

Am I just like them?

Tisiphone, her wings quivering, reaches for me with her taloned hands. "Finish it!" she urges, the sword appearing in my hand. I fall backward, away from her and out of Their reach. The sword clatters to the floor and lies there for a second before disappearing.

"No," I say, my voice more certain than I feel. I remember Niko's expression, the disgust and revulsion when he figured out my secret. Lethargy seeps into my limbs, making me feel heavy. I'm so done. "I won't kill for you anymore."

Megaera reaches for me as well, but her ghostly hands pass through me without injury. They both howl in rage as I crab-walk away from the doctor's form. Pain claws behind my eyes and radiates down my spine as They try to force me back to Their side. I scream, and my eyes water, but I continue to scoot toward the front door. They fade from sight, losing Their foothold in this world.

Kill him! Seek your vengeance. You owe it to us.

You are one of us.

"No. I'm not like you. I don't want to be a killer." I hold tight to the memory of Niko's sorrow-filled eyes. I will be the girl he thought I was.

You will be our Third.

"No."

Think of it, Megaera cajoles. *It will be like Savannah all over again. It'll be like last night. We'll stand by your side and keep you going until your body gives out. And when that happens, you will be like us. Eternal.*

There's the soft rustle of wings, and the winged one echoes the serpent's wheedling tone. *Do you really want to be just another human, just another piece of meat? Do you want to flash brightly before burning out? Wouldn't you rather be a force of nature?*

Maybe, once upon a time. But something has changed. I've changed. Now I don't want revenge. I want happiness. I want love. I want a normal life.

I want Niko. He saw something worthwhile in me, once. I want the opportunity to show him that the goodness in me truly does exist.

"No. I told you no."

Nausea churns my stomach, and when I put the back of my hand to my nose, there's blood. Fear and adrenaline make my skin feel like it's a size too small, but I push through the feelings. I lean against the sofa and try to take shallow breaths, breathing through my mouth in panting little gasps like a woman in labor. They are tearing through my mind in Their attempt to fight free, to make me kill, and I'm afraid my head will split apart like a ripe melon.

Now's a good time to start screaming.

The pain grows as They fight for control, but I still manage to stay huddled against the couch. At times I writhe on the floor, shrieking as They try to claw Their way out of my head. I cry and curse and mentally try to push Them back. It feels like slamming my head into a wall. At some point I vomit from the torture.

Slowly I come back to myself. I sit on the floor, leaning against the couch. I'm shivering even though the apartment is warm, and my sweater is soaked through with sweat.

"Don't worry about how you look. I hear funeral homes are very good at putting people back together."

Goodhart stands over me with a smirk. His left arm hangs twisted at his side, but he holds the gun in his right. He points it at me and fires. Heat and pain lance across my left bicep, and I howl. Blood traces a path down my arm, and my mind floods with panic, stealing my sight. I take shallow breaths until I can see again.

The Furies are quiet. I can feel Their smugness.

I hate Them.

Dr. Goodhart stands over me. "On your knees. The only reason you're still alive is because I want to hear you beg for your life. Maybe if you're nice, I'll take you with me. I'm always looking for a subject for my clinical trials, and multiple personality disorder is so hard to find."

Anger courses through me at his tone, the rage all my own. "Fuck you," I grit out. I'm done. They aren't coming to the rescue this time, not after my rejection. I don't want Their kind of rescue, anyway. The price is too steep.

"That's not a very nice way to ask. You'd better hurry before I lose my patience. If you lived in a better neighborhood, I'm sure someone would have been here by now, but a gunshot will have the police en route even in this miserable pit. If you want to live, you'd better start begging."

He's lying. No matter what I say, he's going to kill me. But if I'm going to die, I'll do it on my own terms. Brave words, since I shake with fear.

Dr. Goodhart has opened his mouth to say something, when there is a knock on the door. His eyes widen comically in alarm, and he gestures with the gun toward my front door. "Open it and see who it is."

"Open it yourself." I fall sideways onto the floor. I am truly fearless for the first time in years. It's probably the blood loss. It flows out of my arm unchecked, and I'm pretty dizzy. I think the doctor may have hit an artery or something. I never thought my life would end this way, bleeding out onto the floor in a cheap apartment.

But there are worse ways to go.

The doctor grumbles something I don't hear, kicking me hard in the ribs as he steps over me to get the door. I groan and roll instinctively into a ball. I wonder what he'll say when he opens it. "Oh, don't mind the gunshot. I was just trying to kill a cockroach."

He inches the door open and sticks his head into the gap. He doesn't say a word before thunder booms through my apartment and the back of his head explodes. He falls backward, and blood pools on the floor. The door slowly swings open to reveal Mindi, a gun clutched in her shaking hands. Her shocked gaze meets mine. She looks down at the dead man on the floor and then back at me.

"I thought he was you," she whispers.

"Dumb luck," I mutter. I look away from the doctor. The sight of his head makes me want to puke. Darkness begins to tinge the edges of my vision, and They flow out of me, manifesting in a burst of heat. Maybe They're here to gloat.

Mindi turns the gun on me, but when she catches a glimpse of Them, her mouth forms an O of surprise. She doesn't look afraid, though. More awestruck. "What are They?"

"The Furies." No big deal, just creatures straight out of mythology.

Mindi holds out a reverent hand toward Them. I felt the same way the first time They appeared before me. Funny how things change.

"Where were you when my mother was killed?" Mindi asks in a hoarse voice. There's a spark of some dark emotion in her eyes. This is not a good thing.

I manage to push myself up on my elbow. "Wait. You don't want to talk to Them, Mindi. They aren't what you think They are." It's too late. Already I can feel Them pulling away from me toward her. I understand why. Her sorrow and vulnerability are so raw, so naked. They are pulled toward her like iron filings to a magnet. After all, she's the perfect candidate. I've seen her violent streak. And she just killed Dr. Goodhart. "Stop that, Mindi. They won't give you what you want. You don't want what They have to offer."

Mindi stares at me, her eyes burning with an eerie light. With horror I realize it's the brown melting away into cobalt blue. "Why wouldn't I want what They offer? Justice, righteousness. I could find the guy who killed my mom, who left her on the floor like trash. My life was ruined the day my mother was killed. If I kill him, maybe everything will be better. I can fix things. I can have the perfect life." She tilts her head to the side, as though listening to far-off music. Her brown locks curl, and bleach out to blond. Her newly blue eyes snap as she looks at me with disdain. "You had your chance, Amelie. Now it's mine. I always lose. I'm going to win for a change."

Silver chains begin to show around Mindi's arms, and I sit up in panic. "No, Mindi. You don't want this. Their price is higher than you think." I try to crawl forward, to slap some sense into her, but a super-heated wind picks me up and hurls me into the bedroom and slams the door behind me. Mindi screams as They take her.

I have to do something.

I sway as I get to my feet. Dizziness almost overwhelms me, but I manage to stay upright. The doorknob scalds my hand when I touch it, and I turn to grab something to use as a barrier.

The room is filled with a golden glow. I blink, and when my eyes adjust, I see Alekto standing near my bed. She's a blinding pillar of light. My eyes water at her strange beauty. "Leave it alone, Amelie. You cannot help her."

"I have to. I summoned Them, and I have to get rid of Them, take Them with me when I die."

"You did not summon Them. They found you, the same way They have just found Mindi. My sisters have been here far longer than you know. They can't be stopped, only slowed. They will always find a bro-ken girl to use." She smiles sadly. "And I will always be there to attempt to put Their vessels back together."

She gestures toward me, and soft warmth suffuses my body. "This is not your fight any longer." The light in the room brightens before fading away. When it clears, Alekto is gone. So is the wound on my arm.

Go live your life, Amelie. Her dulcet tone echoes in my mind. You are free. Go after what your heart truly desires. Go find your love.

I run across the room, open the window, and take the fire escape down to the alley below. When I look up toward my apartment, smoke billows out of the window I just exited. An explosion rips through the room, and I cover my head. Bricks and bits of ash rain down from above, somehow missing me. I shakily walk out of the alley toward my car.

In front of the building my neighbors gather, a few stragglers running out of the building in a crouch. My clothes are a mess, so I stand off to the side and watch the inferno rip through the structure.

I stand with my shell-shocked neighbors for a long while, wondering if Mindi got out alive. I have no doubt she caused the wreckage. The memory of her appearance changing to a pale imitation of Alekto's makes it pretty clear that They accepted her as Their new Third. I only hope everyone else was able to get out in time.

There's a soft pressure near my ankles, and I look down to see Odie. He's covered with soot, and he meows plaintively at me. I smile and scoop him up, hugging him close. "Sorry about that, but I didn't think I was going to make it." I'm not sure what to do. My apartment has just exploded, and very soon cops and firemen will be showing up. They will have a lot of questions that I have no answers for, so I decide it's a good time to take a walk. I stroll down the block to where my car is parked.

I climb in and dump Odie onto the passenger seat. He sits up high, like the co-captain of a ship.

I flip down the visor and examine my eyes. They're gray, like the sky during a rainstorm. And no matter how I stare at my irises, there isn't any movement. Even my hair is different, dark and straight. All except for a golden streak near the front. A memento from my time with Them.

Odie meows loudly. I scratch him under his chin. For once the only thing I hear is his contented purr. My mind is finally, blissfully silent.

"Let's go home, Odysseus."

JUST LIKE CINDERELLA

NIKO ANSWERS ON THE SECOND RING. "HELLO?"

"Hi. How are you?"

He takes a sharp breath. "Jesus, Amelie, where are you? Are you okay?"

I look out over the beach, at the waves crashing upon the sand. The Pacific is different from the Atlantic. The waves are bigger and the water is ice-cold. Still, families frolic in the surf, and couples hold hands and walk along the water's edge, their toes dipping into the foam. I envy them their closeness, when the one I want to be with is more than three thousand miles away.

"I'm good. Better than good, actually. I'm fantastic."

"Where are you?"

A flock of green parrots flies overhead, calling out raucously. I smile at the sight. "San Diego. I'm sitting on the beach, watching the waves. Did I ever tell you your eyes remind me of the ocean?"

There is a heavy silence on the other end, and Niko takes a sharp breath. "Are you okay?" The pain in the question makes me laugh a little too loudly, and a few people turn to give me looks. I just wave at them.

"I'm fine. I told you, I'm doing wonderfully. How are you?"

"Mindi's missing."

People around me point and exclaim at something in the water. I shield my eyes against the sun and look out toward the horizon. In the distance a school of dolphins breaks the surface, their curved dorsal fins distinctive. The sight makes me happy. "I know. She's gone."

"Did you kill her?"

I snort. "No. Under that sweet exterior she was full of rage over her mother's death. She wanted a way to get revenge. They gave her what she needed. I imagine she's out there somewhere ripping criminals to pieces."

Another silence. "The Furies."

"Yes. She wanted Them; They wanted her. I tried to stop Them, but . . ." I trail off, a familiar heaviness in my chest. I'll probably always feel guilty about letting Mindi take Them, despite what Alekto said. I don't think Mindi's strong enough to control Them.

I hope I'm wrong.

"Did you really try to save her?" Niko asks softly.

"Yes. She was my friend." The weight in my chest has moved up to lodge in my throat, and I swipe a tear away before it can fall past my sunglasses. Maybe I didn't do enough. What could I do? She had to make her own choice.

Niko sighs, and I wonder if he believes me. "Who shot Dr. Goodhart? The newspaper said he was in the apartment. It also said he suffered a fatal shooting."

I remember the sight of his head and swallow my nausea. "Mindi, but I doubt you'll believe me if I tell you that it was an accident. It was Their way in. If she hadn't killed him, we wouldn't be having this conversation. I'd be dead."

I don't add that she was trying to shoot me at the time. Let him have some untarnished memories.

The silence stretches between us, seconds ticking away to minutes. I swallow hard, and ask, "How are you?"

"I miss you," Niko says. His voice is rough with emotion, and my eyes fill with fresh tears.

"I miss you, too."

"I still love you, you know. That day in the diner, I walked to my car and immediately changed my mind. I walked back to talk to you, to tell you that we should work through things together, but you were already gone."

I was already gone. Dumb luck. I don't say anything.

Niko continues. "A couple days later I went to talk to you, but your building was destroyed, and one of your neighbors told me they hadn't seen you since the day of the gas explosion."

I push a lock of stick-straight brown hair out of my eyes, and smile. I don't miss the blond curls at all. "Explosion? That was Mindi. I guess the change is different for everyone."

A long silence on the other end. "Are you coming back?"

"No. I'm done with Pennsylvania. I bought a house out here, on the beach." When I went to check on my trust fund, it was larger than I'd expected. A ridiculous amount of money was added from my grandmother's estate when I turned eighteen, plus unrestricted access to what my parents left me. I own the house in West Chester, but I think I want to sell that. I don't want to be anywhere near Mindi. I have a feeling she's still in Pennsylvania.

I continue. "I'm going to college in the fall." I don't tell him how I hacked into Brighter Day's and Saint Dymphna's databases and erased my medical records. My uncanny computer skills have come in handy. Thanks to them, I look like I've had a pretty normal life, even graduated high school. "I think I'm going to study to be a psychiatrist," I joke.

Niko laughs, but the sound is bitter. "That's great. It looks like everything is working out great for you."

"It could be better."

"Yeah?"

"Yeah." I hold my breath. "You could come out here and live with me."

"And do what?"

It's my turn to laugh. "Manage my investments? Go to school? Get a tan?"

"There's still a week until graduation."

"You can come out here afterward."

I can almost hear his indecision through the line, and I stand to stretch. I pick up my beach towel and begin walking through the sand to the path that will take me home. I think about how much better it would be if Niko were here holding my hand.

"Tell you what," I say. "I'll send you a round-trip ticket, open date, open location. If you want to fly out here to be with me, you do that. If not, you can go see Europe or something." The sentence sticks in my throat, clogged with yearning for him. I swallow past the lump. "I still love you, Niko. I always will. But I'm not perfect. I never will be. My past, no matter what I do, will always be a part of me."

Niko laughs, and a teasing tone enters his voice. "Are you seeing a shrink?"

I can't help but smile as I walk up the narrow sandy path. It gives way to the sidewalk quickly enough, and I head toward my house. "Maybe." I don't tell him about the woman I see once a week, a middle-aged psychiatrist who specializes in victims of abuse. She helps me work through the memories, which seem so fresh. The first couple of weeks driving out West, I had trouble dealing with them, but now that a few weeks have passed, they're fading quickly. Getting real professional help is really letting me work through things.

I've learned, though, that there are parts of me that I will never be able to share, no matter how I want to. That's why I don't open up to her about the Furies; I have no desire to see the inside of another mental institution. Still, our talks help.

I stop on the sidewalk and tilt my face to the sun. My mind is quiet, and even though talking to Niko has set fire once again to the longing that burns in my chest, I'm okay. For the first time in years, I'm actually okay.

I clear my throat. "Think about my offer. You have my new number now, and the ticket's already in the mail. I love you, and nothing would make me happier than to have you here with me." I hang up before he answers. There's nothing left to say. I've already had my happy ending, and hoping for anything more seems greedy. We may love each other, but Niko has to come to terms with what I was on his own. When he can do that, we can be together, no matter what the cost.

The choice is his to make. I've already made mine.

ZEPHYR MUST EMBRACE HER DESTINY
AS A DARK GODDESS . . .
OR ALL THE WORLD WILL BE LOST.

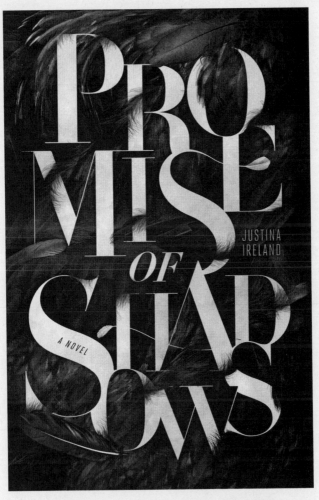

I MOVE MY SHOVEL, PUSHING THE MUD BACK

and forth at a glacial pace. Next to me, my friend Cass moves just as slowly. They have a saying down here in Tartarus: There's no need to hurry when you've got forever to get the job done. The saying is just one of many. It's easy to be clever when you're staring eternity in the face.

I've just dumped a load of dirt on top of my steadily growing pile when Cass speaks.

"I think you got a visitor," she says, looking past me toward the guard shack at the far edge of the plain. We work on the line with a few hundred others, digging a ditch the same way we have every day since I got to the Pits. The lowest point in the Underworld, the

Pits of Tartarus is a bleak place. A muddy plain edged by a forest of black trees, the sky a constant twilight, it's a place reserved for criminals and lowlifes. All we do here is dig, moving the mud into long rows. I'm not sure why we dig all the time, since no one ever tells us anything except when to work, when to rest, and when to eat. I'm not even sure the work serves a purpose beyond keeping us from killing each other, and we still manage to do that just fine.

Cass elbows me hard in the side, and I wince. My ribs are still bruised from our most recent attack. A couple of Fae who thought kicking me to death would get them out of Tartarus or at least get them some respect. Thanks to Cass, all it got them was dead.

She nudges me again, and this time I groan. "That hurts."

"It's the Messenger this time," she says, jutting her chin toward the figure at the far end of the line. "They're getting serious." I don't look up. The last thing I need is the guard taking his whip to my back.

Panic rises, tightening my chest. I take a deep breath and force it down. I cannot freak out. "You don't know that he's here for me," I tell Cass. The words are more for me than for her. One of the guards, who are all minotaurs, starts to move in our direction, and I lower my voice. "If he's here for me, they'll let me know." I hold my breath until the half-bull, half-man creature heads back the other way. I don't want to get in trouble for talking. Cass doesn't really mind the punishments the bulls hand out. I do.

I'm not as strong as she is.

"Mourning!"

The bull's voice echoes across the plain, carrying down along the line of prisoners toiling in the dirt. I keep my head down and my shovel moving, not bothering to acknowledge the shout and buying some time to compose myself. It starts to rain, and I sigh. It's the least of my problems, but the downpour gives me something to focus on besides my visitor.

Rain in Tartarus means a lot of different things. Today it's a fine mist of excrement falling from the sky. It's like having an outhouse upended over your head. Cass keeps telling me that at some point I'll get used to it, but she's been here longer than anyone else. There's no time in the Underworld, but from what I can tell of her penchant for togas, she's been here a while. Like, centuries. I don't think I'll be kicking around here that long. Too many people want me dead.

And the weather sucks.

The best way to keep the muck out of my eyes and mouth is to keep my head down and wait until it passes. I'm a smart girl, so that's what I do. Deep down, I'm hoping that the guard won't call me again.

"Mourning. Zephyr Mourning. Get your lazy carcass down here, Godslayer."

I wince at the tone in the guard's voice. I've waited too long to answer, and now I'm in for it. The bulls down here are no better than the prisoners, just as violent and rude. What do you expect from a minotaur? I'm not very good at taking a punch, and I have no desire to provoke the guard any further, so I plant my shovel in the mud and jog in the direction of the shout.

I slow down to a walk when I see a familiar figure walking beside the bull, a whip-thin man with a shock of white-blond hair. The

"Messenger" Cass called him. But she's old school, and most vættir these days refer to him by his given name, Hermes. The Messenger of the Gods. He carries an oversize golf umbrella and picks his way around the larger muck puddles. The wings on his ankles flutter in agitation. His blue eyes glow in the constant dusk of Tartarus, their metallic blued-steel sheen denoting his Æthereal blood and causing the other prisoners to subtly shift away from him. There's too much shine to them for him to be anything but Exalted, and even the dumbest vættir knows better than to cross paths with one of the favored sons and daughters of the universe. Their powers are so vast that they are gods among gods.

Still, all the æther in the universe can't keep the rain from splattering Hermes. His impeccably tailored dove-gray suit has several dark spots. It serves him right. Only Hermes would wear couture to hell.

A few feet still separate me and Hermes when a fight breaks out on the line. A couple of Fae grapple, their wrestling match carrying them right into our path. The scent of their rage pushes away the stink of the rain, and for once I'm grateful for my ability to smell emotions. Their anger is the acrid aroma of burning flesh, which is better than the bathroom scent of the rain. Whatever they're fighting about, it's clear that the Fae hate each other. This is more than a normal Tartarus scuffle.

The Fae are more intent on their fight than on the Æthereal walking toward them. They go down a couple of feet away from Hermes, landing in a deep puddle. The contents splash up and across the legs of Hermes's pants, soaking them with crap and mud. I swallow the hysterical laugh that threatens to bubble up.

This can't end well.

Everyone freezes for a moment, even the fighters on the ground. They're all waiting for Hermes's wrath, for the outpouring of æther that follows any Æthereal temper tantrum. But this is Tartarus, and there's no æther here. Hermes is as powerless as the rest of us.

That doesn't stop him from closing the umbrella and swinging it at the nearest Fae. The fiberglass snaps as it catches the slim man across the face, snapping his head back with an audible crunch. The other Fae tries to scramble away, but Hermes is much faster. With one hand he hauls the Fae up by the scruff before slamming him face-first into the soft mud. Then, with the detached expression of a man buying groceries, Hermes holds the flailing Fae down until he no longer moves.

Bile burns the back of my throat, and it's hard to breathe. I push down the fear that makes me want to run away, to keep running until I can forget the coldness in Hermes's eyes as he killed a man.

Cass appears next to me with a sigh. Even though I can smell the mixed fear and relief from the rest of the vættir, I get nothing from her. Cass's emotions are always a mystery. "Great, now I'll never get that food ration he owes me." She's serious. Cass never jokes about anything.

Life is cheap in Tartarus.

A couple of bulls run over to haul away the two Fae. Their bodies will be thrown beyond the tree line so that the unseen things that live in the woods can feast on them instead of on us. I relax so my expression doesn't reflect the horror I feel. Hermes straightens, tossing away his ruined umbrella. "Hey, Zephyr," he says as he adjusts his suit.

Cass slides back into the work crew as I cross my arms. It feels like a lifetime since I last saw Hermes. Time passes differently in Tartarus, so I have no idea how long it's actually been. A month? A year? Some days it feels like it was just yesterday that I landed here. Others, it feels like I've been here my entire life.

No matter how long it's been, I can't forget that he's the one who put me in Tartarus. I thought he was more than just my sister's boyfriend. I thought of him as family, the big brother I never had. And he turned me in to the Æthereal High Council. That's what I get for trusting an Æthereal.

Never trust the gods.

Reminding myself of his betrayal centers me. "Hey, Hermes. If it isn't my favorite psycho . . . pomp." My voice is even. I've learned a few things down here, especially from Cass. I won't let him know how his presence fills me with a burning rage that blurs my vision and makes me want to scream.

He gives me a wide smile, his chiseled cheekbones looking even sharper. "Funny. Did you think of it yourself?"

I sigh, feigning boredom. "What do you want? Can't you see I have a very important ditch to dig?"

Hermes's lips twitch. At least he still appreciates sarcasm. He clears his throat. "I'm here to speak with you on behalf of the Æthereal High Council."

I shrug. "Okay." I'm not sure what else I'm supposed to say. I was never important enough to garner the High Council's notice before they sent me to Tartarus. Not many of the vættir are. We're second-class citizens, lucky to avoid the gods' notice.

"This is a private interview," Hermes says. He eyes the nearest bull. The minotaur straightens, steam puffing out of his bovine nostrils as he snaps to attention.

"You may use the nearby gatehouse, Exalted, if it suits your needs." The minotaur executes a clumsy bow, muck flying off one of his massive horns and landing on Hermes's pants.

Hermes sighs and pinches the bridge of his nose before he remembers that his hands are covered in crap. Rage tightens his mouth as he gives the half-man, half-bull creature a limp-wristed wave to lead the way. We follow the guard to a nearby outbuilding in silence. Only the set of Hermes's shoulders belies his utter disgust.

This would be hilarious if I wasn't sick with dread.

We make our way through the steady rain to the gatehouse, where the bull remains outside while we go in. The room is small. It's little more than a shack, really. Rough-hewn boards keep out the storm, and the floor is made of hard-packed earth. Dark fire flickers in the hearth, casting no light but warming the room nonetheless. A rickety table and chair lean against the wall opposite the fireplace, and a handful of pixies sealed in glass globes cast the only light in the room. The pixies emit a sickly yellow glow when they see us, one of them tapping on his prison insistently.

"Hey. Hey! Let me out before the bull comes back. I'll pay you."

I ignore the bug. Anyone foolish enough to try to bribe me must be new to hell. He must not know who I am, or that I don't care about his money, because there's no way I'm ever leaving Tartarus.

Godslayers don't get parole.

I try to scrape as much of the sludge off my face as I can, before I see the well in the far corner of the room. The water has the same sulfurous rotten-egg smell as all the water here in the Pits, but at least it doesn't smell like an outhouse in August. There's a grate near the well, and I upend the bucket over my head while standing on it. I repeat this two more times before I'm satisfied I've gotten the worst of the mess off. No sense in trying to get completely clean. This is Tartarus, after all.

I hold a full bucket out to Hermes. He shakes his head in distaste before thinking twice and dipping a lemon-yellow pocket square into the water. He gingerly wipes the dark streaks off his pale skin. I dump the rest of the water over my head before tossing the bucket back in the corner.

"The Underworld seems to agree with you," he remarks as he starts to put away the handkerchief, thinks twice, and throws it on the sad-looking table.

I squeeze the excess water out of my blue, ropy locks and snort. What does he see? The front I keep up so the weaker inmates won't mess with me? Just because I've learned how to hide my fear doesn't mean I'm not scared. "It's hell, H. I don't think it agrees with anyone."

He purses his lips. "No æther, which means no real magic, it's perpetually dark, the sky rains excrement, and there are monsters waiting for a chance to devour the unwitting. I honestly don't see what your problem is."

His sense of humor is still as dry as the Sahara. It's too bad I don't find him funny anymore. I extend my talons and growl. "Give me one reason why I shouldn't turn your face into confetti, Betrayer."

Hermes's blued-steel gaze flashes. "Because it's the last thing Whisper would've wanted you to do."

Agony arcs through my chest, and I look away so he won't see the pain of my loss in my gaze. Whisper. I can't think of my sister without remembering the last time I saw her, her chest a gaping wound, her blood soaking into the concrete of the patio. She was my best friend and now she's gone. My talons slide back under my fingernails. I wasn't really going to attack him, anyway. "She loved you, you know. Even though she knew you'd eventually leave her."

He clears his throat and looks away. I'm glad that I've managed to make him uncomfortable. Some of the water from my hair has managed to find its way into my mouth, and I spit onto the floor. "You didn't come here to discuss my sister. What do you want?"

He sighs. "Still just as ladylike as ever. The High Council has sent me down here to inquire how it was that you managed to kill an Æthereal."

I smirk. This is the third inquisitor the Council has sent down since I got here. The first two left with nothing, and Hermes will too. Just because he used to screw my sister doesn't mean I owe him anything. "Just lucky, I guess."

His lips thin in irritation before he sighs. "I bear this message for you." He takes a shining white rock from his pocket, and I take a step back in surprise. He holds an æther stone, a magically charged rock that would fetch a good price in the Pits. Before I can ask what he plans to do with it, he drops it on the ground between us. Light surges upward and snaps into sharp focus. I can't help the hitch of breath in my chest.

Standing before me is a too-real image of my mother. The last time I saw the form before me, she was leaving for a battle, her claymore propped on her shoulder. Ruby-red hair knotted into locks that reached her waist, skin the color of midnight, and wings of deepest red and black. "Blood on coal," Whisper used to call them when we'd watch her fly off to battle. I know that it isn't really her. She's dead, her shade somewhere in the Elysian Fields, enjoying eternal happiness. The projection is the Æthereal equivalent of Princess Leia's plea to Obi-Wan. Still, I can't stop myself from reaching out to her like I've always wanted.

My mother's voice cuts through my mind after all these years, an unwanted phantom. *You're the daughter of an Æthereal, Zephyr. Try to stop being such an incredible disappointment.* I can even see the way her dark face would scrunch up at me, as though I was the one problem in her life that she couldn't solve.

The memory is the opposite end of the emotional spectrum from the woman gazing at me lovingly from the projection. "Zephyr, I know you probably aren't happy to see me, but I need you to answer Hermes's questions. It is of the utmost importance that the High Council be able to understand how you killed Ramun Mar."

I swallow dryly. Who is this woman? There's love shining in her eyes, and she seems gentle and affectionate. This stranger is nothing like my mother. That Mourning Dove once flew me up to ten thousand feet and then dropped me, all to teach me how to fly.

"There's no room for mistakes in battle," she called as I fell, screaming until my sister, Whisper, flew up to catch me. It's amazing I ever learned to fly after that terrifying introduction to the sky.

The message plays, but I'm finished listening to the lying image before me. I fight back angry tears before I kick the æther stone toward the corner. It falls into the well with a wet plunk. I fight to keep my words steady. "If you think that's going to get me to talk, then you don't know me at all."

"Do you think that's what your mother would want?"

I turn around once my eyes have stopped burning, the threat of tears avoided. "That woman doesn't exist. Never did. I don't know how you did it, but it's a pretty sad attempt to get me to talk. Why don't you just tell me what you want from me?" The words come out as a plea. I bite my lip, my eyes sliding away from his all-too-knowing blue ones.

"Aw, Peep," he whispers, and the pet name cuts through me, the pain sharper and fresher than the ache of his betrayal. He reaches for me but at the last moment draws back, and I know he's thinking about our last meeting.

He's remembering that I might not have been caught by the Æthereals if he hadn't tricked me.

I hate him even as I love him with all my heart. He made my sister so happy, and that made me happy. Deep down I'd always hoped he would stay with Whisper, marry her like people do on television. I had this idea of a huge wedding, one that everyone in the Aerie would attend. There'd be cake, and I'd be Whisper's maid of honor. It would be just like a movie.

I made the mistake of telling her that one time, and she just laughed, the sound high and brittle like glass breaking. "Zeph, you know that Æthereals don't marry vættir. Especially not Exalteds like Hermes. I'm just grateful for the time that we have together. One day you'll understand that."

Hermes sighs and leans back against the wall of the gatehouse, drawing me out of the memory and putting a physical distance between us that's a match for the emotional one. "The High Council needs you to cooperate because a war is brewing over you, kiddo. The kind of war that the vættir might not survive."

"Why me? What did I do?"

A bark of laughter escapes from him. "What, besides kill an Æthereal? No big deal there, Godslayer." He shakes his head, a small smile playing around his lips before he turns serious again. "You killed one of the unkillable. People want to know how. They want to know if it can happen again. And if they're next."

I smile tightly. "Sounds like Hera's been working overtime." At my trial she'd advocated for my death more than any of the other gods.

Hermes nods slowly. "That's putting it mildly. She's been on the warpath since you were sent here last year, and things are only getting worse."

The air whooshes out of my lungs. I feel like I've been punched. "A year? I've been here a year?" I imagine all the things I've missed in a year. If I'd been in the Mortal Realm, I would've finally gone to high school, a real school with norms. Homecoming, prom, football games, all the things regular people get to do. That's what I would've spent the last year doing. Not digging ditches and fighting to stay alive.

After I failed my Trials, I thought a normal life was finally in my reach. Harpies who cannot pass the Trials are either given menial positions or expelled from the Aerie, forced to spend the rest of their lives trying to blend in among the norms, full-blooded humans. Most Harpies dread the modern world and opt to work in the Aerie's laundry or kitchens, but I dreamed of the day when I'd no longer have to live in the Aerie. Freedom seemed like a blessing, not a curse.

But then I accidentally killed an Æthereal and ended up in Tartarus, ruining all my plans. And now I find out that I've lost a year in what felt like a few months.

Hermes's eyes dart away from mine, and he shrugs in response. "Time passes differently down here."

"You think?" I begin to pace as his words sink in. I'm finally realizing that my imprisonment is permanent. I'm not going to go to high school, or college, or anywhere else in the Mortal Realm. I'm going to be forever stuck here in Tartarus, covered in sludge and pretending to be brave. A year has passed, and I feel just like I did the last time I saw Hermes. Desperate, confused, and incredibly lost.

I stop pacing and cross my arms, trying to school my face to blankness. *Arrows are useless without a bow.* It's an old Harpy saying. No sense wallowing in might-have-beens. "Are we finished?" I snap.

Hermes startles, my sharp tone unfamiliar. "What?" he asks in surprise. I've never raised my voice at him. I've always given him the deference that the Exalteds demand, even as he snuck into the house late at night to meet with my sister. But now I'm not thinking about class structures and the proper forms of address, or even the way my sister lit up when she saw him. I'm just thinking about the year of my life that I lost.

"Are you done with me or what? I have to get back before someone steals my shovel."

His expression goes from shocked to sad, and I have to turn away from the pity on his face. "What happened to you, Peep? You're different. I almost didn't recognize you when I arrived. You're rougher now."

I sigh and sit in the room's only chair, leaning my head back against the wall's rough wood. "Tartarus happened to me, H. That's all. Just Tartarus."